The
COMET
And The
THIEF

RUTH MORGAN

The
COMET
And The
THIEF

Gomer

First published in 2019 by Gomer Press,
Llandysul, Ceredigion SA44 4JL

ISBN 978 1 78562 310 3

A CIP record for this title is available from the British Library.

This book is published with the financial support of the
Welsh Books Council.

Printed and bound in Wales at
Gomer Press, Llandysul, Ceredigion
www.gomer.co.uk

*To my lovely folk family
at Halsway Manor*

ACKNOWLEDGEMENTS

I want to give huge thanks to my editor at Gomer, Rebecca John, who has provided such a wealth of understanding and encouragement. Rebecca, you have brightened many a dull and daunting day for me in this process. As ever I want to thank my wonderful family for their constant love and support.

A NOTE ON LANGUAGE

In *The Comet and the Thief* the way the characters speak reflect the times in which they live, so for example in Zannah's time, 'thou' and 'thee' were used for the singular 'you' and the word 'you' was only used when speaking to a group of people. Also, it was more fashionable in Kit's time to say ''Tis' for 'It is' and ''Twas' for 'It was'.

Here are translations for non-English words in the story not otherwise explained:

Italian

perbacco! .... (literally) *by Bacchus! – goodness me!*

cavolo! .... (literally) *cabbage!* (insult)

buongiorno .... *good morning/ good day*

con brio! .... *with energy!* (musical term)

diavolo .... *devil*

certo .... *of course*

sicuramente .... *certainly*

bravo .... *well done*

Welsh

bychan yw e .... *he's a lad*

yn wir? .... *indeed?*

Duw .... *God*

diawch erioed! .... *goodness me!*

dere 'mlaen 'ychan! .. *come on lad!*

nos da .... *goodnight*

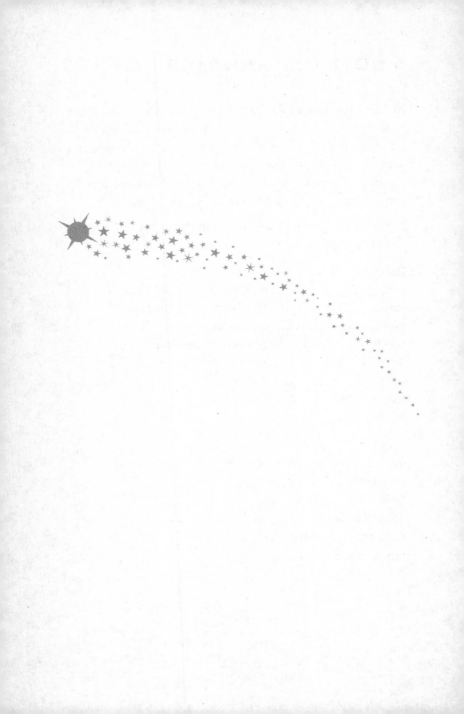

Kit was nearly bursting but he'd been summoned three times and couldn't remain in his hiding place much longer. To laugh now would spoil everything. Yet peeping through the gap in the wood panelling, watching the men's expressions of awe and fear grow to a point at which they seemed in danger of doing themselves an injury, the need to laugh out loud made his belly ache.

'Great demon Ashentoth, we call you from the underworld. Come among us that we might worship you!' pleaded Mr Steen, his eyes squeezed shut and his hands clasped in prayer. Candlelight glinted off the jewelled rings on Steen's podgy fingers. He was rocking so much his magical-looking sultan's hat had nearly fallen off. It was hilarious. Kit breathed deeply and tried to control himself. This was his moment to leap into view.

First, he tossed in a smoke pellet. A blood red column of smoke rose to the ceiling, disguising his entrance via the loose section of panelling which he just had time to close before the smoke dispersed. The smell of burning incense filled the stuffy chamber with its windows shuttered up to the night.

'Ashentoth is HERE!' exclaimed Kit, throwing up

his arms, flinging back his head. As usual, he'd painted every inch of visible skin blue, drawn on thick charcoal eyebrows and his hair was slicked up with a paste of flour and dye, like an orange flame. When they saw him, the men sitting around the table groaned and bowed their heads as though unworthy to look upon their infernal guest. Idiots! Giggles bubbled up from Kit's aching belly and it was too late to do anything but make it part of the show, so he shrieked with evil laughter and began cavorting around the table.

'Ashentoth comes among us in a good mood,' gulped Mr Steen.

'Ye-as,' replied Kit in the strange, strangulated voice he always used when he was being Ashentoth. He stopped right in front of the host, opened his eyes frighteningly wide, pointed a finger at the floor and spat out the dread words – 'I've been torturing souls in the underworld all afternoon!' – prompting gasps of horror all round. From the pockets of his Moorish pantaloons, Kit pulled a couple of firecrackers then tossed them into the corners of the room.

'HahahaHA!' he laughed.

Now lost in the enjoyment of his performance, Kit bounded onto the polished mahogany table with his filthy bare feet and continued to dance wildly around the dishes of meat, cakes and pastries which had all been laid out as offerings to Ashentoth, kicking the silver dishes around like a naughty goblin before squatting to gorge himself on a game pie whilst wiggling his eyebrows at the onlookers. Some of the food he stuffed into his pantaloon pockets, to take back to the attic.

Kit needn't have worried about laughing in front of this lot. It didn't matter what he did, these rich men wanted to believe he was some demon called Ashentoth and nothing in the world was going to put them off. It had all started a couple of months earlier when Kit, returning from a job and covered in grime from head to foot, had taken a wrong turn behind the panelling and found himself in this room where Mr Steen's Thursday Occultist Club was in full swing. The men, dressed in flowing robes, had their eyes shut so hadn't observed him enter. They had been attempting to conjure a demon and were amazed and horrified to achieve success at last, so much so they'd knelt and not really studied him properly. Kit hadn't known what a demon was supposed to do so he'd made it up, acting weirdly and leaping around. Amazingly, it had worked.

Better to be thought a demon than caught as a thief.

Since then, Kit had returned to Mr Steen's week after week to put on a show for the Occultist Club and was always rewarded for his efforts. He recognised a few of those present, all wealthy men well known upon the streets of London: great merchants, lords and judges who rode around with po-faces in sedan chairs and visited the theatre of an evening. This was just a different kind of theatre really and tonight, Kit was giving the performance of his life.

Having eaten his fill, Ashentoth jumped from the

table and performed a dance before the fire, jerking his knees and elbows, clapping, spinning and letting out the occasional chilling shriek. All very demonic. The fire in the grate and the candlelight threw manic jolting shadows around the walls and ceiling. Kit was sweating so much he was afraid his body paint might melt, but what he noticed next made him sweat even more. Surely there were seven pairs of eyes watching him instead of the usual six? Yes, someone new was sitting beside the fireplace – a brown-wigged man, dressed richly but in a more everyday fashion and holding a silver-capped walking stick between his knees. It was the look on his face that was most troubling. Whereas the others viewed him with fear and wonder, this stranger was studying Kit's antics with a shrewdness in his eyes and a sneer about his lips. It was horribly clear that he did not believe in the demon Ashentoth. Not one bit.

Kit hesitated. He just stopped himself from bolting back behind the panelling. The others believed in Ashentoth, even if the stranger didn't, but running away in such an obvious manner would cast doubts, even in their simple minds. Kit would have to carry on with the performance. He plastered an even bigger grimace on his face, showing all his teeth and continued to dance until he regained confidence. Then Ashentoth fell into a trance as usual. Kit fixed his eyes upon the brass chandelier hanging from the ceiling, in the great ball of which he saw his own mighty-eyed, distorted reflection looking really devilish. This was the part when the men got to ask the demon questions about magic, the underworld and even for advice, mainly about what to do with their vast wealth. Kit always enjoyed this part; he could let his imagination run wild and they swallowed everything he said.

'Great Ashentoth,' began a hook-nosed, raven-like man called Mr Watts. 'A mighty comet burns brightly in our sky, the one predicted by the late Sir Edmond Halley. Despite what scientists say, is it a portent of evil?'

Kit swayed from side to side, giving himself time to concoct an answer. 'The comet is good for some and bad for others,' he said, holding his finger at an angle. 'Heed the direction the tail points. Let not dogs within your house point their tails thusly and all will be well.' It was a typical bit of Ashentoth nonsense. Kit loved to think of these important men chasing their dogs about, desperate to ensure they did not point their tails the same way as the comet's.

'Ashentoth, I have been thinking of adding a new wing to my house, Grenworth Hall.'

It was Lord Snitherton speaking. His Lordship always sat in a high-backed armchair directly opposite the fireplace. He wore a fanciful hat like Steen's but his had a peacock's feather sticking up in front. He wasn't as grovelly as the rest of them but he still spoke in hushed tones.

'To east or west?' asked Ashentoth.

'West.'

'More difficult.' Ashentoth shook his head. 'You will

have to prepare. Take a white goose feather and dip it in honey. Bury it at midnight by a full moon where you intend to build. Bury it yourself, mind, a servant will not do. You must be naked when 'tis done but for a pair of green silk breeches and a bird's nest crown. Dance three times widdershins round the plot and spell your name backwards. Then all will be well.' For a moment, Kit thought he might have overdone it with the green breeches and bird's nest crown. Ashentoth was being cheekier than usual. He held his breath and was relieved when Lord Snitherton spoke again, in a slightly puzzled way. 'I shall do as you say, Ashentoth, if it is absolutely necessary?'

'Oh, 'tis indeed.' Kit conjured up the image of his Lordship burying the goose feather in his silk breeches and had to bite the inside of his cheek hard to stop himself laughing again.

There were several more questions and Ashentoth replied with similar nonsense. Kit was so carried away by his performance, he had all but forgotten the stranger until a new voice spoke. Ashentoth was still in his trance so Kit couldn't look directly at the speaker but he recognised a coldness in the voice.

'Ashentoth, I believe I have detected an annoying little troublemaker,' said the stranger. 'Someone who pretends to be something he's not. What, in your opinion, should I do?'

Kit swallowed and again, fought his urge to dive behind the panelling. He swayed giving himself time to answer but decided he could only respond with the usual made-up rubbish. He would certainly not give the stranger the chance to explain his question.

'Write down this troublemaker's name,' said Ashentoth. 'On a strip of cotton. Fold it three times. Put it in a box. Lock the box with a copper key. Throw it in a river, beneath a willow tree.'

'I'll try that then,' said the stranger. Kit hoped the others could not detect the sarcasm in his reply. 'If only I knew this person's real name? Perhaps that should be my first task, Ashentoth? To discover his name?'

Kit saw the mistake he'd made, mentioning the name. 'Indeed,' he croaked, 'And that's best done on a Sunday in June.' He was drying up and decided to cut the session short. Ashentoth awoke from his trance then danced around the table some more, during which Mr Steen passed around a dish to which each man added a silver coin. This was a parting gift for Ashentoth to take back and present to the Dark Lord of the Underworld. As he whirled about, Kit saw how the stranger paused when the dish was passed to him, how he smirked as he tossed in a coin. How he made it his business to catch Kit's eye and nod meaningfully.

After pocketing the money Kit threw another smoke bomb and disappeared, exiting through the gap in the panelling and closing it carefully behind him. He sighed with relief to be out of that room. As he squeezed along the tiny passages between the panelling and walls of the different apartments, climbing from floor to floor and clinging onto the batons and brick with his fingertips, he struggled to remember his usual route. That he was giddy and shaking with fright made the climb more difficult and dangerous. One false move might find him trapped. Kit had to hold his breath to make his way through some sections and the risk of suffocation in these tiny spaces was all too real. He was desperately disappointed. It was a crying shame but after what had just happened, he couldn't risk returning to Mr Steen's Occultist Club evenings. Ashentoth was going to have to retire and Kit would be forced back into a way of life he despised. Above all, he hated being a thief.

CHAPTER 2

In total darkness, the only maps were those of touch and turn and smell. Kit could never completely work out, from the outside of the building, the location of Mr Steen's apartments but reckoned they must be at least two houses along from the one above which he and Gabe lived. The gorgeous decorations of the rooms Kit stole past, the dainty plasterwork and painted wood panelling concealed a whole labyrinth of gaps, chimney flues and forgotten passages which joined the apartments together. Kit was small, quick and skilled in finding his way around the multi directional maze. The pretty decorations were like a wig, disguising the baldness, scabs and decay of these buildings although Kit didn't like to think of it this way. It made him feel like a crawling louse.

Back in the attic and by the light of a guttering candle stub, Gabe looked worse than ever. His colour was ghastly, as pale as his shirt, and his whole body shook with the rattling cough which had been going on for weeks. Kit's stomach heaved with the fresh shock of seeing his love like this. He had tried stuffing more straw sacks under Gabe's half of the moth-eaten carpet which served as a bed, to raise him up from the dusty floorboards. Yet nothing he did seemed to stop Gabe's cough or ease the pain.

'A good haul tonight at Steen's. Look at the shiners!' Kit put on a bright voice and let the silver coins cascade from his palm onto the bed. If they were the last they'd see for a while, Gabe need not know it.

Kit crouched beside the bed, pulled a chicken leg and some gingerbread from his pocket and placed them beside the coins. As he chattered on, he stripped pieces of chicken from the bone to offer the patient, like you might feed a kitten. Gabe barely had strength to open his mouth, let alone chew and swallow the small pieces. A cracked cup of water stood next to the bed and after a few morsels, Kit helped him take a couple of sips, after which Gabe slumped back exhausted, as though he'd completed a twelve-course meal.

'I'll away to Whiting's first thing and buy more medicine. There's better stuff to be had than the last lot. More pricey but that don't matter, it'll get you well again my dove, I promise. And some beautiful hot steaming chops for breakfast, that'll put the spark back in you.' He stroked Gabe's brow. Gabe smiled, closing his eyes as though he only had enough energy to use one part of his face at a time. 'Lovely,' he whispered, and Kit had to put his ear very close to catch the word. He kissed Gabe's forehead lightly.

Despite the fire in Steen's apartment, it was a warm spring evening and the attic was stuffy. Kit felt his way along one of the boards resting across the joists, to the part of the roof directly opposite the bed, where he removed a square of eight loose roof tiles, stacking them carefully below. Gabe loved to see the stars but as the fresh air blew in, it triggered another bout of coughing.

'The air'll do you good in a moment when you're used to it,' said Kit. He spent a while tidying up, which included throwing old scraps of food and the contents of the chamber pot out of the hole in the roof. His work done, Kit sat at the foot of the bed and looked up at the stars. The comet sat right in the middle of the hole he'd made, like a framed work of art. It flew in the velvet blackness like a pale ghost, its tail the length of Kit's little finger up to the second joint. Gabe spotted it, raising his own finger weakly to point.

'Comet's bright up there,' said Kit, working his way back to Gabe's side.

'Bad luck,' mouthed Gabe.

'That's what them lot downstairs was just saying,' said Kit, determined to hang on to his natural good sense. 'Know what? I don't believe it. Why would something as beautiful be bad luck? How could it make any kind of luck, anyway? 'Tis so far away.'

Gabe's fearful eyes were like watery moons and for a moment, Kit considered replacing the tiles. He changed the subject instead.

'You should have seen them old boys tonight; I laid on such a show and they swallowed it all, straight. I doubt Garrick could have outdone me at Drury Lane!' Kit recalled his earlier performance, leaving out any mention of the stranger but mimicking the voices of all the others brilliantly. 'Lord Snitherton goes to me,

"Ow, Ashentoth, I'm wanting to build a new wing on ma' house in the country, how can I get that to work ma' fine demon?" And guess what I tell him to do?' By the time Kit had told the whole story, Gabe was wheezing with silent laughter, after which Kit wrapped up the performance quickly.

'Magic?' said Kit, wiping his own tears of laughter away. 'No such thing my dove. They're a bunch of idiots, that lot downstairs, I don't care how much money they got or how important they are. The only magic in life is the magic we make for ourselves, Gabe.'

'Comet... looks... magic.' At least Gabe returned to the earlier subject with a smile.

'Well then, go to sleep and dream of you and me up there, riding the comet across the heavens like a fine, white stallion, visiting all the bright stars and gold and silver angels.' The smile was still on Gabe's face as he closed his eyes and Kit brushed the damp tendrils of hair off his brow. For the first time in a long time, Gabe looked at peace and Kit carried on telling the story of their wonderful comet ride until he was sure he was asleep.

Kit buried the coins under the sacks on his side of the bed. Even though no one else set foot in the attic, he'd lived in too many rough and rotten places to trust leaving so much money lying about. He returned to the hole in the tiles. Noises drifted up from the street and he guessed that Steen's guests were departing. A carriage would arrive for Lord Snitherton, whose fine stockings and bright buckles were never soiled by common road muck. Further south, people with money, maybe not as much as Snitherton but enough to keep them comfortable, would be departing the theatre where they'd spent the evening watching the play. Whatever they'd seen couldn't have bettered the plays he put on night after night in their attic. The collection of props he'd amassed lay in a heap by his side of the bed. Most had come from a room in the same building where the travelling conjuror Chi-Keen had been staying before his disappearance. Kit had seen Chi-Keen's show several times, in the courtyards of inns, even sneaking into theatres to watch the mesmerising performances of levitation and mind reading. He knew it was all tricks but that didn't matter, the performances captivated him, body and soul. When word got about that Chi-Keen had disappeared, some said to avoid a brutal moneylender, Kit found a way into his apartments and made off with the costumes, make-up, smoke bombs and firecrackers he'd been using at Steen's ever since.

It wasn't stealing really. Chi-Keen's stuff would only have been sold to pay back his debts. If he ever returned, Kit would give it all back except for what had been used. He felt sorry for Chi-Keen. When his own father, a wheelwright who'd been teaching Kit his trade, died of smallpox, moneylenders had swooped and removed everything before the final funeral hymn had even been sung. Kit's mother and baby brother had died several years before and with no other family, he had found himself homeless and alone. At the time, his best chance seemed to be to set off from their village in Kent and walk to London. Too late Kit discovered that, for a poor nobody like himself, the city was at best an uncaring place and at worst a cesspit of hell. He would never have lasted if he hadn't met Gabriel, a born Londoner and orphan like himself who'd shown him how to survive. They'd met by chance but the instantaneous bond they'd experienced had developed over time into a love that felt as natural as any goodness Kit had ever known. Life was always going to be hard, but they had each other. 'You and I agin the world, Kit,' Gabe had a fondness for saying.

Riches. Wealth. Were he as rich as Lord Snitherton, Kit would have swapped it all to have his precious Gabe well again. That evening, when he'd said there was no real magic in the world, he'd meant it. Yet, as he gazed up at the night sky, trembling, Kit whispered a prayer to any Maker who might have been listening. Maker of comets, Maker of poor lads like them. The words caught in his throat.

'Please let Gabriel live.'

★ **CHAPTER 3**

Gabe was still asleep when Kit left the next morning, having woken early to replace the tiles before anyone in the street could see them missing. He always left the house early if he intended using the quick, outside route.

Their attic was the topmost triangle of the roof and you could only stand up to full height in the middle. The garret rooms directly below were occupied by servants. This empty section ran the entire length of the terrace without any break and Kit and Gabe were the only inhabitants. When they'd moved in the previous year, they had nailed old blankets around the roof trusses to section off their living space from the rest of the empty corridor. It was cosier that way, easier to keep out rats, and neither of them particularly enjoyed the empty views on either side racing off into ghostly darkness.

There were several ways down to the street. Kit could descend on the inside of the building from floor to floor, but it was quicker and easier to take the outside route. If he crawled along the attic joists for about twenty yards and removed another section of tiles to the rear of the building, he could squeeze through. Outside, there was a dip where the bottom of the roof fell below the balustrade and there was a deep stone gutter so no danger of being seen from below. Descending to the back garden was more hazardous. Kit was sixteen but particularly small, light and agile. He could swing over the balustrade and drop five feet onto the flat roof of a sticking out window. He could then shin down sections of drainpipe and jump from flat roof to flat roof of a variety of windows and extra bits of rooms which the builders had cobbled on. Whereas the front of the building was perfectly balanced and orderly, the builders hadn't cared a hang about the back. No one was supposed to see it, so it didn't matter.

Busy tending to Gabe, Kit hadn't left the house for days and he was still blinking, unused to sunlight, as he jumped from the yard wall, kicking up the dust where he landed in the road. He scrambled to his feet but there didn't seem to be anyone around. Good. He would head to Golden Square and kill some time before Whitings and the chop house opened. London was waking and stirring itself. Dogs barked. Good-for-nothing rich boys staggered home from gambling dens while street traders cranked up for business. The ragtag, jig-along daytime bustle was beginning again, a brutal and haphazard ride for those who couldn't afford the trappings of respectability. Kit walked around the corner to the pump on Portland Street. He bent to drink and wash his face and the fresh, cold water made him gasp and blink some more. Up in the attic, they had to make do with rainwater for drinking and washing and it was never this refreshing. A yawning boy pushing an empty handcart bowled past and even though he didn't know the lad, Kit crouched so the pump concealed his face. He didn't like being seen in the area and could breathe easier the further he was from home.

Strangely, it was only when the streets became busier and street traders' cries merged into the usual cacophony that Kit realised he was being followed. Feeling hungry and with the giddying jingle of coins in his pocket, he'd halted on Broad Street to buy a small beer from the back of one cart and oysters from another. Having finished the beer, Kit was just downing his third oyster when from the corner of his eye, he noticed a shadowy figure. As he turned his head, the figure ducked sideways into a doorway. There was no mistaking what this meant. Kit moved along the street, dodging traders crying out at the tops of their voices, selling cherries, baskets, mackerel, slippers and geese and whenever he glanced round, the swarthy man who was dressed in a dark great coat and greasy-looking cocked hat still followed. Forgetting Golden Square, Kit flung away the last couple of oysters, rounded a corner and broke into a run. He didn't have to look behind now, he could hear a second set of footsteps pounding in pursuit. Kit knew the area and pushed on through the crowds, weaving this way and that, up and down streets and lesser known lanes until he was completely out of breath and his pulse was thudding inside his skull. He rested against a wall in a dank and crooked alleyway whose only other inhabitant was a gin-soaked wretch asleep against the wall. Kit was still seeing stars as he struggled to regain his breath and listen hard at the same time. The second set of footsteps had ceased. Whoever it had been, Kit had lost him.

He couldn't let himself panic. He had to get home but not without the medicine. He would carry on to Whitings, taking a roundabout route to avoid Broad Street, buy the stuff and return to Gabe as quickly as he could. He licked his hand, flattened it against the filthy stonework, then rubbed muck and slime onto his freshly washed cheeks. He turned his jacket inside out, changing it from brown to grey, and dragged his hair forward, covering his face as much as possible. He raised one shoulder to give himself a stoop. In this impromptu disguise, Kit would still have to be quick and careful. And of course, lucky. Setting off down the alley and along another shadowy back street, glancing left and right, he continued to wonder about the stranger. Was it someone he'd stolen from? Yet the swarthy stranger didn't look the wealthy type, someone who kept a fine set of rooms with plenty of extras he didn't really need. Those were the kind of people Kit stole from. Imagine if the stranger had caught him? Imagine if he'd taken Kit and thrown him in a cell ready for hanging the next day! All he could think about was Gabe alone in the attic, wondering where he'd gone. The thought was chilling, and Kit quickened his pace.

At Whitings, Kit took the small blue bottle of medicine from the apothecary's assistant, who stared suspiciously at the silver coins he received in return but made no comment. This was the most expensive cure-all Whiting's sold: '*A safe and speedy restorative, favoured by Lords and Ladies, Kings and Queens all over Europe*'. A week before, Kit had seen this very assistant standing on the mounting block at the street corner like a travelling preacher, making the most amazing claims for what the medicine could do. He would have liked to ask the fellow to repeat those claims, but time was short. Believing that what he cradled in his hand amounted to his darling's last chance, Kit tucked the bottle inside his shirt, sliding it under some ragged strips of cloth fastened round his chest. Back at Portland Street, Kit would have to climb up one of the secret panelled routes and he would need both hands. He would take no chances with the precious mixture.

The journey home was nerve-wracking and three times longer than usual but right up to the end, Kit was confident he wasn't being followed. Almost overcome with relief, he turned the corner from Portland Street which was now full of its own street traders. All he had to do was use his trusted foot and handholds to get back over the yard wall, squeeze between some broken boards into the back passage of the third house along and he was in.

Kit was in the act of climbing the wall when, before he knew it, he'd been grabbed and was falling to the ground. He leapt to his feet ready to bolt but the same stranger who'd followed him earlier caught hold of the front of his jacket and shunted him hard against the brickwork, knocking the breath out of him.

'Well, well,' said the man with a voice like a rasp on a wooden plank and breath that stank like the river at low tide. 'Here he is, the little squib. Thought you'd lost me, didn't you? If you'd only popped up from that coal hole in front of the house, the way I'd been expecting, I'd 'a nabbed you earlier. But I got experience of rats like you and they always come back to they's nests eventually.'

Kit gave up trying to wriggle out of the hefty grasp. He hung limp and tried putting on an accent even though he couldn't stop his voice shaking. He didn't know where the accent came from but had picked it up from a street entertainer he'd seen once. 'Sorry, sor,' he said, 'But yer've picked the wrong fellow, whoever it is yer looking fer, yer mekkin a big mistake, sor.'

'Oh, I don't think so,' the man gave a hoarse laugh. 'Not unless there's two such vile vermin inhabiting this building.'

Kit had come to the end of his options. He panicked and made one last effort to evade the stranger's grasp but the more he struggled, the more the man gripped until Kit's sleeves were so tight, his arms were numb and useless through lack of blood. Terrified, he began to cry. If this was the end of him, it was also the end of Gabe.

Sensing the fight had gone out of his prey, the stranger spun Kit around and shoving from behind, marched him round to the front of the building and down the street, keeping tight hold of the back of his jacket. Kit was exposed, caught out for the first time ever, unmasked in public. Yet not one passer-by gave him a second look. Why should they? They'd seen it all before – youths arrested in the street for petty theft. Kit hung his head, ashamed of his tears. He could picture his life's candle burning low, on its way to being snuffed out. What if a scaffold awaited him around the next corner? He was half-expecting it, such was the determined way the stranger was leading him from behind. All the time, in his mind's eye he could see Gabe alone in the attic. Gabe, waiting in vain for him to return. Waiting for days then dying alone.

They marched on for about half a mile, with the man giving no hint as to where they were going until they turned down a side street next to a church and the man pulled Kit to a halt next to a parked sedan chair. The chair's box was covered in studded black leather with dark green velvet curtains at the windows. The two chairmen who were sitting on the churchyard wall looked at Kit disinterestedly. The swarthy stranger rapped on the door of the chair with his knuckles and the curtain drew back.

By daylight rather than candlelight, Kit recognised the gentleman at once. His face wasn't that memorable, but the shrewdness of his stare certainly was. So was his silver-capped walking stick. For the second time, Kit felt as though that piercing stare could fish deep into his soul and dredge up all kinds of shameful secrets swimming about at the bottom. The gentleman nodded over Kit's shoulder and the swarthy man relaxed his grip.

'Could I possibly be addressing Ashentoth, demon of the underworld?' The gentleman smirked.

Kit considered denying it. He opened his mouth but closed it again.

'Answer!' the man behind growled, shoving him hard in the kidneys.

'Yes,' Kit said in a small voice. 'I'm sorry. 'Twas only a jest. I won't do it again ever, I swear.'

The gentleman laughed, his eyes dancing with merriment. 'Oh, a jest it certainly was. I've not witnessed such an impressive performance for many a day. As for not doing it again, well, that depends on you. But, I can't keep calling you Ashentoth now, can I? What is your real name?'

'Tom,' said Kit.

'Real name?' The gentleman leant forward, suddenly serious. He thrust the cold silver ball handle of the stick hard under Kit's cheekbone while there came another sharp prod from behind.

'Kit.'

'Good.' The gentleman nodded. He removed the cane and his smile reappeared. 'Now I know yours, Kit, I shall tell you mine. I am Lord Colewich and I live in a large, rather beautiful house over there. Do you see the stone lions at the gate?' Kit followed the direction in which his Lordship was pointing and nodded. A pair of white stone lions flanked an impressive set of iron gates, though from where he was standing, he couldn't see the house. 'I could have asked Pinches to bring you there but that would have given you too much advantage. You see, I have a small job for you, a job that relies not upon your acting skills but certain other skills you certainly possess. Do it well and you shall be rewarded handsomely, Kit.'

This was such a different outcome from the one Kit had been expecting, he stared from Lord Colewich to the gates and lions and back again several times.

'You're a thief, Kit, first and foremost, yes? A thief? You're small, you're quick, you're silent and you can find your way into a house and through all the tiny little spaces, can't you?' Colewich tapped his stick on the wooden floor of the box as though to wake Kit from a dream. Had this been a trap after all? Should Kit agree with his Lordship? He didn't have to. Colewich wasn't waiting for a reply. 'Here's what I want you to do. Tonight, at midnight, I want you to break into my house. I won't tell you how, I just want you to find a way in and meet me in the library. Do you understand?'

Kit didn't really. His Lordship's request was bizarre.

'If you don't come tonight, Kit, I will contact my good, if misguided friend Mr. Steen and tell him he has been hoodwinked. He's bound to be upset and he's a Justice of the Peace you know, a very important man. Wherever you dwell in that building, you'll be flushed out. Meanwhile Pinches here, together with some friends of his, are going to keep an eye on your street, so there's no escape. You'll be taken and hung as a petty thief. Do you understand me, Kit?'

Although stunned, Kit managed to nod and say, 'You… you wish me to break into your house at midnight? And meet you in the library?'

'That's right. You think you can do it?'

'Yes, sir.'

'Then we have a deal.' Beneath Colewich's confident air, Kit detected relief. 'Pinches will return you home and I will meet you tonight as we've arranged. Oh, and you can't tell anyone about this. Not a soul, right?' Without waiting for a reply, his Lordship waved the stick out of the window and the two chairmen jumped to their duty, positioned themselves between the handles at the front and back, lifted the sedan chair and began to walk off in the direction of the gates and lions. Lord Colewich nodded once more at Kit before closing the velvet curtain with the ball of his cane.

'Come on you.' Pinches shook Kit roughly by the arm. 'Back to Portland Street. I've a colleague waiting to take over while I gets me breakfast.'

CHAPTER 4

Kit was still shaking as he climbed through the boarded hole which connected with one of the chimney breasts. The events of the afternoon, the fear and the shame of being marched through the streets, had torn his nerves to ribbons. The attic seemed gloomier than usual, lit by the few faint rays of light stealing through gaps between the tiles. When he saw Gabe, Kit recalled the small bottle still strapped to his chest, the medicine for which he had risked everything. He helped raise Gabe up and encouraged him to take a swig of the medicine, but the patient broke into an uncontrollable coughing fit which sent the brown mixture running down his chin. Kit could have cried but he gave up trying to catch the precious liquid and held Gabe until the coughing subsided, praying as ever that no one below might hear. It was unlikely the busy servants would be in their chambers by day, but you never knew. They wouldn't believe it was rats coughing their lungs up. Gabe eventually managed to swallow a little of the medicine before slumping back on the bed.

'What's wrong?' he mouthed, perturbed by Kit's silence.

'Nothing.'

'What's wrong?'

Kit put his head in his hands. He told the whole story

before he could stop himself. '…So you see, I have to go back to that house at midnight. One of his Lordship's men is outside all the time, watching. He's bound to follow me.'

'If it weren't for me, you could find a way to escape from them,' Gabe made a huge effort to whisper hoarsely. 'Why don't you just go, Kit?'

Kit stared at him in horror. 'I'd never leave you, you know that!' he said fiercely. 'Don't you ever think I would! It was a shock, that's all, being caught in the street, I didn't know what was happening.' He tried softening his tone. 'Look Gabe, it seems like this Lord Colewich means what he says. He wants me to do this one small job, dunno why, but he says he'll pay handsomely. I don't think he gives a damn about what's been going on at Steen's, or he'd have said something last night, wouldn't he?'

Gabe was shaking his head, only slightly but Kit took his meaning.

'I won't lie, we're in a tight spot,' Kit went on. 'But it'll come right, you'll see. Leave it to me. All you must do is concentrate on getting well. This medicine cures everything and especially what you've got, that's what the apothecary told me again this very morning. When Lord Colewich pays up, we'll buy more. And I won't perform at Steen's again, to be on the safe side.'

All afternoon, Kit cursed himself for telling Gabe what was going on. He didn't want him to worry. Gabe took a little more of the food from the night before, a few more sips of water. The rest of the time he slept, moaning from time to time. Kit hoped he wasn't troubled in his dreams but more than anything, he hoped the medicine would soon start to work.

Kit removed the tiles as it was another warm evening. Around ten o'clock, or so he judged by the noise of patrons leaving the theatres, he slipped from the attic. Outside, he spotted Colewich's man but held his nerve and didn't run. When he reached the street of the gates and lions, the church clock was telling a quarter to eleven, so he sat on the wall in the shadow of some young ash trees, to avoid the attentions of the nightwatchman. He waited. The man trailing him sat some distance away. When the clock chimed half past eleven, Kit jumped down and made for the house without so much as glancing at the fellow. This was one job he was keen to be over and done with.

For the first time, Kit could see the house itself, standing at the end of a fine garden of lawns and box bushes which were trimmed to look like obelisks and castles. The gates weren't locked but entering from the front was something Kit would never do. Also, he spotted two enormous hounds lying asleep between the bushes, one on either side of the central path. The chains attached to their collars were long enough for them to attack anyone coming up the path. Perhaps Lord Colewich had other traps set for Kit and if he was going to succeed in reaching the library, he should continue to take less obvious routes.

Kit walked past the gates and stopped at a passageway running between other, humbler-looking houses and parallel to the side of Colewich's house. He turned down the passageway and before long it divided. Kit took the right-hand branch which led to a small, neglected yard. Ahead stood a wall, above which he could see the roof of Colewich's house. Kit climbed the wall and found himself overlooking the side yard of the house, an area used by servants. Down below, a door which probably led to the kitchens had been left open. Just like the unlocked gates, it was another invitation Kit thought it best to ignore. Should he find any back windows open, he wasn't going to waste time exploring the possibility of entering those either. Instead, Kit walked along the top of the wall until he came to another, running at a right angle and joining the house, the purpose of which was to separate the side yard from the fancy front garden. Kit got to the house and began to climb, giving thanks for the moonlight which helped him find the best hand and footholds. Having shinned up a few feet of drainpipe, he stretched out to balance his left foot on the triangular porch capping the door and, gripping onto the brickwork, slid his whole body across to balance on the porch. Being careful took time but he couldn't help that. Sweat trickled down his brow. Inch by inch, Kit made his way up the side of the house like a creeping bat, from drainpipe to windowsill to balcony until he arrived at a section of roof where there was a small skylight. He prised the skylight open with his fingertips and squeezed through.

Kit landed on the squeaky wooden boards of a narrow corridor in what he guessed were the servants' quarters. Immediately, he backed into the shadows and held his breath but there was no movement behind the closed doors and no sound of voices. No one had been disturbed. He tiptoed to one end of the corridor and opened the door a chink. Inside was a small bedchamber but its window shutters were open and the bed was empty. Closing the door, he tiptoed to the other end of the corridor and when he opened that door, he found what he was seeking.

It was a landing overlooking a grand hallway with a panoramic staircase, a forest of twisted wooden spindles. The whole place smelt of lavender and beeswax. Never in his life had he trodden on carpets so thick he felt he was sinking but an even stranger sensation was the mighty heartbeat which resonated through the house. Even the tapestries on the walls and drapes at the windows thrummed to its steady beat; he could feel it in his fingertips as he stroked the rich cloth. Kit crept down the stairs and at the bottom, came upon the source of the sound: an enormous longcase clock at least twice the size of any he had seen before. It was emitting a beat so strong, the vibrations passed right through his body, demanding his own pulse fall in time with it. He couldn't shake off the sense that this clock was what was keeping the house alive and if it ever stopped, the whole building would drop down dead. As he passed the clock, it struck a quarter to midnight.

Kit had no idea where he might find the library. He tried the doors on the ground floor, but they were all locked. He was just about to go back upstairs when he noticed a small shadow flitting along the skirting board. It was a mouse. Kit was touched by the sight of the small, lowly creature, unworthy to set so much as a foot in this grand house yet having the nerve to do so. Not knowing which direction to take, he decided to follow the mouse who seemed quite at home. It ran to the back of the hallway and disappeared under an arch. Kit followed, turned a corner and descended the stairs to the kitchens. All at once, an almighty clattering crash bit into the air like acid on metal and echoed for several seconds. Tiny as the mouse was, it had somehow set off the trap which had been teetering above the door Kit had seen from the outside, the one opening onto the yard. Yet again, he had been right not to take the obvious way in. Spears, swords, daggers and even an axe had dropped onto the stone flagged floor. Anyone coming through that door would have been killed or grievously wounded. Anyone? No, Kit knew the trap had been meant for him. He almost cried with joy when the mouse re-emerged from the pile of weapons and ran past him unhurt. The noise should have woken the entire household, but no one had come running and Kit guessed that Colewich must have banished his servants from the house for the night. But why would he? Why should Kit breaking into his house be such a major event that his Lordship needed to be rid of his servants? Why set traps at all if he wanted the house broken into? Although he felt sick with fear, it was too late to back out. He must find the library, meet the odd and perverse Lord Colewich, hopefully for the last time, and get out of the house as quickly as he could. If he got paid, so much the better. If he could escape with his life, that was enough.

CHAPTER 5

By the time he got back to the hallway, Kit's fear had turned to anger. One day, he would learn a trade and be an honest man like his father, living the kind of life he had been born to, not skulking around in the shadows. One day, he would be able to walk through any front door with his head held high and strange devils like Colewich wouldn't get the chance to play games with him. That's what he'd decided this was, a game. In some sick, twisted way, Colewich was enjoying himself by making a poor boy fear for his life. Now Kit was carrying several of the more useful looking weapons that had fallen onto the kitchen floor. He was armed and more than ready to defend himself.

The heartbeat of the house thumped louder than ever but something else was different too: the fanlight window above a door to his right was glowing. Someone must have lit a candle inside the room and guessing that this was the library where his Lordship awaited, Kit approached warily. He raised the tapestries and tapped along the wall but there were no loose panels. There seemed no way into the room except through the door, unless he was prepared to return to the garden and deal with the hounds, which he wasn't. Also, he wanted the job over and done with as soon as possible.

When he'd tried this door five minutes earlier, it had been locked. Now he put all but one of the weapons down on the black and white tiled floor and rested the tip of the longest spear on the door handle. Keeping well back, he forced the handle down. It gave and the door creaked open. The light inside was peculiar. Smoke-like curls of it were radiating from some source he couldn't see. Kit jabbed the end of the spear into the room several times but nothing happened. He poked it up above the doorframe but there didn't seem to be any traps. Fetching a brass candlestick from the hall table, he hurled it into the room. The candlestick clanged across the tiles but nothing fell on top of it or exploded beneath it. Preparing to enter, Kit sorted through his weaponry. He tucked a dagger into his belt and picked up a sword with his right hand, keeping the spear in his left.

Kit had never been in such a large, impressive room which took up the whole of that side of the ground floor. The shelves upon the walls were lined with row upon row of books, more than he could ever have imagined being written in the history of the world. The rich smell of well-handled leather mingled with the lavender and beeswax from the hall. The only wall spaces not smothered in books were at either end of the room, where two enormous arched windows faced one another. Although the curls of light barely reached these windows and their colours were dim, Kit could make out the stained-glass picture in each: the one ahead was a cheerful sunrise with swallows skimming the air and rabbits cavorting on a daisy strewn hillside. By contrast, the window beside the door showed a gloomy sunset, the dying of the day, with flitting bats and snakes twisting around gnarled tree roots.

All this was surprising, as was the absence of Lord Colewich, but most surprising of all was what lay on the table in the middle of the room. A book lay beside a wooden box, like a Bible box. In size and shape, the book was like any from those on the library shelves, but it was also very different. This book was the source of the strange light he had seen from outside. Its front cover was open, revealing blank endpapers and light-curls drifted upwards and outwards from it at measured intervals, like wind from a blacksmith's bellows. Kit had the strangest impression that the room was expanding and contracting along with it. If the longcase clock was the heart of the house, the library was its lungs.

The beating of the clock and the breathing of the room had a hypnotic effect upon Kit and he was drawn to the table and the book which contained such energy and mystery. At the same time, some small part of his brain still held fast to the notion that Colewich wanted him to find it, probably wanted him to turn the pages and this was enough to make him fear it. He circled the table three times. Would the book burn his fingers? Touching it with a weapon seemed disrespectful. In the end, Kit stood before the book. He placed the sword and spear down on the table on either side of it. He pulled the sleeve of his shirt over the fingers of his right hand and rested his left hand on the handle of the dagger. He stretched towards the book and with a quick movement of one protruding finger, flipped over some pages. Light streamed out in all directions, flooding the room as in the moments following an explosion. The light battered Kit backwards but he gripped the edge of the table and squinted to see what was on the exposed pages. Nothing was visible until the light evened out and settled.

There was a face on the page, an old woman's face. White hair poked out from the dingy scarf covering her head and wrapped around her throat. Her cheeks were raw and ruddy, as though she was used to a hard, outdoor life and the paper was rough and stained brown at the edges. It took a few moments for Kit to register that the woman was looking at him just as though she were before him in the flesh. Her eyes blinked and her scowl deepened. Kit's whole body shook, and his teeth chattered with fear. He didn't know what on earth he was looking at. Was the woman standing beneath the table, with her head caught in the book or wearing it like a collar? For a couple of seconds, he broke eye contact with her to check but there was nothing beneath the table. He waved his hand but there were no obvious mirrors. The woman followed Kit's movements with her eyes as he tilted his head and looked sideways at the page to check it was made of paper. It absolutely was.

The blinking and staring was bad enough but when

the woman opened her mouth to speak, Kit bolted for the door. The croaky voice called him back to the table:

'Whoever are you?' the woman said. 'And where's he?'

'Who?' asked Kit.

'The old 'un. The usual 'un. Oh, I'm heartily glad thou art not him. Fie upon him, I hates him. Goin' on and on about his odjek. How do I know where his precious odjek is? I told him, I did. "Leave a poor ol' body alone," says I. He don't let up, though, do he? Askin', askin' all times o' day an' night.'

The woman carried on in the same manner, moaning about this other person. It was difficult to understand everything she said but Kit made out enough. Even though she didn't name Colewich, Kit guessed this was who she must mean. Had he the power of speech, Kit would have agreed with the woman regarding his detestable character. At another time and place, he and she could have compared their experiences, even had a bit of a laugh about his Lordship. Kit was sure he'd be able to do an impression of the man, his sardonic look and slightly lisping way of speaking.

But talk to a book? What was Kit thinking? The old woman's face was just some trick, like one of Chi-Keen's tricks and he had nearly fallen for it. What if he turned another page, would there be any more faces?

Kit tightened his grip upon the handle of the dagger and prepared to turn the page when a hand reached over his shoulder and closed the book, resting firmly upon the cover with flexing fingers and cutting off what the woman was saying. The room grew dim. Kit looked up at Lord Colewich. His eyes were cold; he wasn't smiling now. The clock in the hall chimed midnight.

'That's as much as you need see,' said Colewich, who was holding a candle in his other hand. For once his Lordship was dressed casually, in a waistcoat and breeches and had removed his wig to reveal a head of mown grey stubble. Colewich placed the candle on the table and flicked his hand dismissively. As instructed, Kit stepped back and watched as Colewich placed the book gently inside the wooden box and closed the lid. Colewich seemed to read his mind and turning to Kit, said: 'This box locks itself. There is only one key with which to open it and I keep it upon me at all times, so don't get any ideas.' He held the candle below Kit's chin almost too close, and the shadows it cast accentuated the cruelty of his face which appeared to float, disembodied upon the air. 'You've proved yourself tonight, Kit. If you'd been killed getting into my house, I would have known you weren't up to the job which still awaits. Oh, you are very good.' This was said in such a way that it seemed less a compliment to Kit and more a boast about his own ability in choosing a marvellous thief.

'I don't understand,' said Kit. 'This – tonight – was what you asked me to do. This was the small job.'

Colewich cocked a half smile. 'This was only "part one" of the job, Kit. Tonight has been partly about testing you, like I said, but 'tis also a way of showing you the book. If I'd simply described it, you would not have believed me. You had to see it for yourself. Amazing, I think you'll agree.'

Kit couldn't agree. He couldn't speak a word. Where was this going? He felt as though he were standing on the edge of a cliff in the dark. He considered the wisdom of making a run for it, but escape was impossible because of what would happen to Gabe if he didn't return to Portland Street.

''Tis a very old book and I haven't had it long. I collect books, Kit. This is a book I had heard of but never imagined I would get the chance to own. You see, even important and extremely rich men like me have ambitions which are not always fulfilled.' Colewich was speaking softly as though, in the intimacy leant by darkness, there was something close to his heart he wanted to share with Kit.

'In the end, I tracked the book down to a Clerkenwell bookshop but eight streets from here. Eight streets, can you imagine? 'Twas in Grey's Inn Lane, in the possession of a bookseller named Polley. Well, I paid handsomely for the book and would have paid twice, three times as much, if truth be told but there was a problem. Is…a problem. The book is incomplete. There's one page missing.'

'Missing?' Kit's stomach muscles tightened with fear. The face of Colewich continued to float above him.

'Well, yes and no. Missing from the book but I do know its whereabouts. That's where you come in. Polley has it. He would not part with it for any amount of money, I have no idea why. I haven't even seen the page, but no doubt 'tis similar to the others, including the one you just saw. Polley has it somewhere in his shop, or where he lives above the shop. He boasted about it to me, the fool, or I never should have known. You have to find it for me, Kit. I must have that missing page or all is lost.' Colewich was growing angrier and angrier, his teeth were clenched and tiny, hellish flames burned in his eyes. Kit hoped they were reflections of the candle flame because at that moment, he could have believed he was staring at the Devil himself. Colewich caught Kit by the arm and shook him violently, as though he had hold of the hated Polley. Spittle burst from his mouth as his words poured out in a frenzy, 'I must have it. You understand? You understand now what you're to do?'

'Get off me!' Kit wriggled from Colewich's grasp. His Lordship ran his free hand over his face and seemed to collect himself.

'Very well,' panted Colewich. He staggered backwards and sat heavily on one of the armchairs which sat around the room like spectators with their hands on their knees. There were beads of sweat running down his Lordship's brow. He took a handkerchief from the pocket of his breeches and wiped them away. 'Of course, you've never been schooled. Can you read?'

He looked up at Kit. Kit shook his head.

'...But if I describe where the shop is, you'll be able to find it?'

Kit nodded, although he didn't really want to.

'I'll give you a few days, Kit. I must have the missing page in my possession before too long. I must. I needn't tell you what will happen if you fail me but there will be no failure in this matter. *When* you succeed, you shall have a purse of gold and whatever else your heart desires. Bring me the missing page and the hard times will be over for you, Kit. I don't care what you have to do, just make sure you return with it.'

Polley had already spent a sizeable chunk of the small fortune he'd received from Colewich, if the shop was anything to go by. It was the brightest and most fashionable establishment in the street and when Kit arrived, a signwriter had just finished painting the bookseller's name in gold letters above the bow window. As soon as he removed his ladder, the crowd surged forward, and Kit had to push between them to get to the front, only to find a row of books staring back at him, like an audience. The words embossed upon their leather spines meant nothing to Kit, but he knew quality when he saw it.

It was easy to pick Polley out from amongst his gentlemen customers. He was the neat little man in a powdered bow-and-pig-tail wig, all elbows, lace cuffs and showy hand gestures. He scuttled here and there, offering different volumes up for inspection with a flourish, leading the gentlemen to shelves and presenting them with fine offerings for their perusal. The shop was small but handsomely furnished with brocade-covered armchairs and a round table where some of the larger books lay open, displaying illustrations of great country houses. The walls were painted primrose yellow and in the frieze between the top of the shelves and the ceiling, a row of chubby cherubs played fiddles and scattered rose petals. Kit had the impression that the four unsmiling customers were keener to be seen by the crowds than they were to buy books. Even so, Polley was doing his best to get them interested.

An errand boy entered the shop whistling and the bookseller pulled him into a side passage although the two could still be seen from the window. The boy gave Polley a package and shrugged his shoulders, whereupon the bookseller raised the package and whacked him across the head with it. The crowd around Kit fell about laughing. The boy ran out of the shop rubbing his head, red faced and fighting back tears. He paused at the entrance and seemed to be deciding whether to re-enter or not. In the end, embarrassed by comments from the crowd, he turned tail and legged it down the street. It crossed Kit's mind that this was a boy who might be bribed for information, if he hated his employer. On the other hand, he couldn't risk Polley getting wind of the fact that someone was interested in the missing page. For the time being, Kit would go it alone.

Despite the front of the shop being so smart, it was no surprise to find the back so poorly built and it didn't take long for Kit to find a way into the building, through a broken panel at the bottom of a doorway up the side alley. He got into Polley's attic through the chimney flue. Finding the missing page was not going to be so easy. Kit began by making a small hole in the plaster ceiling and balancing on the joists on either side of the hole, put his eye to it. Of course, by day the bookseller was downstairs in his shop so there was no activity in the bedchamber into which Kit peered. Also, a large four-poster bed took up most of the room and its wooden canopy obscured much of Kit's view. The bed and room seemed grand enough to belong to Polley himself, rather than a servant, which was something at least. Kit spent most of that day in the attic trying to work out what to do and even ate his dinner up there: a meat pie from a stall in the street. As he ate, he thought about the events of the night before. If only he could persuade himself he'd been dreaming but he knew he hadn't been. The speaking face seemed beyond explanation. For the first time Kit wondered whether magic might really exist, after all?

The next day, after checking that Polley was busy in the shop, Kit took a huge risk by lowering himself from the attic trapdoor onto the landing and stealing into the bedchamber. The bookseller had spent money here as well: the bed was hung with rich red damask drapes and the rest of the furniture was tasteful, with brass handles that gleamed. Interestingly only one drawer was locked, and this was in the bedside table. It was a large, ornate padlock which didn't really belong to the drawer. Kit tried but failed to force the lock and searched for the key without success. Gabe knew how to pick locks, but Kit wasn't as good at it and in any case, the padlock looked too complicated. If he had to bet on it, this was the place where Polley was hiding the precious page he wouldn't part with for love nor money.

Kit waited until evening to see if he was right, hoping Polley might unlock the drawer before going to bed. He wasn't disappointed. Disgusted, yes, but not disappointed. Although he couldn't see much, he heard everything: Polley muttering to himself as he changed into his nightclothes, the rattle of the padlock and the squeak of the opening drawer. There was a flash of light, which died down quickly and Polley began to speak. It was silly old love talk, about how much he had missed this person all day and how much he wanted to kiss her now. Another voice began to protest: a young woman's voice. Kit imagined the speaker must be a face upon the missing page, although the voice was so three dimensional, there might easily have been a real girl in the room. Kit listened and felt like he was going to be sick. The girl was pleading with Polley, insisting that she didn't want to be kissed and it sounded like she was putting up some kind of struggle. When Kit had first come to London as little more than a child, he soon discovered that powerful men could have the cruellest desires and Polley reminded him of them. Although he had managed to escape the worst, friends of his had not been so lucky.

The girl he couldn't see kept asking to return to her village: why was she being kept here against her will? She wanted to return to the people she knew, to the place she knew. The protests carried on, punctuated by the nauseating slurping, kissing sounds until eventually, Polley returned the object to the drawer, locked it and fell asleep. Having searched the entire room that afternoon, Kit guessed Polley was another man who kept the key to his secrets on his person at all times. In the silence, in the dark, Kit breathed deeply, trying to steer a safe passage through his own bad memories and vowing he would help this girl if he could.

On his way home through the darkened streets, Kit found himself grabbed by Pinches, which wasn't totally unexpected. From what he said, Pinches knew that his master had instructed Kit to find something, but it was clear that he didn't know what that something was. Perhaps this put him in a worse temper than usual because he squeezed Kit's arm harder than ever, making him yelp with pain. Kit had to swear that he was closing in on the object and would have something to give Lord Colewich soon.

Kit really was desperate to get on and find the missing page, also because Gabe was in such a bad way. When he returned to their attic that evening, he thought his darling looked paler and more feverish than ever. Whiting's medicine hadn't worked and if anything, seemed to have made him worse. 'Whatever your heart desires', that's what Colewich had promised. Well, once he'd delivered the page to his Lordship, Kit was going to ask for a safe passage out of the attic for Gabe and a soft bed in a respectable house in which he could recover with the best of doctors to attend to him. Time was running out. Kit had to find the missing page without delay.

He'd told Gabe about the book, finding it impossible to keep the information to himself. Gabe had laughed, or what passed for a laugh these days, and treated what Kit was telling him as just another story. Kit hadn't gone into details about the last part of the job and Gabe hadn't asked any more questions. Kit encouraged him to buck up and not worry, assuring him that everything would be all right again when he got paid.

Kit had a plan and the next morning, he rifled through what remained of Chi-Keen's props for what he needed to carry it out. In his act, Chi-Keen had made objects float in the air but only when Kit got hold of the props did he find the invisible hooks and strings and realise how the trick was done. He also discovered the phosphorescent paint which gave the objects a ghostly glow when the lights went down, and some of the objects themselves. Best of all was a small, stuffed monkey with yellow glass eyes and a terrible, toothy grin. Its limbs were articulated so it would jiggle around on the strings in a ghastly fashion.

Kit spent most of that day creeping around Polley's bedchamber and the attic, rigging up a nightmare for the evening to come, making small holes all over the ceiling and threading them with invisible strings which he then attached to various objects in the room below. He was going to haunt Polley. He would wait until the bookseller unlocked the drawer at bedtime, then frighten him out of his wits and seize his chance to steal the missing page. It would serve the bookseller right and, after what Kit had witnessed the night before, he would be doing the young woman a favour.

Kit listened as Polley prepared for bed, hoping it was his custom to take the page from the drawer each evening. With relief, he heard the drawer open and saw the flash of light. Just as before, the bookseller talked the most appalling pretend baby talk to the girl, peppered with foul kisses. Kit winced with horror and embarrassment. As before, the girl was angry, ordering him to stop and insisting upon returning home. The creak of the bed-ropes told Kit that the man had lain down and he guessed he'd placed the page on the pillow beside him. He had to act quickly, before Polley grew sleepy and locked it away again.

Kit felt his way across the joists and pulled hard on a string threaded through one of the holes in the chamber ceiling. He heard a candlestick jump off the mantelpiece and because he'd wrapped the string around its base several times, felt it spin in the air. There was a shriek from below and he continued pulling the string, imagining the spinning candlestick floating higher and higher. Kit had painted the back of the candlestick with phosphorescent paint so Polley would see it flickering, appearing then disappearing. Finally, Kit let go of the string altogether and heard the candlestick crash down upon the hearth. It was important to keep the shocks going so he moved swiftly but with care from joist to joist, pulling the strings. Polley continued to cry out in terror as all manner of objects began to jump from their places and rise to the ceiling, emitting a pale, ghostly, flickering light, before dropping to the ground. Now it was time for one final fright that should send him racing from the room and down the stairs, after which Kit would jump through the trapdoor, race to the bedchamber and grab the missing page. He caught hold of a handful of strings and pulled. The monkey which had been resting on the top edge of the four-poster bed just out of sight, lowered itself in front of Polley and began its skittering dance. The bookseller gave a bloodcurdling scream, and Kit heard him leap from the bed, but with dismay he also heard the drawer being yanked open. After all Kit's efforts, Polley was about to lock the precious page away again. Kit didn't know what to do. He was balancing on a single joist, his arms spread wide, holding several strings at once. He lost concentration, took a sideways step and one foot smashed through the lath and plaster. Before he knew what was happening, his whole body followed, crashing through the ceiling but the top of the four-poster bed broke his fall. Kit was covered in white plaster from head to foot. For the first time, he came face to face with Polley who was clutching the page to his scrawny chest. He looked as though he were about to die of fright.

Though shocked, Kit was unhurt and his Ashentoth performance kicked in automatically. Crouching on the edge of the canopy like a cat preparing to spring, he opened his eyes and mouth frighteningly wide, a colourful contrast to the rest of him, and roared at the top of his voice:

'POLLEY!'

That did it. The page fell to the floor and the bookseller raced to the door, flung it open, blundered along the corridor and tumbled down the stairs. Kit jumped down, snatched up the page and rolled it into a tube without even looking at it. He tucked it down his shirt and there was no time to do anything about the girl's cries of protest. Flinging back the shutters, Kit threw up the sash window and swung himself out into the night, his route down to the street already planned.

CHAPTER 7

The girl's protests continued and even though Kit
stuck to the shadows, the noise carried, and the front
of his shirt glowed as though he were trying to conceal
twenty candles beneath it. He begged her to be quiet, but
this only seemed to make matters worse. Pinches wasn't
around but Kit was right to be fearful. The main streets
were still full of carriages, mainly rich, spoilt young men
who spent each night roaming from one gambling den
to another, while the backstreets were full of dangers,
drunken gangs and desperate thieves. The girl's cries
were bound to attract someone's attention before too
long. Should he run straight to Lord Colewich's house or
make a small detour and rest at Portland Street? Back at
the attic he could wrap the page up in one of Chi-Keen's
scarves to muffle the sound before continuing on his
way. It didn't take Kit long to decide what to do.

'Gabriel? Gabe! You won't believe what I've got here.'
Kit was so glad to have reached the attic safely, he was
nearly exploding with delight at the thought of showing
Gabe the page and admitting that magic did exist after
all. When Gabe didn't move, Kit decided to let him
sleep. He was burning with his own curiosity to see the
page properly and also wanted to try and calm the girl.

Kit drew the rolled page from his shirt and flattened
it out on his side of the bed. A flash of light filled the

attic and Kit shut his eyes for fear of being blinded but the light died almost immediately. For the first time he saw the girl's face.

It was certainly the sweetest girl's face he had ever beheld. She blinked at him with clear green eyes brightened by tears of frustration. This was probably the kind of girl's face he'd heard ballad sellers singing about. Her cheeks were like roses and her mouth looked as though it were made for eating strawberries. Her dark, flowing hair was lost in the edges of the page and delicate freckles spread over her nose and cheeks. Kit only had an instant to admire her before she started shouting: 'Who art thou? And to where hast thou brought me? I demand to go home, right now.'

'Hush, hush.' Kit put his finger to his lips. 'I'll take you home, first thing tomorrow morning, I promise. I know where the book is.'

'Book?' the girl cried. 'Of what book dost thou speak? I will go back to my village! Why talk in such riddles?'

'Please be still,' said Kit. 'My friend is sick and you'll wake him up.'

The girl stopped for a moment, her mouth twitching as she stared distrustfully at Kit. 'Don't start with thy kissing and such. I givest thou warning, I bite,' she said.

Kit was flummoxed.

'I will bite,' she shouted. 'If thou dost try and kiss me. Where be that other man? Fie upon him, I'd like to kill him.'

'No, no…' said Kit. 'I don't want to kiss you, really

I don't. I saw what Polley was doing. How horrible that was for you. I would never take you back to that old devil, I swear.'

The girl swallowed, and new tears of relief began to flow. 'Just as well. I cannot bite, not properly so it hurts. I did try. I did.'

'Don't upset yourself,' said Kit. 'I was sent to fetch you. First thing in the morning, I'll take you back to the boo– I mean I'll take you home.'

'Back to my village?' she said.

'To your village, yes.' Kit didn't want to distress the girl who obviously didn't realise she was only a page in a book. Maybe being in the book was like being in a village to her? There was nothing about this situation that made any sense, so it seemed best to agree with her.

The girl started to relax a little. She was looking around and her eyes fell on Gabe.

'That's thy sick friend? What hath he? Plague?'

'I think not. 'Tis a fever that comes and goes. I don't like to wake him, but we must leave soon, and I know he'd like to see you.' Kit leaned over. 'Gabriel? Gabe!' he raised his voice but there was no movement from the bed. Gabe lay facing the other way. Kit got up and walked around the bed. He crouched and gently shook Gabe's shoulder.

There was no movement. Kit put his hand on Gabe's cheek. It was cold. He put his hand on Gabe's chest. There was no rise and fall. He put his cheek to his mouth. There was no breath.

'Oh no. Please God no!' Kit whispered. He sank to his knees. He was too late. It was all too late.

'Whatever's wrong?' said the girl but for a long time, Kit was crying too much to speak. She guessed why. 'Oh, God rest his soul,' she said. 'I'm sorry for thee, truly I am.'

'No, no, no,' said Kit. He started to cry, to howl Gabe's name over and over. He buried his head in the rough blankets to stifle the sounds he was making, for fear of waking the servants sleeping below. Then again, what did that matter now? What did anything matter? What did he have in the world without Gabe? It was too much. The girl tried her best to offer words of comfort and condolence but for a long time, he couldn't bear to listen to her. He cried and cried until he was cried out of the bigger tears.

When Kit raised his head again, he found the girl waiting patiently. 'Prithee, thou dost not cry that way for a friend?' She spoke from the other side of the bed, softly and with great compassion.

'You're right,' whispered Kit. 'More than a friend. Much more than a friend.'

'A brother?'

'More than that.'

'Thou lovest him, in thy deepest heart?' she said, and Kit nodded. 'It be a natural thing, faith. We have our own paths to follow in life, so Grandda's always taught me.' Instead of commenting further, she began to talk about herself. She told Kit about her mother, who had died when she was small and her father who had died before she was born. After a while Kit told her how he'd come to London and how meeting Gabe had saved his life. His revelation that he and Gabe had been thieves came as a shock to her.

'Thou dost not look like a thief,' she marvelled.

'I'm not really,' said Kit. It took him five times as long to say anything while he was still sobbing but he wanted to explain. 'I hate being a thief. I'm going to jack it in, soon as I can. I can't stay here any more. Soon as I get my reward for finding you, I'll leave London, buy some tools and set up in a small way as a wheelwright. An honest man. I still remember some of what my Da taught me. I always meant to do it, only my dream was to take Gabe with me. We'd talked it over, before he got sick. He never hated thieving as much as me, but he said he was willing. That's the life I was meant for, not this.'

'There'll be a burial for Gabe?' asked the girl.

Kit looked at Gabe's poor scrap of a body. That wasn't him any more, Kit knew that. The body was like the house where Gabe had lived, in his short time on Earth. Now he had gone to the Maker, he might look different Kit supposed. On the other hand, when Kit left the attic the next morning, he didn't intend coming back and there would need to be some kind of funeral to mark poor Gabe's passing. Kit recalled how Gabe had loved looking up at the stars, even during the worst part of his illness. Suddenly he knew what he was going to do. He explained it all to the girl and then, softly and slowly because he was still numb with grief, he spent the next couple of hours getting everything ready. He would lay Gabe's empty body to rest outside on the roof.

Shaking and sobbing, Kit prepared a place beside the stone gutter at the back of the house, sheltered from view by the balustrade. He wrapped Gabe's body in Chi-Keen's long, brightly coloured silk scarves, tying them firmly in place so he looked like a swaddled baby with his face alone showing. Slowly and gently, he pulled the body which seemed light as a bird, along the boarded joists and through the hole, onto the roof. Carefully he laid Gabe to rest, facing the sky, and placed more scarves below his head like a pillow. Kit wanted to imagine that Gabe's soul was now up there, riding the comet for real through the vast mysteries of space and up to heaven. He tucked Chi-Keen's colourful paper flowers around the body, so they were held in place by the folds of the scarves. He was glad that Gabe looked so colourful and finally at peace. Just as the sun was rising, Kit went to fetch the girl and holding up her page, Kit knelt beside Gabe for the last time. Kit sobbed his way through a story from the Bible, about Daniel in the lion's den, which didn't seem particularly suitable for a funeral, but it was the only one he could remember properly. Even though his heart was breaking, he said a prayer, asking the Maker to look after Gabe's soul and both he and the girl said 'Amen'. The ceremony over, they left Gabe and went back inside. Kit replaced the tiles.

CHAPTER 8

'We're here,' whispered Kit.

They were at the end of the passage next to Colewich's yard. Colewich had told Kit to use the side door upon his return; there would be no more traps. Although he didn't trust Colewich, under the circumstances Kit didn't see why he shouldn't believe him.

He had barely begun to cry all the tears he had for Gabe and there was a tight knot in his chest, but he had a job to finish and there would be plenty of time for grieving after that. As terrible as grief was, he knew deep down that it wouldn't kill him. There was a toughness about Kit which he'd learnt from all the terrible experiences of his young life. He had promised this girl he would return her to her village, as she called it, and he would keep that promise. With the purse of gold as his reward, he would then leave London for good and give up being a stinking thief once and for all. A few of his worldly possessions lay tied in a bundle at his feet; he would never return to the Portland Street attic again.

'We're here,' he whispered louder. There was no response from inside his shirt. He and the girl had said one lot of goodbyes before leaving the attic but now he was on the point of never seeing her again, he felt the need to speak to her once more. He pulled the page from his shirt and unrolled it. The flash of light was not as shocking in the sunlight and the girl looked as though she were just waking.

'We've nearly reached your village,' Kit tried to smile.

The girl smiled back and little lights danced in her eyes. 'Thou art so kind,' she said. 'I thank thee. I never will forget thee... I was going to say thy name, but I know it not.'

'Kit,' said Kit. 'I never knew yours neither.'

'Zannah,' she said. 'Least, that's what they do call me now. Suzannah was my name as a child.'

'I won't see you again, Zannah, but I hope you're happy when you're back among your people.'

'I fear for thee, Kit,' she frowned. 'After Gabe dying and so. It is hard.'

'I'll be all right,' Kit nodded and tried to smile again. 'Well goodbye then, Zannah.'

'Goodbye, Kit.'

It was an odd way to part from someone, particularly one with whom you'd shared such a terrible experience, but Kit rolled up the page again.

A servant answered his knock on the door. She looked Kit up and down disapprovingly then muttered something about his Lordship wanting to speak to callers personally and ushered him inside. Kit followed her up to the hallway. It was strange to be back in Colewich's house in the daytime. The clock seemed normal; there was no thunderous heartbeat making the house vibrate, just a steady tick tock. The servant knocked on the door of a room opposite the library, spoke a few words around the door, then stood aside for Kit to enter. His Lordship was taking his breakfast in this small yellow sitting room and was wearing a long, richly embroidered dressing gown and tasselled cap. He rose the moment he saw Kit and nodded to the servant, who tutted at Kit before leaving.

'Have you got it?' asked Colewich.

Kit nodded and felt inside his shirt. Energy fizzed through his hand as he passed the rolled page to Colewich. Colewich walked to the window, where he unrolled it partway to take a brief look. With a small smile of satisfaction, he rolled it up again briskly and used a key from his pocket to unlock a drawer in the writing desk which stood in the middle of the room. Colewich placed the treasure inside, exchanging it for a small leather purse. He closed and locked the drawer.

'Well done, Kit,' said Lord Colewich, walking around the desk and holding out the purse. 'Here is your payment, gold sovereigns, just as you were promised. Did you have much trouble getting hold of it?'

'A little, sir.'

'Oh well,' Colewich broke into a grin. 'News travels fast. I expect I shall hear something of what happened. You're sure you weren't seen coming here today?'

'No, sir,' Kit couldn't take his eyes off the desk. 'Will she be all right, sir? I mean, you'll return her to that book in your library?'

Lord Colewich raised his eyebrows as though Kit were overstepping the mark. 'Yes,' he said. 'Although whatever I choose to do is no concern of yours. Now mark you, Kit, I have eyes everywhere.' His own eyes narrowed. 'I employ several men like Pinches. If I hear that you have spoken, publicly or privately about this matter to anyone – *anyone* – I shall send them after you. Like a pack of dogs, they will hunt you down, close in on you and rip you apart. Do you understand what I am saying?' He emphasised each word of the question, to hammer it into Kit's brain. 'I don't want you back at Portland Street either. I've changed my mind about that. I don't want you performing for Mr Steen or seeing any of those gentlemen again. Not after this. It would be better if you simply disappeared. You can do that yourself or I can do it for you.'

'I'm leaving London today,' said Kit. He was annoyed. Surely his Lordship owed him a bit more gratitude, after what he'd done?

'Good.' Colewich smiled, gesturing to the purse in Kit's hand. 'And now you have the means to do so. That's it, you may go.'

After this blunt dismissal, Colewich rang a little bell sitting on the breakfast tray. The same servant appeared, and his Lordship returned to his newspaper. Kit tucked the purse down the front of his shirt and was shown out without another word.

Kit hoped Zannah would be all right. He felt dazed as he walked along the busy streets, heading west. With no real plan in mind, he followed Oxford Street to the Tyburn Road and the outskirts of the city, placing one foot heedlessly ahead of the other, each sad step taking him further from the life he'd known. He passed Tyburn tree and its lifeless, hanging bodies as quickly as he could, knowing how lucky he was not to have ended up the same way after all his and Gabe's exploits. At that moment, the knowledge offered no relief. On the other side of Tyburn village, he stopped to rest. He couldn't risk bringing out his sovereigns in such a place, but he still had a few coins from his final evening at Steen's. He bought some slices of meat and a small loaf, which he forced himself to eat although he didn't really want to. The journey ahead was long and he needed to keep up his strength. Barely able to keep his eyes open, Kit fell asleep in the long grass by the side of the road, with the morning sun on his face.

It was late afternoon when he woke, stale and cloth-headed. For a moment, he wondered where he was. Then he remembered and he also remembered that Gabe was dead, and he cried bitterly. He turned his back to the road, even though no one was watching and nobody cared. There were still a few people buying from the carts, mainly travellers about to set foot in London perhaps for the first time. Kit was more than happy to be leaving. He thought about all the times Gabe and he had spent together, good and bad. Lodgings in odd places, escapes from the watchmen, many a freezing night spent on the streets before the wonderful discovery of the Portland Street attic. All the stories and all the plans they had made in that attic, all come to nothing. Kit felt so empty. He knew he would go on missing Gabe wherever he ended up. He wouldn't return to his old village in Kent which held such unhappy memories; no, he would start afresh. The purse of gold was a golden chance, his opportunity to settle down, buy tools and get back to his trade, return to the honest life he longed for. At least his final act in London had been a good one, rescuing Zannah from the clutches of that awful bookseller and making sure she returned safely to her people in the village.

Is that what Kit had done? Had he really returned her to safety?

Ahead, the road ran between the green fields and somewhere along it lay his future, perhaps at a great distance. Behind were the building works on the dusty edge of London. Heaven knew how big this city would become eventually because it was growing so fast, spreading like an infection. Here he was, poised with one foot in the past and one in the future and no one else to care a hang about what might happen to him. When he set off again along that road, there'd be no turning back. Yet there was a niggling something, like a flea jumping around in his brain, causing him to hesitate.

One person had cared, and he would always remember that human warmth at a time when all seemed so bleak. He'd poured his heart out to Zannah and although she was only a face on a piece of paper, she had listened and spoken kindly and lamented with him. When he'd cried over Gabe, she'd offered words of comfort. When she had shed tears, he had promised to get her back to her people.

And what had Kit done? What had he *actually* done? Handed her over to Colewich, one of the most evil-minded men he had ever met, that's what. Not having witnessed Zannah's page being placed in the book, how could he be sure that's what the old devil had done? What if, right at that moment, he was taking the same vile liberties as Polley, kissing her while she pleaded with him to stop, forcing himself upon her in the most disgusting way? For the first time, Kit remembered the old woman in the book. What had she said about Colewich?

I'm heartily glad thou art not him. Fie upon him, I hates him.

It echoed what Zannah herself had said about Polley.

Where is that other man? Fie upon him. I'd like to kill him.

Despite the sunshine which had warmed his tired bones as he'd slept, Kit broke into a cold sweat. What had he done? Was Zannah back in the book or not? If she was suffering because of his mistake, how could he ever forgive himself? From now until the day he died, the not knowing would torment him. He had to go back, just to check, just to reassure himself that all was well. Then he could continue his journey with an easy mind. He had to go back and check.

CHAPTER 9

Under cover of darkness, Kit stuck to the shadows and made sure he wasn't seen approaching Colewich's house. There was no sign of Pinches, but if his Lordship believed he'd seen the last of Kit, his henchman would hardly be lying in wait. It was late enough for the servants to be in bed but one splendid window at the front of the great house was all lit up. Kit knew exactly why the sunrise window was glowing so brightly: Colewich was in his library, studying the book of faces. This wasn't enough for Kit, he had to know for sure that Zannah's page was back inside the book. As soon as he knew that, he would leave without any fuss and retrace his steps to the Tyburn Road.

From across the street, Kit observed the sleeping guard dogs chained up in the front garden. He padded past the gates and ducked down the passageway. After mounting the wall overlooking the side yard, Kit turned left instead of right and once he'd made it over the roof of an outbuilding, found himself in the smaller, back garden which was enclosed on all sides by high walls. There were no dogs round the back and Kit knew the heavy smell of roses and lavender would help disguise his own human scent upon the air.

After scaling a few feet of the back wall of the house, Kit found he could see clearly through the green glass beneath a badger's foot in the sunset window. Colewich was standing with his back to Kit and having a conversation with the open book which lay on the table. The night was still, and Kit could hear some words being spoken. Voices came and went, young and old, male and female, but they all sounded either fearful or complaining. Colewich seemed to be questioning the inhabitants of the book and when he didn't get an answer that satisfied him, he would turn to the next page. All at once, Kit recognised one of the voices as that of the old woman.

'Art thou there again, old goat?' she cried out. 'I've told thee a thousand times, I know not where thy odjek is. Wherefore dost thou ask me agin? I never seen no odjek! Canst not thou give me a bit of peace instead o' askin', askin' the whole time?'

'One day,' Colewich shouted her down, sounding genuinely angry. 'Mark my words you haggish old draggle-tail, I shall find my way into your village, for I know some way exists, and when I do, it will be the worse for you. I shall find the magical object myself rather than relying on a bunch of dullards. And when I do… when I do…' He seemed to be struggling to come up with the worst threat imaginable.

'Stayest thou away from me,' the woman shrieked. 'Go hence and never return! I never met such a saddle-goose lubberwort. Stay away from our village, bobolyne!'

Colewich and the woman continued to trade insults

and if Kit hadn't had his own worries tormenting him, he would have enjoyed the show. It was obvious Colewich wasn't used to being spoken to like this and he was livid. Finally, he cut his losses and turned the page. Some of the people he bullied weren't as good at defending themselves as the old woman and Colewich reduced one or two to tears with his threats. Kit gathered that Colewich had been searching for some magical object since getting hold of the book but was no closer to finding it. He remembered his first night in the library, the way Colewich had seized him with such manic force and the frenzy in his eyes. It was certain that his Lordship would stop at nothing to get what he wanted, and his ambition was only matched by his cruelty and ruthlessness. Kit realised how lucky he'd been to escape from this place with his life, so far at least.

Kit was roused from these thoughts when he heard another voice he recognised. It was certainly Zannah speaking. He pressed his ear to the glass, desperate to hear what she was saying.

'Not again,' moaned Zannah. 'Faith, I know not of what thou speak'st. What is it I need look for?'

'I don't know. That's the trouble.' Colewich sounded weary now. 'Just keep an eye open for anything around the village that seems at all... magical. It should be obvious, surely.'

'But if it be impossible to find, then...'

'You are grateful for my returning you to the village, my dear?'

'Certainly,' she said, '…and the boy who helped me escape from…that other man.' Kit could only imagine Zannah's disgusted expression at the memory of Polley. Although she hadn't named Kit, he was glad she hadn't forgotten about him so soon.

'You wouldn't wish to return to that other man?' There was a new freshness in Colewich's voice now he'd found a weakness to exploit. 'You wouldn't wish me to return you to Polley? Because from what I hear he is very, very keen to get you back. Would pay good money to have you back. You wouldn't want to go back, I take it?'

'Oh God, verily I would not,' cried Zannah, suddenly panicked. 'Sir. My good lord. I beg of thee, send me not back to that foul man. I couldst not bear it.'

'If you do not manage to find the magical object, I may have to send you back to him.' Kit's teeth clenched. He had been at the end of one of his Lordship's blackmailing threats and it was clearly a weapon Colewich relished using. 'Consider it awhile, what it would be like to find yourself with him again. Then get looking.'

He cut off Zannah's reply by closing the book, then placed it in the box and closed the lid. The room darkened instantly.

Kit jumped to the ground. The situation was almost as bad as he'd feared. Yes, he knew Zannah was back with her people but for how long? She'd sounded terrified and even if Colewich didn't intend sending her back to Polley, the threat was bad enough. Through a window high above, Kit saw the light of a single candle ascending the stairs. He only had the time it took for Colewich to get himself to bed and fall asleep to decide what he was going to do. Could he really continue his journey to a new life, knowing that Zannah was in such trouble? There was also the complication of her not wanting to be separated from the village. Kit realised that it wouldn't be enough to steal her page. If he was going to get her away from Colewich, he would have to steal the whole book.

The village, what was that all about? Although the faces spoke from their pages, did they also exist in a place that really felt like a village? Zannah didn't seem to realise he was seeing her as a moving image on a page. How did this magic work and was the magical object sought by Colewich a part of it?

And yet another worry was rattling him. What if Colewich succeeded in getting his wicked hands on the unknown magical object? What kind of powers would it give him? Though new to the idea of real magic, it was easy for Kit to imagine that in the wrong hands it would be extremely bad. No: making off with the book was his only course of action, which meant stealing the whole box, locked as it was, and finding a way to open it later.

Kit had a good memory for places he'd been before, especially when his life depended upon it. After dropping from the skylight and landing softly on all fours like a cat, he managed to avoid the squeakiest floorboards in the servants' corridor. He descended the stairs, swiftly and silently. The clock's heartbeat was at full blast and it shuddered through him, right down to his fingertips as he tested the handle of the library door. It opened. Perhaps with all the outer doors locked and dogs on the prowl, Colewich didn't feel the need to lock the library itself.

He approached the box on the table and lifted it. Despite its heaviness, Kit saw something he should have noticed before: the box was secured on either side with iron chains which were riveted to the table itself. There was no way he was going to be able to take the whole box, instead he would have to find some way of removing the book.

Kit hadn't any tools to try and force the box open and it didn't seem to have any weak points as its wooden sides and lid were reinforced with iron bands. He put his eye to the keyhole but couldn't see any light. He tried whispering through the key hole: 'Zannah, 'tis I, Kit!' but there came no reply. Obviously when the book was closed, the magic slept.

He was going to have to try picking the lock. Hampered by the darkness, he couldn't find anything lying around which might help. What about the sitting room where he'd met with Colewich that morning? Feeling like he was treading on the toes of his luck, Kit crossed the hall and soon returned with items from

Colewich's desk: a long, thin-bladed letter opener and a sharp quill cutter. He held his breath and got to work. He'd witnessed Gabe perform similar feats; if only he'd been paying more attention at the time, especially since the lock itself didn't look that hard to pick. Kneeling in front of the box, he placed the tip of the letter opener into the hole and detected the slight give of a spring, then holding the spring tense and inserting the quill cutter at the top, wiggled it. Surely this is what he'd seen Gabe do? Nothing happened at first but Kit tried to stay calm, wiping his forehead on his sleeve when drips of sweat trickled into his eyes. For a full ten minutes he persisted, removing the tools, taking a few deep breaths and inserting them again. His heart leapt when he heard a click inside but fell when the lid still refused to open. The next time he inserted the letter opener, the spring wouldn't budge. Gabe had told him about puzzle locks and he feared that this was what the box contained: nothing much to see on the outside but inside, a fiendishly cunning mechanism of springs and bolts impossible to pick in any normal way. No wonder Colewich didn't bother locking his library door.

Kit stared hopelessly at the impossible lock. He was going to have to give up and leave before he was caught. He knew that the rest of his life, long or short, would be haunted by the fear that he'd let something terrible happen to Zannah. If only he could unravel the hours and be back with her in the Portland Street attic. Why didn't he explain how evil Colewich was? Why didn't he try and persuade her to remain with him rather than return to her people? Once Gabe's funeral was over, they could have left the house by a different route, given his Lordship's men the slip and fled London. She would have been safe. They both would have been safe. If only, if only, but now it was too late.

Kit put his mouth close to the keyhole. He doubted she would hear but whispered anyway, 'Pray forgive me, Zannah. I came back for you because Colewich is a bad man. I should have warned you about him and now 'tis too late. This time I can't do anything about it and I am so sorry.' His words whistled through the keyhole, which was as tall as half Kit's thumb. If it were only slightly bigger, he could have inserted his finger. With a nervous gasp, Kit placed the letter opener in the keyhole but not just the tip. He thrust the long, thin blade straight through the hole and felt it dig into something inside the box. Pivoting the blade in the hole, he managed to lift the something. He felt the riffle of pages. A curl of light shot out of the hole, blinding him momentarily in one eye, and he heard distant, angry voices which sounded as though they were howling at the end of a tunnel. He had just opened the book! Pivoting the blade amongst the pages again, he shut his eyes and put his mouth to the hole.

'I don't know who's listening,' he whispered as loudly as he dared. 'But I'm your true friend. You're locked in a box in his Lordship's library. He's a very bad man.'

More curls of light broke through the hole, more

distant shouts and Kit saw that the room was beginning to breathe again, the walls expanding and contracting.

'He's evil,' Kit went on. 'He'll do bad things with your magic, I just know it. Is there anything you can do to help me get you out of this box? Anything at all?'

Light curls were swirling around the room like escaping souls and the room itself was breathing more deeply. Kit was alarmed to see the bookcases rocking violently backwards and forwards, one almost on the point of toppling over.

'We must be quick,' he whispered. 'Help me and I can get you away from him. You can all come with me.' One book after another fell from the tops of the shaking bookcases and thudded onto the tiled floor. Before long, the noise would certainly rouse Colewich and his servants. Each passing second made it less likely that Kit would escape in one piece, let alone escape with the book. He didn't know for sure if the magic could do any more than put on a light show, but it was all he had left to gamble on.

'Now!' he pleaded, his hands shaking and almost out of his mind with fear. 'It has to be now. Just do something. Do it now!'

The box leapt a foot into the air, sending the letter opener spinning past Kit's head but then came crashing down onto the table, held fast by the chains. An intense beam of light from the keyhole illuminated the whole room and Kit fell backwards. The shelves were shaking violently and more and more books were raining down all around. Kit tried to shield himself as best he could from the light and the falling books, but he felt a sick kind of relief when from inside the box, he heard the drawing back of bolts, the whirring of cogs and twanging of springs. The lid flew open, cracking against the table like a thunderclap and a firework fountain shot up into the air. At the same time, the library door burst open and in came Colewich and his servants who staggered backwards when they beheld the strange sight.

Kit lifted the book from the box, wrestled it open and flattened its cover against his chest, like a weapon pointed at Colewich and his servants. It was a huge task to hold it while it throbbed with such energy, but the blinding light acted as a defence, battering them back against the sunset window wall. Sounds of raw anger blasted from the pages. Something else was happening too: when the light curls touched any object, that object changed and became animated, if only for a little while. Weighty volumes which had fallen from the shelves took off from the ground and flew around the room like a flock of leather-winged birds. When the light curls struck the empty fireplace, it became a laughing giant's mouth while the sunrise and sunset windows turned into real, moving scenes: at one end of the room, rabbits danced for real around the windswept grassy bank while on the other, bats flitted and snakes slithered in the twilight. Several of Colewich's servants panicked and bolted but his Lordship struggled forward with one arm across his face as though he were entering a burning building. At one point he got close enough to lunge at Kit with his sword. A light curl caught the sword in mid thrust and turned it into a sunflower. Even though the book's energy was scorching his fingers and it was as much as he could do to hold on, Kit continued to use it to force Colewich to stay back, along with a couple of the braver servants who remained, while he made his way across the room and towards the door.

Unfortunately, Kit hadn't realised that many of the wailing, cursing, loudly protesting pages weren't secure within the book. They began to fall out and he had to snatch them up and try to stuff them back in as best he could. It made his progress across the room slower and his fingers tingled horribly when they touched the pages, as though they were being stabbed with hot pins. Kit cried out in pain while Colewich raged and shouted but each time he attempted another attack, the book set up some kind of defence. The whole room was in uproar. Kit reached the door but so had a mighty curl of light which slammed into the large rectangle of wood and turned it into a tree with roots that rumbled across the floor, cutting up the black and white tiles, and branches which shot up and smashed through the ceiling. Great chunks of wood and plaster rained down upon their heads and clouds of choking dust filled the room. Kit somehow managed to keep hold of the book although he was doubled up with coughing. He was waiting for the tree to turn back into a door but remaining so close to the light source, it didn't. Of course, the tree had no handle. He was going to have to find some other way out of the library.

Colewich spotted his advantage and ran at Kit, but two fist-like curls of light punched their way from the book, caught him by the ankles and upended him, throwing him head over heels. His Lordship rolled along the floor until he was nearly swallowed by the laughing fireplace. Kit seized his chance. He ran past Colewich and pointed the book at the sunrise window which had reformed and changed back to glass while the book had been at the other end of the room. One of the library bookcases had fallen over and was lying at an angle right in front of the window. Holding the book like a shield, Kit ran up the shelves and into the scene which was now fully alive again. For a moment, there was a lovely, slow motion pause in all the hellishness. Kit could hear the swallows calling, feel the early morning sun on his face and smell the fresh green grass. He landed on the lawn in front of the house, in the middle of the night but in one piece.

Kit heard a scream behind him and turned around. If he'd had time to think, he might have expected Colewich to follow him. Unfortunately for his Lordship, the sunrise window had decided to reform just as he was climbing through. Now Colewich was stuck, half in and half out of the rising sun, grimacing as the crackling glass panes bit into his face and around his chest and one protruding knee. The arm which had made it outside dropped its sword and hung limply. Colewich looked like an actor playing the part of sunrise, except for his agonised expression. He tried calling for his servants but it came out in a wheeze, like a seized up old bellows because the window held him so tightly in its grasp. Kit couldn't hang about but still felt like making a point. Men like Colewich sickened him. Forcing the book closed and holding it under one arm, Kit brought out the purse of sovereigns and hurled it at his Lordship, hitting him squarely in the face. The golden pieces fell and scattered across the grass.

'There!' screamed Kit, his voice hoarse and full of fury. 'You can have that back. You can't buy me "Your Lordship" and I'm not thieving this book, see? I'm rescuing it.'

Kit turned. The hounds were standing in front of him, snarling. Kit opened the book again and held it up with numb, shaking hands. The cursing voices from within sounded angrier than ever. When the magical curls touched the dogs, they began to grow. Their powerful muscles strained under their skin and their fangs grew long and sharp as carving knives. This was bad. It was another example of what Kit had suspected in the library: now the magic was at its height it didn't seem to know what to do with itself and would cause mayhem wherever it went. Even though Kit was trying to help the book, the magic was lashing out at everything and that didn't necessarily help him.

Holding the book above his head, Kit ran straight

through the legs of one of the monstrous, giant hounds. The other tried to follow and the two became tangled in their chains and one another, giving Kit precious seconds to reach the gates, which turned to ice and melted on the book's approach. Behind, Kit heard the chains snap and massive paws thudded across the lawn but the magic had also woken the stone lions which, grown tenfold in size, pounced from their plinths to challenge the dogs. As Kit ran out into the road, all hell erupted in Lord Colewich's front garden. Neighbours roused from sleep could not believe their eyes as they stuck their heads from their chamber windows to witness two enormous stone lions taking on a pair of devil dogs. By the time the magic had died down, the whole garden was in ruins.

CHAPTER 10

'Please quieten yourself. Hush! The danger's passed.' Kit had uncovered a small section of his jacket which was wrapped around the book. He was speaking as loudly as he dared, although the trundling of the cart's wheels, the juddering of the boxes he was squashed between and the rain hammering on the oilskin covering him made it unlikely he'd be overheard by the driver.

Kit could hear the mixture of angry voices as though they were at the other end of the long tunnel again. The cart went over a stone, jolting the book open and a light curl shot out, formed itself into a miniature fist and punched him on the chin. He covered the book again quickly. It was early morning and without his jacket, he was stiff with cold, could barely feel his fingers or toes and didn't dare move beneath the oilskin for fear of giving himself away. He could only hope that the book would eventually calm down.

The journey from Colewich's house had been a nightmare, with Kit doing his best to keep the noisy book shut as he ran through the streets. The magical light curls continued to escape and wreak havoc, causing oil lights strung over the main roads to explode and melting shop windows to quicksilver puddles.

As Kit ran past these shops, hats and coats left their stands to dance with one another before dropping lifeless onto the cobbles. Coffee pots and tea-bowls flew out, smashing to pieces as they hit the ground. Frameless prints of castles, churches and fountains folded themselves into paper arrows and came sailing through the air, trying to catch him up. Cutting down the dark alleys had been just as bad: the book brought to life the tavern signs, so the *King's Head* went rolling down the cobbles, chased by a RAMPING CAT while a live and slippery looking *Mermaid* dropped into the lap of a drunken sailor asleep in the tavern's doorway. It was after this last event that Kit had stopped to remove his jacket and cover the book, smothering the magic like you'd smother an object on fire. He had no plan and no chance to retrieve his bundle of belongings from the lane beside Colewich's house, so he was desperate. When he came across a yard where a cart was being packed with goods, he didn't hesitate; he slid in between the boxes and fortunately, escaped the notice of the man doing the packing. As soon as everything had been loaded and an oilskin thrown over the top, the cart began to move, and Kit had remained in this cramped position ever since, trying to talk sense into the book but failing.

Squinting between the boxes and a gap in the side of the cart, he could tell it was growing light. If only he could have found Zannah's page and explained the situation to her, she might have helped him quieten the others down, but he couldn't even turn the pages, his hands were so numb. Having been burnt by magic then frozen all night long, Kit wondered if they would ever work again.

In a while the rain stopped and a little further on, the man ordered the horse to stop in an unfamiliar language: *'Ferma Donatello!'* Through the gap in the cart's side, Kit could only see bushes and grass. Nearby, he could hear chickens clucking and scratching the earth. The cart shook as the driver climbed down and Kit heard him walking away. The arm he'd been lying upon felt dead through lack of blood and the rest of him felt like a lump of wood, but he managed to squeeze around the boxes and pull up an inch of oilcloth to see where he was. It was the yard of an inn and the sign hanging over its gateway showed a picture of a half moon. The driver was leaning against the doorpost of the inn and talking to a woman who was wiping her hands on her apron. As he leant closer towards her, she smirked at him.

Kit weighed up what to do. If he got off the cart and made a run for it, where would he go? They were in the countryside, far from any town so there wasn't much sense in the idea. He cursed himself for throwing the purse in Colewich's face, even though it had felt so good at the time. That purse had contained a small fortune. Back in everyday life, Kit was down to his last farthings and that left him with few options. Why had he been such a paperskull? Well, wishing and regrets could not change what he'd done and for now, it was probably best to remain on the cart. With any luck, they would reach a town, park up again and he could sneak away. The driver entered the inn and Kit imagined him sitting down to a delicious breakfast of bacon, bread and ale, while his own rumbling belly echoed like a bear growling in a cave. He was at his lowest ebb, his heart still pining for Gabe. At least the driver's absence gave him a bit of time to rearrange himself. The feeling was seeping back into his dead arm and he could flex his fingers slowly, although they still hurt. He squashed up an old blanket to form a pillow and made himself comfier. The book lay quietly at last beneath his jacket. If Kit was carrying on with this journey, at least he would try and get some sleep.

He'd expected to wake and find the cart on the move again. Instead he half woke to the sound of several different voices all jumbled together. Still drifting on the margins of sleep, he thought he was at the theatre, up in the gallery amongst an audience calling out and cursing some poor performer on stage. Suddenly, the oilcloth was thrown back like a sharp slap in the face and he recalled exactly where he was. He sat bolt upright. The driver stood over him, glaring angrily.

'Where are the others?' the driver demanded in his rich and wonderful accent. He wore a stripy red waistcoat, which must once have been an expensive garment but was now threadbare, and the sleeves of his shirt were rolled up for work. His hat was decorated with a cockerel's shiny tail feather, black and tinged with green.

Kit swallowed. From the corner of his eye he could see that one side of the book was sticking out from beneath the jacket. Several pages were hanging out, which explained where the voices had come from, but the driver was more interested in Kit than anything else. Kit found he could hold the man's stare while using one hand to casually rearrange the jacket over it. The driver had removed some of the boxes and other objects from the cart, during which the jacket must have been pulled off the book. At least there were no more magical light curls. Perhaps the magic was just as exhausted as Kit.

'Where are they?' shouted the driver, waving his hands wildly. 'I hear many, many people under there. Where did they go?'

'I'm here alone,' said Kit.

'What do you mean?' the driver opened his eyes so wide, his eyebrows disappeared under the broad brim of his hat. Every time he said something, it sounded so dramatic.

'I did all those voices,' Kit nodded.

'You?' said the driver folding his strong, bare arms. '*Perbacco!* I don't believe it. You are just a boy!' He continued poking around in the cart, looking for more stowaways while Kit shuffled sideways, so he was practically sitting on top of the book.

'Did you hear someone like this, sir?' Kit did a

gruff old man voice. 'Or was it someone like this?' He switched to a sweet young woman, finishing off with, 'And this is the voice of a demon called Ashentoth!' Adding quickly, 'I made him up.'

The driver studied Kit dubiously. 'What are you doing in my cart? Are you a thief?'

'No, I swear,' said Kit. 'If I had any money, I'd pay you. In fact...' he felt inside his shoe and brought out two farthings, offering them to the driver. 'Here, that's all I have. Take it.'

The driver waved away Kit's offer impatiently and sighed. 'You running away from someone, huh?'

Kit nodded.

'Old, old story,' said the driver. To Kit's surprise, he carried on unloading. 'Well, you can at least help me with this. Poor Donatello, having to pull your extra weight all the way from London.' The chestnut horse paused from drinking at the water trough and looked round, resentfully. 'Pardon me, Donatello,' said Kit. He climbed down from the cart and went to rest the book, now bundled up tightly once more, in the long grass at the foot of a large oak tree in the middle of the yard. He came back and began to help with the unloading.

'Dobbin, his name when I bought him,' said the driver over his shoulder. 'But Donatello suits him better, yes?' He rubbed the horse's nose, talking to him lovingly in that other language while uncoupling him from the cart. He took a moment to look Kit up and down once more with a puzzled expression. 'Come on,' he said, leading the horse and pointing to the barn which stood beside the inn. 'You help me carry all this over there, huh? My horse, he goes to that field.' Kit picked up the nearest box and followed.

Throughout the morning, Kit expected the driver to tell him to leave. Instead, he was given one job to do after another. When he finally introduced himself by name, the man merely grunted although perhaps he was distracted by the heavy boxes he was humping about at the time. At one point the woman keeping the inn re-emerged with refreshments for the pair of them and when she spoke to the man, she called him Saroni. Kit wolfed down the bread and honey, sensing that Saroni was studying him closely again. He'd never been so glad to see food in all his life. They were sitting on what looked like a small stage which they'd been erecting at one end of the barn: a rough wooden frame decorated with colourful triangular flags and bright paintings of a town next to the sea and a smoking mountain.

'Correct. It is a stage.' said Saroni, when Kit asked. 'I am doing a show here later this afternoon. This is what I do, put on the marionette shows. You would like to see?'

'I would, Mister Saroni.'

'*Signor* Saroni,' the man corrected. 'I am from Napoli.' He could see this didn't mean anything to Kit so he gestured towards the scene painted on the front of the stage. 'You see here? *Versuvio*? Volcano?' Kit smiled and nodded; he understood that Saroni came from a foreign land but had never before seen or heard of a volcano. Saroni rooted through a box and pulled out a large puppet, the type known as a *marionette*, the size of a three-year-old child, which dangled from a rod which was joined to the top of its head. It was dressed all in black with a mask painted on its huge face and a large moustache. It held a sword and by using a wire attached to the hand, Saroni made the sword swish backwards and forwards. It was very simply made, with drapery hiding its bottom half. Some of the marionettes Kit had seen in shows on the streets of London were far more sophisticated but the face of this one was so well painted, Kit couldn't take his eyes off it.

'*Buongiorno!*' Saroni altered his voice so it became smoother and deeper. 'My name is Scarramouccia! I steal money from rich noblemen and give it to the poor. Nya-ha-ha!'

Kit felt uncomfortable. Was Saroni hinting that he still thought Kit was a thief? But no, Saroni discarded the first marionette and brought out a second, a soldier with a tall helmet on its oversized head.

'Me, Il Capitano!' Saroni barked out the words. 'I am an oh-so brave and oh-so handsome soldier. Uh-uh-uh... unless I see a mouse. You tell me if you see one, yes?' The marionette glanced around nervously and while he held the rod and wires in one hand, Saroni pulled a toy mouse from his pocket and wiggled it. Kit pointed at the mouse. The Captain turned, saw it, screamed and ran away. Kit laughed and immediately felt guilty. He was still grieving for Gabe after all. Yet, laughing did make him feel better and as he told himself, Gabe wouldn't have minded.

Saroni did not pause but brought another marionette out of the box, a rosy-cheeked, smiling girl. 'I am Columbina, a serving girl, and I look after my mistress. Sometimes I have to trick her would-be lovers.' Although he lightened his voice as much as possible, it was unconvincing. Saroni peeped around her large head at Kit. 'You see my problem?' he asked in his own voice. 'How would *you* say it?'

Kit coughed and repeated what Columbina had just said but in a fresh, young voice which seemed just right.

'Ha, I knew it,' chuckled Saroni. 'Have you ever worked a marionette? Can I show you how?'

Kit tried out several of the marionettes: there was a doctor, a nobleman and his daughter who was Columbina's mistress. There was a terrifying-looking devil painted red from horns to hooves and Saroni seemed to enjoy doing his voice very much indeed. He didn't ask if Kit wanted to take part in the show that evening, but everything seemed to be pointing that way. Saroni explained the main story and taught him the lines spoken by the younger characters, which Kit rehearsed, while the man who seemed to be his master for the evening made final preparations. Kit hadn't forgotten about the book of course. After unpacking, he had retrieved it from the long grass beneath the oak tree and buried it in the hay behind where the stage now stood.

In the late afternoon, people started drifting into the barn and before long, a fair-sized crowd had amassed. They were mainly farm servants, but chairs were carried from the inn for the better-dressed local farm owners and their wives. As he waited behind the painted backdrop, Kit heard Saroni welcome everyone to the show in his flourishing way. Then the play began.

The main story was about three young men – played by the same marionette wearing different coloured hats – who wanted to marry the nobleman's daughter and how the first two were thwarted in funny ways by Columbina's tricks. Kit operated Columbina and was pleased to remember all her lines perfectly, coming in at the right moments as they'd rehearsed that afternoon. He enjoyed taking part, just as he'd enjoyed putting on shows for Mr Steen's Occultist Club and better still, for Gabe in their attic. Now he discovered that making a whole audience laugh was the best feeling in the world. There was a lot happening behind the scenes and Kit was impressed by the way Saroni darted around so lightly and energetically, playing many different parts and responding to the crowd with perfect timing. He could understand why the marionettes were constructed so simply. Saroni often had to hold two at a time, leaning over the backdrop and hovering above the stage.

The play was broken up with lots of smaller scenes involving characters who had nothing to do with the main story, including Punchinello who was always sticking his hook nose into everyone else's business. Saroni could operate this puppet differently, with one hand inserted in the character's back, because from time to time he would come out from behind the backdrop and use Punchinello to play with the audience, his speciality being to chase and tease the women and children. In truth Punchinello was a cruel fellow and back on stage, he would batter other characters with his big stick, especially the cowardly Captain. Kit could see that Saroni was slipping an object into his mouth which made Punchinello speak in a strange, squeaky way. The crowd loved Punchinello better that all the other characters and if he sensed they were growing tired, Saroni would whip him out and a cheer would go up immediately. This didn't stop him closing the show with the Devil dragging a shrieking Punchinello to hell accompanied by painted canvas flames which rose eerily at the front of the stage, prompting gasps and groans from the onlookers. They were soon cheering again when the genuine lover got to marry Columbina's mistress. At the very end, Saroni stepped out as himself and passed his black feathered hat amongst the crowd for payment before they left.

The woman from the inn brought them a supper of bread and broth and Saroni handed over her share of the money, then gave four pennies to Kit before stowing the rest in the pockets of his waistcoat and breeches. Kit could not thank him enough. He felt he had learnt more about performing that day than he had in all the years he'd lived in London and that included sneaking into the Drury Lane theatre to watch the great actors in Garrick's company. He tried to explain but grew tongue-tied. Saroni smiled at Kit for the first time, patted his shoulder and told him there was still work to be done. After supper, Kit helped pack away the marionettes and dismantle the stage which took another two hours. He was still half expecting the marionette master to ask him to leave but instead, Saroni tossed a sack over to him, telling him to stuff it with straw for a mattress and leant him a blanket. When Saroni went outside, Kit retrieved the book and hid it at the bottom of the sack before adding the straw. The puppet master returned with Donatello, instructed the horse to lie down and covered him with another blanket. Finally, Saroni stuffed his own sack with straw and lay down. He kicked off his boots, folded them and placed them beneath his head as a pillow.

Kit was exhausted. His final thoughts before falling asleep were of Gabe and how much he would have enjoyed that afternoon's performance.

CHAPTER 11

When Kit woke it was very early morning, with the darkness giving way to a misty grey light. Saroni lay fast asleep and Kit saw his chance to go somewhere private and try to talk to Zannah. Carrying the book which was still tucked up in his jacket, Kit stole from the barn and crossed the yard. He walked a third of the way up the field which was wet with dew, keeping close to the hedge, then stopped and when he was sure no one was about, unwrapped the bundle in his arms. Crows in the nearby trees set up their startled cawing and flew off as soon as the light flared from the book but although its brightness made him shield his eyes, it seemed that much of its angry energy had burnt itself out. He used the jacket to cover his head and the book, concealing as much of the light as possible. Kit couldn't risk attracting attention, even at such an early hour. Was it too soon to do what he was about to attempt? 'What do you think, Gabe?' he whispered. He had to stop a moment and wipe away the fresh tears which began to flow at the thought of Gabe. It took some effort and deep breathing to steady himself again.

The pages were in a mess after the many occasions when he'd shoved the loose ones back in, sometimes upside down or the wrong way around. Each page was printed, or however it might be explained, on one side only. The first page he came to revealed the face of a lad somewhere near his own age who immediately launched into complaints:

'I din't get no wink o' sleep with all that stormin' an' wind. Broke two of the shutters on the house but I cannot mend it 'cos my tools have gone missing. My Alys won't talk to me. And she's vexed cos I forgot to ask the priest to read the banns in church afore our wedding...'

Kit turned the page. A woman glowered at him:

'Hast thou seen my dog? He ran off in the middle o' the windstorm and I ain't seen him since. Summat's wrong with this village, things is bad and gettin' worse...'

Kit turned again. It was the same story everywhere. There was much repair work to do following a terrible storm, which he suspected was these people's interpretation of the events in Colewich's library. Several of them were worried about what affect it would have upon the wedding which was soon taking place. When Kit tried explaining that he was looking for Zannah, the faces became suspicious. If Zannah wasn't at home, how would they know where she was? Why ask them?

'Zannah came back to the village a couple o' days back,' said the old woman Kit had first met in Colewich's library. Although she remembered Kit, she didn't look at all pleased to see him. 'She been away awhile but don't say where. Strange wench. Now she be back, look what do happen!'

'I'm sure it's not her fault,' said Kit but the old woman just sniffed and started moaning that her hens had been laying soft eggs since the storm.

Kit was beginning to worry he might have lost Zannah's page altogether in Colewich's library or since escaping the place. Maybe at that moment Zannah was lying in a gutter somewhere, to be rained on and ruined or taken and used badly by another man like Polley. He felt so relieved to turn a page and find her green eyes focusing upon him.

'Kit!' she said, breaking into a nervous smile. 'Thank God. Glad I am to see thee. I thought it was the end of the world or summat. Such a storm!'

'You're safe,' said Kit. 'Thank God is right! I had to get you away from that wicked man. I think that's what the storm was about. Me and him had a fight.'

Zannah frowned. 'All is... well now?'

'Yes,' said Kit. 'I've got you. Your whole village in fact. Tell me, Zannah, what is the name of your village? It feels odd calling it "the village" all the time.'

Zannah looked around as though the answer lay on the edges of the page. In the end, she shrugged her shoulders. 'It be just "the village",' she said. 'That's all anyone ever calls it.'

'But surely every village has a name?' said Kit. 'Same as towns and cities?'

'Not ours. It just be "the village",' she nodded.

Kit found it strange. His own village had been called

Little Stepney. He'd never heard of a place not having a name before.

'What's it like there?' he asked.

'Ordinary,' said Zannah, wrinkling her nose. 'Anyway, dost thou not know? I would have thought dream people could know anything they wanted. Dost thou really need ask me?'

'What do you mean?'

Zannah chuckled. 'Kit, I like thee,' she said. 'But I'm only dreaming thee, in't I? I mean, I had that nightmare and dreamt I could not get back to the village and was there with this horrible man for days and days. Thou camest for me in that dream, Kit. Even though, I s'pose I would have woke up in the end.'

By horrible man, she meant Polley. What she was saying was very peculiar, but Kit's instinct told him it was best not to probe too much. Clearly Zannah thought Kit was part of some dream while she was a real girl living in a village. Maybe in some magical dimension, she really was. That's unless it wasn't Kit dreaming this whole adventure.

'Then there was that other mean man dream, the night of the storm,' Zannah went on. 'I'm sure I heard thy voice then, too. Yes, I definitely did, thou came for to rescue us all. And now look, here thou art again. Even though thou art not real, glad I am to have a good dream person to help in times of trouble. Thou art like some guardian angel.'

The sun was beginning to rise, its rays spreading

across the field in a fan shape. 'I'll have to go now,' said Kit.

Zannah nodded and he closed the book, noticing how her eyes closed at the same time. The book looked perfectly ordinary now, not bleeding light or magic any more and yet whenever he opened it, he was staring through a window at another world. For the first time, Kit could inspect the cover and his eyes were drawn to some figures on what remained of the leather spine. Someone had inscribed '1456' on it but that was all. If it was a date, that made the book just over three hundred years old. Kit swallowed. This was becoming stranger and stranger. Questions flooded his mind and he would have opened it up again and searched for answers, only there was no time. He had to return to the barn before Saroni woke up.

It was very cold, and Kit's teeth were chattering. He held the book against his chest as he shrugged on his jacket. As he retraced his steps down the field, the questions kept coming. Was the village a real place, somewhere in England to judge by the sound of the voices? Was it possible to really go there? He remembered what Colewich had said about there being a way into the book and he wondered if this were true. Kit walked into the yard, clutching the book. For the hundredth time, he wished Gabe could have been with him to share in the strange adventure but perhaps now Zannah and her village were safe, the adventure was over anyway? Kit had done what he'd set out to do. If only there was somewhere secure where he could leave the book, but there was nowhere. If only there was someone he could trust completely, he might have given it to them. There was no one. For the time being he still had the burden of looking after the book, of making sure it didn't fall into the wrong hands.

Saroni was already loading the cart. He frowned when he saw Kit but didn't stop what he was doing. 'So you're still here?' he said gruffly.

'Sorry, yes. I just needed...' Kit pointed at the field but didn't really know how to end the sentence.

'What's that?' Saroni nodded at the book and Kit mentally cursed himself for not having hidden it better.

''Tis a Bible,' he said, knowing exactly how unlikely this sounded. What a penniless boy would be doing with such an expensive object was difficult to imagine, but he was going to have to imagine something quickly.

Saroni stopped what he was doing. 'A Bible?' he said, all the creases in his face demonstrating his amazement. 'You stole a Bible?'

'I didn't steal it,' said Kit, tucking the edges of his jacket around the book although they wouldn't quite meet in the middle.

'But you can read it?'

'Not quite well,' said Kit, trying to look gentle and holy. 'I am teaching myself.'

'Where did you get it from?' pressed Saroni.

'Well... you see...' said Kit, his brain trying to catch up with his mouth. 'There was an old preacher I worked for in London who sickened and died. Just before he left this world he made me promise I would become a preacher, same as him. That's why he gave me this holy book on his deathbed. I study it every morning and learn the words and the stories. Like Daniel in the lion's den. That's what I was doing up the field just now.'

Saroni blinked several times but Kit looked up into the sky, as though he could see the gates of heaven.

'And this is why you are running away?'

Kit nodded slowly and sadly. 'A wicked man said it belonged to him and tried to take it off me. He beat me but I wouldn't give it up, not for nothing. All the time, I kept hanging on to it and saying to meself, "He meant you to have it, Kit." The preacher actually said to me these words with his very final breath: "Don't you never show this Bible to no one, Kit, not until you've learnt every word of it off by heart. Then you can show 'em but not 'til then." You can't go against the wishes of the dead, 'tis terrible bad luck if you do. I ran off and never showed that wicked man. I never show no one this Bible book, not ever, 'cos of what the preacher said before breathing his last.' Now Kit looked at the ground. He had moved himself so much, he could feel tears in his eyes and hoped Saroni could see them too.

Saroni whistled through his teeth. He didn't exactly look like he'd fallen for Kit's story but he returned to packing up the cart. Kit went to rest the book against the tree in the yard, being sure to cover it with the jacket again, and joined him.

'So my little *Angelo*, you want to come with me, huh?'

'Please,' said Kit. 'I'd like to. I can be helpful. I work hard.'

'No running out on me, right?' Saroni shook his finger in Kit's face. Kit nodded and promised and Saroni carried on, 'You do that to me, I never will forgive you. But I could use someone like you. I'm not getting any younger. And you are good at the young voices, girls and boys. All right. We can make it for a week or so and see how you get on. There's lots of travelling and most small places like this, we only stay a night. Life on the road is rough. Right now, we are working our way toward Bath. Lots of people arrive there soon, many wealthy people. We will stay there longer.'

Bath! Kit was thrilled at the mention of the name. So much of the talk amongst the high and mighty of London was about that elegant city, even if Kit usually caught it second hand from their servants as they jawed together in the streets. Rich people went to Bath to 'take the waters' and to live a high kind of life, going to balls and entertainments, to see and be seen by others. It was a golden city, a fashionable heaven on earth.

'I always wanted to see Bath,' said Kit.

'Humph. Get ready for hard work,' was all he got by way of reply.

So began their journey west. Most of the time, Saroni stopped at places where he was a regular visitor but occasionally he would halt at some unfamiliar wayside inn to enquire if the keeper was interested in putting on a show for the locals and sharing the profits. Sometimes he was taken up on the offer, sometimes not. Occasionally they would travel off the main road a little way towards some village but the next morning the sun was on their backs as they joined the Bath Road again. As Saroni had said, the inns and villages were normally one-night stops, but they might stay for two in the coaching inns of towns like Newbury and Marlborough. Occasionally, they spotted familiar faces, fellow travellers heading in the same direction but most other vehicles went quicker than their cart. Saroni wasn't in any hurry. Travelling was his life and the road was his home. In the sunshine, he would greet fellow travellers with a shout and a wave; he sang Neopolitan songs in his rich, baritone voice and chatted to Kit – who now sat up in front beside him – telling stories of his boyhood on the streets of Naples. At times, Kit took the reins while Saroni lay in the back of the cart and snoozed with his feathered hat covering his eyes and his boots up on the tailboard. Then there were the rainy days when his master's expression turned grim and he didn't say much as the two of them tried to stay dry, water rolling off the oilskin covering their heads. In every weather, Donatello kept up the same steady, plodding pace and Kit became used to viewing the countryside with the gentle rise and fall of a pair of brown ears and a mane in the foreground.

If Kit felt he'd learnt a lot from that first show at the Half Moon, he discovered so much more about being a performer over the next few weeks. There was little time to stand and stare while you were putting on a show, yet although he was so busy, Kit studied his master at work behind the scenes. In the late afternoon or early evening, often in a dark corner of a courtyard and by the light of a single candle stub, it was fascinating to watch Saroni change from one character to another, his exaggerated facial expressions coaxing out the drama of the various voices while his pauses were timed just right to trigger ripples, then waves of laughter from the audience. Saroni concentrated so intently and worked with such furious energy, sometimes Kit feared his master would drop dead from exhaustion. The sweat dripped from his dark, handsome face as Scarramouccia threatened and the cowardly Il Capitano begged for mercy. The squeaky voiced Punchinello was forever the crowd's favourite. Saroni had shown Kit the *strega* he placed in his mouth to do the voice and had let Kit try it for himself. Punchinello was the only character to emerge from behind the drapes screening the sides of the stage and he did so chiefly to tease the women, although Saroni always reined in the wicked marionette's behaviour before it got out of hand. A strong and powerful man, Saroni would caper about like a spring lamb at these times.

The basic story of each performance was always the same, yet every night was different as Saroni improvised with the audience or dropped in jokes about the locals present, having gained information about them from the innkeeper. It was always done in such an innocently cheeky way, no one ever complained; in fact the more he did it the more they loved it. Kit would peep from behind the stage and was amused to see the audience enthralled by his master's performance, their expressions altering as he played with their feelings almost as though they were puppets too. In some of the coaching inns, the crowds were squeezed in rows several deep along the balconies as well as down in the yard.

For his part, Kit found himself growing more and more into his new role. With his lighter voice, not only did he act the younger male and female parts with great spirit and timing, he also began to improvise just like his master. The first time he did it, he happened to catch Saroni's eye. The older man was sitting on a beer cask, seizing his chance to rest while Kit took over from him. Although Saroni was out of breath, he smiled broadly and nodded his approval. After this, Kit began to improvise a lot more and he and Saroni fed off one another's jokes so well, they would make each other laugh. They were developing into a great team and at the end of each performance, a sweat-drenched Saroni would call for 'Angelo', as he always named Kit, to step out in front of the audience and take a bow before the cheering crowd.

Kit loved his new master and his new life, hard going though it was. Saroni continued to give him a cut of the money the audience threw into the hat at the end of a performance. Kit saved his share and in Marlborough, bought himself a pair of new boots in the same style as his master's. He didn't have to worry about where his next meal was coming from, even though Saroni himself had some strange eating habits. He would eat raw fruit whenever he could, and Kit didn't know anyone else who did that. A couple of the inns they stopped at were kept by widows with whom Saroni appeared to be on very good terms and in these places Kit didn't see as much of him, but apart from that they spent all their time in one another's company. Except when Kit was off studying his 'Bible'.

Saroni seemed to accept that Kit needed to go and spend an hour poring over the good book early in the morning and again before bed. Occasionally, when Kit returned he would get teased a little: *'Hey Angelo, did Daniel find his way out of the lion's den yet?'* but otherwise, Saroni seemed to take little or no interest. It was often difficult for Kit to find a quiet enough place in which to study the book, particularly when they were staying in town. He had to make sure he was out of earshot of everyone and wouldn't be disturbed. Once or twice he paid a penny for the use of an upstairs chamber of some inn for an hour, much to the suspicion of the landlord. There he would lock himself in, sit on the bed, take the book from the oilskin bag he'd bought to carry it in and immerse himself in the magic. He remembered what he'd overheard Colewich say, that night in the library, that there was some way of getting to the village. Kit had started wondering if he might be able to find it.

CHAPTER 12

Kit would dive into the book at every opportunity. Although he enjoyed his everyday life as Saroni's apprentice, he was beginning to think of the people in the book as a kind of family. They had no idea how vulnerable they were, and this made Kit want to protect them. He continued to hide the truth from his master. He might trust Saroni with his own life but trusting him with the villagers' lives was another matter.

Kit spent most of his time with Zannah and noticed how she started replacing her 'thees' and 'thous' with the word 'you'. He said he didn't expect her to, but she said she wanted to. On the other hand, she found it difficult to get used to saying ''tis'. Over time, Kit also got to know other villagers, mostly poor peasants who eked out a living working the land: Aldith and Hamon, Joan and Grisel. There was one very salty old character named Coswonked Jem. When Kit turned the pages, the villagers were usually awake but sometimes they appeared to sleep. Most he warmed to, for all the gossipy tales they would tell of one another, although sometimes he struggled to work out what they were saying because their speech was thick with unfamiliar words. Most of the women wore the same kind of head covering as Meggy, the old woman he'd encountered first, the one who'd given Colewich such a hard time.

She was the village baker and one of those moaning-but-heart-of-gold types. She was always talking about the preparations underway for the wedding of Col, the farm servant and Alys, her blushing niece. Meanwhile, Judd the Blacksmith gave him regular updates on his progress in making a fine new suit of armour for his Lordship who would soon be stopping by the village to collect it, along with the villagers' taxes. He didn't speak fondly of his Lordship who owned all the land thereabouts, but he was proud of his own workmanship.

Kit was still no clearer about whether the village really existed or not. None of the villagers appeared to know its name, or the name of the lord to whom they paid taxes. When Kit asked difficult questions like these, they would appear perplexed, as though the answer were somewhere just out of reach. It became clear that like Zannah, they believed Kit to be some kind of dream person or even a heavenly angel and he often found himself in the strange position of acting as a confessor. The villagers would unburden all kinds of personal secrets which Kit would sometimes have preferred not to know. John Farmer who proudly described himself as a 'freeman' and the wealthiest man in the village, admitted that he turned a blind eye to the odd sheep wandering onto his land from another man's flock. Kit also learnt that Col had originally wanted to marry Zannah and, even though folk had started calling her a witch, he still liked her. When they were young, Meggy had let Coswonked Jem kiss her behind the church one Sunday and he'd never let her forget it. Worst of all for wanting to confess his sins was the Priest, Father Bernard, who drank mead when he should have been fasting and secretly coveted the priest in a neighbouring village's fancy new robes.

Kit had learnt that Zannah lived with her otherwise hermit-like grandfather, Awl Robin, in a cottage on the edge of the village. He was in the book too but was so deaf Kit couldn't communicate with him beyond nods and smiles. Zannah had been encouraged to read by her learned and free-thinking grandfather and could write her name. She had refused more than one offer of marriage and, even before her disappearance, the other villagers had thought her odd. When her return was accompanied by the most devastating storm anyone could remember, the villagers had begun to suspect her of witchcraft. Kit had tried sticking up for her, but it was no good, their minds were fixed. If they began calling her a witch, he would either change the subject or turn the page.

Even though they'd got so messed up that night in Colewich's library, from the way they were discoloured and rubbed at the edges, it looked as though the pages had been parted from the cover for many years. Now Kit began trying to rearrange the pages of the book into their proper order. He had noticed something: little scratches at the edge of each page, which in a certain light and with a bit of imagination, looked like a small stick man climbing a ladder which grew as he ascended. On one page he was at the bottom of the ladder, on the next at the top, and on the next, somewhere in the middle. Kit wondered if anyone had ever noticed the scratches before. He decided that if they were as old as they looked, they might provide a key as to how the pages should be arranged, with the man starting at the bottom of the first page and climbing steadily to the top of the last. Kit could only rearrange one or two at a time because the faces would kick up a fuss if they were taken from the book for more than a second and then the magical light curls would appear and threaten to do damage. It was slow work.

About six weeks after leaving London, Saroni and Kit arrived in Bath. It was the middle of June and the weather was fine and warm. When he first saw Bath, Kit wondered if the buildings really were made of gold and Saroni had to explain that it was actually a pale, yellow stone quarried locally. There were many fine buildings with more expected to be built. Up and down the wide streets sauntered the most elegant and expensively dressed gentlemen and ladies in their silks and ribbons, embroidery and feathers and devastating wigs. The ladies had wide sleeves and even wider skirts while the gentlemen's long satin waistcoats shone like iridescent beetle wings. Kit laughed to imagine them dropping onto their backs and scurrying off down the South Parade. Most of these gentlefolk came from London and Kit felt a pang of fear that Colewich might be somewhere amongst them but then he reminded himself how different he looked these days in his splendid boots, new cocked hat and velvet coat. Not at all like the thief he'd once been.

Saroni found them lodgings above a coffee house which was attached to the Abbey, with a tall chimney which snaked up the Abbey wall. Donatello and the cart were housed in stables a little further along the same row of buildings. Saroni announced that he was going to a barber surgeon for a haircut and shave and would then bathe in the famous waters, which was a ritual of his whenever he arrived in Bath. With the book safe in the oilskin bag on his shoulder, Kit decided to explore the city.

The west side of the Abbey was a splendid sight with its great arched window but what really caught Kit's attention were the golden angels, peeping cautiously over their shoulders as they climbed the tall ladders on either side or came down head first, in which case they looked more like creeping bats. He shielded his eyes from the sunlight and marvelled for a long time: this was almost like a sign from heaven that he was on the right track with the book, and his way of rearranging the pages to get that little scratched stick man to climb his own ladder was the right way. Kit was drawn to enter the Abbey through the enormous wooden doors which were wide open. Inside, worshippers knelt and prayed while ordinary-looking sightseers like himself strolled up and down the aisle and chancels. There weren't many of the fashionable, wealthy types present, possibly because in the shadowy interior their costumes would not have been shown off to their best. Despite the air of holiness, the smell of incense and thin drift of organ music, the inside seemed more like a public road with people on foot crossing from one side to the other across the middle, exiting through the side doors with baskets of wares to sell. Kit saw that this was a convenient short cut from the North side where his lodgings were, to the South, although the people cutting through seemed respectful enough. In their way, they looked like the busy angels outside.

Kit sat in the aisle and hugged the bag to his chest. He gazed up at the high vaulted ceiling and wondered if the book's magic might not have been summoned by the late Sir Edmond Halley's comet after all? Perhaps Kit should not have mocked those who claimed the comet had some effect upon events on Earth, bringing good luck, or bad. On the other hand, the comet had recently disappeared from the sky, yet this magic remained. Would he ever get to the bottom of what it all meant?

Kit studied the marble memorials attached to the tall Abbey pillars and although he could not read the words, guessed the numbers referred to the ages of the people who'd died and the years they had been born and left this Earth. It hurt him to think of Gabe without any kind of physical monument to mark his life and passing. There were carvings of skulls and angel faces, flowers and shipwrecks. Could the pages of the book be like these memorials somehow? To Kit's ears, the names of the villagers were strange and their accents were odd, yet they'd told him they were English. What if they were people who'd died hundreds of years before, spirits who didn't realise they were no longer alive? Maybe the plague had rampaged through their village and carried everyone off at once, like the empty villages Saroni said he'd encountered around the country. If this were the case, the pages were like speaking tombstones. If they didn't realise they were dead, wasn't Kit's job to persuade these spirits to stop clinging to this world and leave for the next? How was he going to break the news to them?

Saroni looked very different short-haired and clean shaven. Kit took his master's advice and visited the King's Bath later that afternoon, joining the other bathers who wallowed in the warm, green salty waters which were said to cure all kinds of ailments. A row of stone seats flanked the edges of the Bath and one was occupied by a painted statue of an old King named Blud. Kit lay on his back and watched the steam rise, though not as high as the clear blue sky above. He tried not to worry about the book, which was safely locked away in his lodgings, yet he could never entirely shake off the feeling of responsibility, as though the villagers were thoughtless children about to stumble into danger without him. It might have helped if he could only have told someone else about the book, but he was scared to reveal the secret, even to his beloved master Saroni. He couldn't risk it becoming known, in case by some fluke Colewich heard about it and tracked him down. This fear was with him the whole time, just below the surface and Kit only really escaped from it when he was performing. That afternoon, Kit stayed in the King's Bath for as long as he dared, then raced back to the lodgings to check on the book.

That evening he helped Saroni build the stage and the next morning, they paid a couple of lads to assist them in shifting it from Donatello's stables into the Abbey Yard, where they pitched it not far from the west window, all ready for their first performance that afternoon. Saroni put on a smart yellow waistcoat and it was the first time Kit had seen him wear a wig. He made Kit tie his own hair back with a black ribbon and insisted he rub his cheeks with a little goose grease until they shone. *'Con brio!'* said Saroni. 'We must look brilliant for this audience. It is different here to playing in these little inns along the road. You and I must give our best performances, my little Angelo!'

It was a different kind of audience and a different kind of performance. Saroni stuck to the story a lot more and the white-powdered ladies and gentlemen with the pink spots painted on their cheeks laughed politely and elegantly when they were certain they were supposed to. Punchinello was still a favourite but when he came out into the audience he was far more polite than usual and only leered cheekily at the children, some of whom checked with their parents first before laughing. The performance was also shorter and at the end, when Angelo was summoned, Kit thanked the audience for their applause with the deep gentlemanly bow Saroni had taught him, placing one leg out straight. It made Kit smile to see how each gentleman strove to outdo his neighbour by putting slightly more money in the hat and understood why Saroni went to such trouble to put on a good show in Bath.

There were two of these polite performances in the afternoon and a more raucous one in the evening. With all the wealthy people at balls and gatherings organised by the famous Master of Ceremonies, Beau Nash, it was the common folk's turn and yet again, Saroni was leaping about the audience, with Punchinello ogling the women. He even turned the old man Pantalone into the strutting character of Beau Nash, who complained bitterly about the lack of royalty in Bath that season and this went down very well with the locals. Kit was relieved to be back playing to a crowd who weren't afraid to scream with laughter. Lanterns were set on the floor to mark the edge of the performance area and they lit up the faces of the audience, showing how much they appreciated Saroni's antics. They loved it when he appeared with his wig on backwards, staring cross-eyed at the pigtail hanging down his nose and the trick in which he got Punchinello to fart out a row of candle flames. What that afternoon's audience would have made of the trick could only be guessed at.

The next five weeks revolved around the performances but in between the shows, Kit got to know Bath well. He admired the Circus, which was only one third complete but where famous people lived including William

Pitt, the MP, and Thomas Gainsborough, the portrait painter. However, he normally only walked as far as the Queen's Square, then into Barton Fields where he would seek out a quiet place in which to study the book. One such morning, Kit was sitting on a tree-covered mound where he could be sure of seeing anyone approaching from the city. He believed he had succeeded in arranging most of the eighty-six thick pages in order so now the stick man began on the bottom edge of page one and ascended his ladder in the margin of every page until the last, where he disappeared in a puff of smoke at the top. Although he had succeeded in rearranging the pages after spending such a long time at it, the question as to why someone would have bothered to scratch the man onto each page so painstakingly still puzzled him. As he was closing the book, and a few of the pages dropped into place, he noticed how the man seemed to move down his ladder. Surely, if he flipped the pages in the other direction, he could get him to climb up? Kit had a couple of tries. Moving the page edges one at a time when the edges weren't at all level proved difficult. Kit was also trying not to disturb the book's inhabitants because they either liked to be contacted and spoken with properly or not at all. On his seventh attempt, Kit partly managed it: he flipped the pages so the man moved from the bottom of the margin to a third of the way up, building his ladder as he went. To Kit's amazement, something else happened too. His hand, the one doing the flipping, disappeared.

The disappearance of Kit's hand only lasted a moment before it was back on the end of his arm again. The book gave a little cough of magic and that was it. Kit's first reaction was not to want to ever do it again. Even after everything he'd witnessed that night in Colewich's library, seeing a part of your own body disappear in broad daylight seemed worse, somehow. It took him a while to summon the courage to try it once more, flipping fewer of the pages this time and keeping his attention on his hand rather than the stick man. This time a couple of fingers disappeared then reappeared. Where did they go in those few seconds? He hadn't felt any pain, but that part of his hand had suddenly turned cold.

The idea hit him: could this be the way into the book which Colewich had been seeking? If Kit flipped the pages in the right order, all the way up to the top where the man disappeared, would he also disappear completely into the world of the book? After taking a good look around to make sure no one was approaching, he carried on flipping the pages, a few more each time and watched his right arm disappear, then his shoulder and part of his chest. He felt one side of his face turn cold and guessed that this had disappeared too, momentarily. Finally, Kit took the bold step of flicking half the pages of the book. The little man reached halfway up the ladder and the world changed.

CHAPTER 13

Kit was flying high and the cold, clear air was stinging his throat and nostrils. It felt like he was about to faint but he relaxed into the feeling rather than try and fight it. Any conscious thoughts were like dice shaking and landing, shaking and landing, so one moment he was riding on the back of a comet while the next he was clinging on to the golden front of Bath Abbey, looking down, over his shoulder at the Abbey Yard. Whereas his top half felt weightless, his lead heavy feet were still anchored to another place. Meanwhile the middle of his body felt like it was being stretched into a rope. It didn't hurt. Kit felt no emotion, no fear or panic or even much wonder because there was no time, only second by second sensations, forces, speed and light. No sound. He halted in mid-air and there below was the village looking more solid and real than he felt himself to be at that moment. He only had time to glimpse it before being sucked backwards again with such force, his clothes were nearly pulled off over his head. He thudded back down on the grassy mound, where he lay gasping for breath and shivering.

The village was real. Even after one bare glimpse, Kit was as certain of its existence as he was of Bath's existence, or London's or any place he had ever been. It was as solid as the earth beneath him. In a couple of seconds, he'd taken it all in. With perfect clarity, he'd seen smoke rising from chimneys and villagers going about their daily lives carrying baskets, tools and young children. There'd been pigs and geese and woven wooden fences, he could still see them clearly in his mind. He'd beheld the churned-up muck beside the millpond and the rickety bridge. He'd seen the squat towered church with a grey goat tethered to the lychgate. There'd been animal dung, buttercups and washing drying on bushes. One man had been digging a trench, another had been mending a thatched roof. He could swear the woman brushing the flour from her skirts in one doorway was Meggy.

As soon as some feeling returned to his frozen, shaking hands, Kit replaced the book in the bag and started walking slowly back to town. His head was spinning, and he was forced to stop every so often to lean against a wall or cling to a railing and regain his balance. He was in shock. When he felt better he would think about what had just happened and more particularly what he was going to do about it.

It was hours before Kit dared open the book again. Saroni had left for the tavern straight after their evening performance but Kit had declined to go with him. He didn't expect to see Saroni until gone midnight but locked himself into their room anyway. Saroni could knock when he returned.

'Zannah, can I ask you something?'

'What is it, my angel?' Zannah smiled. It was a coincidence that she had taken to using the same nickname for Kit as his master.

'I'm no angel and I'm being deadly serious,' said Kit. 'What if I could come and visit you in your village? Would you like that?'

Zannah looked surprised, then she threw back her head and laughed.

'In faith, it is not possible,' she said. 'How can you come here? You are not...'

Kit knew what she'd been about to say: you are not real.

'What if I am, Zannah?' said Kit. 'What if I'm as real as you or your grandfather or anyone you know? Wouldn't you want to see me properly?'

Zannah stopped laughing. She frowned and spoke more slowly, as though an uncomfortable truth were dawning upon her. 'I don't know Kit. I mean, I never thought of it. Yet I know what people in the village say about me, ever since I came back. I know they call me a witch and blame me for the storm.' There was a spark of fright in her eyes.

'You are not a witch, you know that.'

'But when you say something like "you can come to the village" I wonder if I am what they say I am? Have I summoned a spirit? Are you a good spirit, Kit? I always thought of you as good but mayhap you are not. You have told me you were a thief. I remember what you told me about being in London with Gabe. I thought maybe you were someone who'd died too. Mayhap your own body was lying in that attic, but you did not know you were dead and what I've been seeing is your ghost-life? I am sorry for finally saying that aloud.'

It was amazing. Zannah had been thinking exactly the same about Kit as he'd been thinking about her and the others.

''Tis all right, Zannah. Neither of us must get upset.' Kit tried to soothe her. With alarm, he saw magic beginning to seep from her page.

'Pray tell, why do I see you Kit? And those other men I saw before you? I must be a witch or you wouldn't all be so ready to talk to me, would you?'

'Zannah, hush. 'Tis not you alone, I talk to all the villagers. I know Meggy and Judd the smith and Coswonked Jem and everyone. And I'm not a spirit, I am a real live person. Just, I live at a different time from you. I live a long time in the future from where you are.'

'You are in the future? Is that why you talk with funny words sometimes, Kit? Forgive me for saying so.' Zannah put her hand on her chest as though trying to still her pounding heart. 'And you say all our neighbours speak to you too?'

'That's right,' Kit nodded fervently. 'I've got to know them all. And I reckon I've found a way I could visit you. I just wanted to warn you first.'

'I suppose 'twould be all right,' said Zannah. 'I like you a lot, Kit. You are the first boy who's never wanted anything from me. Your first thought isn't to kiss me or marry me or own me. And right now, you are my only friend.'

'And you, Zannah, you are my best friend. Since Gabe died you're the only one I can really talk to.' There were tears in Kit's eyes. 'I need to know more, we both do, if we're going to find out what's going on. When you speak to me, where do you see me? Am I up in the sky or where?'

'Not in the sky,' she said. 'I see you in any scrying place, any place where there is a reflection. We've a small mirror beside the cottage door, where I do see you at this moment. Yet it could be a puddle in a ditch or yonder in the duckpond. Marry, even a bowl of water! I was washing muck off the carrots the other day and there you were in the bowl. It feels like being in a dream; it is not frightening.'

'But what makes you look in the mirror or the pond or wherever?' Kit had never ventured to ask about this before.

'I get drawn to the scrying places, like you start calling me. I feel the pull of you, somehow. It can be any time of day, I am drawn to look. It stops me feeling so lonely. I like it.'

'I do, too.' Kit almost reached out to touch the page.

'Come to think on it,' she went on. 'I did notice John Farmer by the pond the other day just staring in the water and muttering. I thought it odd. Was he talking to you?'

'I don't know. P'raps.'

Zannah's face clouded over. 'It vexes me, that they do call me witch,' she said. 'While they've been freely talking to spirits too.'

'Not a spirit,' Kit reminded her. 'Real flesh and blood, remember?'

'What? Oh yes, forgive me. But fie upon them.' To Kit's surprise, she spat at the ground to signal her disgust. 'Blaming me when all the time they are as bad. I should go right now and tell them what I do think of them.'

'I wouldn't,' said Kit. 'You're different, Zannah. You're special. And if things have been going wrong, they're going to blame it on someone different. That's what people like that always do. You're better off laying low awhile.'

'That's what Grandda says.' Zannah still looked resentful. 'But I'm tired of keeping to meself and being made to feel like I've done summat wrong. It wasn't my fault I got took away, was it?'

'Of course not.' Kit wondered where she'd thought she was when her page was removed from the book and he asked her.

'It was more like a nightmare.' Her eyes began swimming with tears. 'I kept expecting to wake up but it went on and on. It was a terrible dark place, like a dungeon but there was nothing to see, nothing. That horrible man's face would appear out of the dark and try and kiss me and – oh, it was worse than I can say.'

'There's no need. Hush.' Kit was immediately sorry that he had reminded her of Polley.

'You came for me, did you not? You helped me get back home. And again, you helped us all on the night of the storm. Oh, Kit, I do want you to come to the village. You can help a third time: it will shame the others, to have to admit they have been speaking with you, too. They will have to stop calling me witch then, will they not?'

It wasn't exactly why Kit had wanted to visit Zannah but before he closed the book that night, she had made him promise that he would try to come as soon as he could.

For the next few days, Kit pondered over when, how and even if he should do it. He began to wish he hadn't said anything to Zannah because she was so excited at the prospect of his visiting her. More than anything, he didn't want to let her down. Even so, Kit was scared. If he flipped the little man right up the ladder and found himself actually there, in the village, his whole body not just a part of him, was he willing to risk being stuck there forever? There was something extremely strange about the place, even more than the obvious fact that it existed in a book. In all the weeks he'd been talking to the villagers, nothing had really moved on. For instance, although Meggy still relished talking to him about her niece's wedding preparations, the wedding itself didn't come any closer. Kit had gone from wondering whether the village existed, to knowing that it did, to thinking that although it was real, there were different rules operating there, rules the villagers themselves weren't aware of. Whenever he asked when the wedding was taking place, the answer was always the same: 'Soon, soon...' Meggy's eyes would crinkle in merriment and she didn't seem to realise she'd been giving him the same reply for weeks.

Kit threw himself into his performances with as much enthusiasm as ever but Saroni noticed how, once they were over, he would become quiet and withdrawn. Once or twice, his master caught him in the Abbey, staring at the marble memorials, lost in thought.

'Is it your Bible studying?' asked Saroni. 'Perhaps you are not destined to be a preacher after all, my little Angelo. Not if all the study makes you sad.'

Kit shook his head and wished he could tell his master the truth. He loved performing in Bath but their time there was nearly over. The audiences were dwindling. Saroni felt he had exhausted the rich visitors staying that season and soon they would be packing up the cart and wending their way up country, then back down to Bristol for the St James' Fair at the start of September. Somehow, Kit felt he should make his attempt to get into the book before leaving the golden city because if he failed to return, or died trying, at least it would happen there. Bath was the loveliest place imaginable, a place he wished he could have taken

Gabe to. He didn't feel sad exactly when he stared at the memorials in the Abbey, just thoughtful. What would be, would be.

At other times, Kit felt quite differently and tried desperately hard to think up some plan for ensuring his safe return from the village. Although he wanted very much to go there and help Zannah if he could, he didn't want to disappear into those strange pages forever! At these times, he would trudge the streets, the oilskin bag on his shoulder, searching for the solution. There had to be some way, there had to be. Eventually, he hit on an idea quite by chance.

There were plenty of other entertainers on the streets of Bath that summer, including musicians and pantomime artists performing in booths or on small stages. One afternoon, Kit's attention was attracted by a crowd which had gathered in Duke Street to watch a comical version of a Greek myth, Theseus and the Minotaur. In order to find his way out of the labyrinth where the Minotaur lived, Theseus tied one end of a silken thread to a post and unwound it, travelling in and out of the ladies and gentlemen, until they found themselves in such a tangle, it was the cause of much blushing and polite merriment. The fight between Theseus and the Minotaur took place behind the curtain and following some blood-curdling screams at which the audience fell silent, the hero reappeared, holding up a very battered and unconvincing papier mâché Minotaur head, at the sight of which everyone cheered. He proceeded to find his way back to the start of the labyrinth by rewinding the thread, causing lots more confusion and well-bred laughter amongst the crowd as well as shrieks when the Minotaur head got too close. There wasn't very much to the performance but Kit threw a farthing at the end and walked back to his lodgings at a quicker pace. He'd found exactly what he'd been looking for.

That evening, their own performances over for another day, Kit again declined Saroni's offer to accompany him to the tavern. Saroni shook his head sadly as he left, as though he considered Kit a hopeless case. Kit rose from the bed and went to the window where, through the small, thick panes of glass, he watched the green-black feather of his master's hat wend its way through the evening crowds. After the hat had vanished from sight, Kit walked to the door of their chamber and turned the key in the lock. His stomach churned, full of nervous excitement for what he was about to attempt. At some stage he would have to try to visit Zannah as he'd promised. This was as good a time as any.

The thread which Saroni used to mend the marionettes was fairly strong but it didn't have to be strong enough to carry Kit's weight or long enough to travel for miles: it only had to provide some connection between Kit's own world and the village, a means of his finding his way home, just like Theseus in the labyrinth. Although he had no way of knowing whether this plan would work, it was the best plan he had, and he wanted to get his attempt over with. He took one end of the thread and tied it with many knots around the wooden bedpost. He unwound the ball to its full extent, around twenty feet, and tied the other end to his wrist. He took the book from the bag and placed it in his lap. His hands were shaking so much and he was breathing so hard, he shut his eyes and took a moment to try and calm himself. When he opened his eyes, he looked around the sparsely-furnished room which had been their home for five weeks, at the brick fireplace and three-legged chair, the battered pewter candlestick and of course, the marionettes which were too precious to be left in the stables. Punchinello grinned at him from the top of the old rope-handled sailor's chest and Kit swallowed hard as he recalled the marionette being dragged to hell earlier that evening.

Kit's first attempts at flipping the pages failed because his hands were shaking too much. The little man started off building his ladder, then suddenly jumped to the top leaving out the whole of the middle section. Kit couldn't bear to look at his hands and watch them disappear, but they did turn freezing cold several times. He wiped his sweaty palms on the bed's quilt and began to think that he might have to leave his attempt to another day. Finally, he took a deep breath and began flipping from front to back, evenly and not too quickly. By now, he knew the wonky way the pages sat next to one another and could take account of it as he flipped.

The little man started building and climbing. He proceeded smoothly up the side of the page into the sky region and then disappeared. At that instant, Kit felt his own body disappear and experienced that same feeling of travelling through the highest point in the sky, the thin blue line before the sky becomes heavenly space and feeling the cold ice-speckled air travelling down his throat. When he landed this time, it was nothing less than a full body landing.

CHAPTER 14

It was dusk in the village and there was no one around except a black and white cat stalking away down a path between trees. A pig somewhere nearby was rooting around and grunting contentedly.

Kit had landed on a low thatched roof of a one-storey cottage. A little way down the track leading off to his right there were other lime-washed buildings. The cottage was closely hemmed in by trees and, from the description she'd given, it looked a lot like Zannah's place. There was no chimney on the roof, but a plume of smoke rose from a hole at one end. Someone was at home.

He put his mouth close to the thatch. 'Zannah!' He whispered once, and then a little louder but no response came from within, no voices, no signs of human life.

Kit felt for the thread around his wrist. It was still there and although the sun had nearly set and it was dark beneath the trees, he could just make out how the thread curved up into the sky and vanished. He would have to be careful not to go too far and risk snapping this delicate lifeline but it was slack enough for him to descend to ground level. He still didn't know whether he would be able to travel back or not but the thread gave him hope: in his mind's eye he could still see the other end tied to the bedpost at the inn.

It wasn't far from the roof to the ground but the thatch was wet and slippery and Kit had to sidle forwards and lower himself over the edge with care. The wooden door had no handle or keyhole so Kit tapped on it softly with his fingertips and whispered Zannah's name as loudly as he dared. He could hear someone approaching the door so he hid around the corner, untangling the thread when it became caught in some foxgloves.

The door opened and Zannah's profile emerged and looked around. He stepped into view and she stifled a cry. ''Tis I. Kit,' he said quickly.

She grasped the doorframe with one hand, as though trying to stop herself from diving back inside. With the other, she clutched her shawl tighter to her throat and peered at him.

'Oh my God,' she said, the darker shape of her open mouth standing out in the gloom. After a few seconds she instructed him to wait and disappeared inside. When she reappeared, she was carrying a pale ember on a stick: a rushlight like those which had lit his own childhood home. She closed the door behind her and held the light to Kit's face, bringing her own face to meet it. In the faint glow, Kit detected her wide, clear eyes, even a few of her freckles. Her hair framed her face like a cloud. She was the same height as Kit so they could stare straight into one another's eyes. Kit saw how she trembled, although the evening was not cold.

'We must not be scared,' said Kit. 'I promised I would come and here I am.'

'I can scarce believe it,' she whispered. 'Thanks be Grandda sleeps already. How came you? Have you a horse?'

'No,' said Kit. The wonder of meeting Zannah in the flesh was still very raw and he could barely get out his words. 'You must prepare yourself for a surprise. I can't even explain it but there is magic involved.' She drew in a sharp breath. 'Not witchcraft,' he added quickly.

'That's what a demon *would* say.'

'You'll have to trust me. There are more things in heaven and earth than we imagine and whatever we've stumbled upon is natural in its own way. We just don't understand it, that's all.' With surprise, Kit felt the truth of what he'd just said, adding his own bit onto a line he remembered being spoken by Hamlet when he'd seen it played at the Drury Lane theatre. Had Shakespeare known of this magic, Kit wondered?

Zannah's expression changed. Her face softened into a smile. 'I'm so glad you're here, Kit,' she whispered, reaching out to him. 'Your hand is freezing cold,' she said. There was a pause as though time stood still, then an owl hooted and it was the cue for them to fall into each other's arms and hold each other tightly. In the dreamlike beauty of the green dusk they stood for a long time, silent in one another's company yet aware of the strength of their solidarity, their true friendship, that the link between them was stronger than the oddness of their situation. It was as though Kit had been holding his breath, ever since the death of his beloved Gabe and now, finally, he was able to let it out again, exhale all the pretence. Here at last was his true friend, one who knew the secrets of his heart and that poor heart was nearly bursting with joy.

A second hoot and Zannah pulled away and broke the spell. 'I know it's late,' she said urgently, 'But let us go now and find those who do call me a witch. Meggy's place is but a stone's throw. Truly, I cannot wait to see the look on her face, having to call herself witch now. She'll have to confess she's been talking to you, just as I have.'

'Zannah, stop!' Kit resisted the tug of her hand as she tried pulling him down the beaten track. The thread tied to his wrist was invisible in the dusk but he could feel it begin to grow taut. 'Listen to me please. I can't move any further from your door; really I can't.'

'But you must, it's the only way they'll believe me.' She clutched at him now, dug her heels into the earth and pulled.

'Stop it!' he said louder. Any moment the thread would break and the link between this world and his own would also be broken. Kit was forced to loosen himself from her grasp and she stumbled.

'Kit!' He saw Zannah's eyes grow round and sparkle with annoyance. 'Won't you do this one thing for me?'

'You don't understand!'

'No, no, no… What's happening to you?' She

stretched out to him but then covered her mouth to stifle a shriek. In the wood, the owl screeched and flew off in alarm.

Kit looked down, newly aware that the tingling sensation in his fingers had been going on for a while. Now he was already looking straight through his hands at the ground. When he looked up again, Zannah was gone and instead, he was sitting on his bed at the inn, facing the window. The book was lying on the floor and the thread around his wrist was still tied to the bedpost. There was no time to regret how he'd left matters with Zannah, for he heard someone running up the stairs. Realising the door of the chamber was wide open, Kit hurriedly stuffed the book into the bag and pulled the thread so it snapped from his wrist, hiding the rest of it under the quilt.

Saroni burst in, out of breath and carrying a lantern. 'You're here,' he panted and shook his finger. 'But you weren't here earlier. Explanation now!'

'How did you..?' Kit gestured to the key in the outside lock, but he could tell from his master's face that he didn't appreciate the subject being changed.

'An old trick,' panted Saroni. 'Never mind that. Where did you go? The door was locked from the inside and the window's too small even for you. I searched the room. Where were you?'

Kit shook his head.

''Tis something to do with that so-called Bible you're always carrying round, am I right? I can see from your face that I am! What is this you've become mixed up with, Kit?' It was the first time Saroni had used his real name. He threw his hat angrily onto the other bed and gestured wildly with both hands. 'Listen to me. There are tricks, like what I did to get into this room. You know what it was? I simply slid a piece of paper beneath the door, poked the key from the outside, heard it fall onto the paper then pulled it towards me, back under the door. Looks like magic but no, not a bit. This is different. Where I come from there is still belief in the *strega*: witch! Not the thing I put in my mouth for Punchinello, I mean a real witch, a wife of the Devil. Now I see what is happening here... you must not get involved with this, Kit. Already I feared that someone had put the evil eye on you.' Saroni waved his hand around in the darkness as though he were trying to grasp the unknown. Kit had never seen his master look genuinely scared before. Over on the sailor's chest, Punchinello smiled horribly from ear to ear.

Kit spent a long time trying to persuade Saroni that he wasn't involved in black magic but when they lay down to sleep at last, he saw how carefully his master placed the lantern on the floor between them, how he crossed his arms over his chest and kept facing Kit's way. It crossed Kit's mind that Saroni would never call him *Angelo* again.

Kit didn't sleep that night and when dawn broke and he began to rouse himself, Saroni's eyes shot open.

Those eyes seemed to follow Kit around all morning. After what had taken place the evening before, Kit was desperate to open the book and talk to Zannah. He remembered how annoyed she'd been and wanted to explain why he'd been unable to leave the cottage door and go with her. It was impossible because all morning his master gave him jobs to do, painting and mending puppets, sweeping around the stage, brushing the dust from coats, the list went on and on. Kit knew the reason: Saroni was keeping him busy to make sure he stayed out of trouble.

Kit tried to act normally but his head was spinning from his encounter with Zannah. In one way, he was elated that he had managed to get to the village and return but, in another, he couldn't imagine when he would get the space and privacy to do so again, even if Saroni stopped being so watchful. All the taverns in Bath were familiar with Saroni and his apprentice and if Kit hired a room for an hour, the way he had in other towns, his master would soon get to hear of it. If only he could have told Saroni the truth and shown him the book but now this seemed the biggest risk of all. Saroni was someone who believed in magic but was deeply suspicious of it and if he didn't accept Kit's explanation, he might even try and destroy the book. Yet Kit loved his master and it saddened him to keep the great secret to himself.

At the end of the first performance of the afternoon, Kit spotted his chance to slip away as Saroni was collecting payment from the small crowd. Their plan was to pack up and leave Bath the next day, but Kit knew well that life on the road would allow him few opportunities to communicate with Zannah. That afternoon, he only had an hour at best to find a quiet spot and open the book, and so he ran up to Queen's Square, heading for Barton Fields. He thought about attaching the thread to a tree trunk and jumping in again. The thread was wound into a ball and in his bag all ready. After weighing everything up, Kit decided against this course of action: what if some passer-by found the book lying there and made off with it? What if they snapped the thread?

Taking up a position upon the grassy mound, under cover of the trees, Kit turned the pages hurriedly until he came to Zannah's. It took a few moments before her eyes focused upon him and Kit could imagine her being drawn to the mirror beside the cottage door, in answer to his call.

'Kit, thank God. You vanished right before my eyes,' she said.

'I couldn't help it. I'm all right,' he said. 'Let me tell you why I couldn't go with you last night.'

Zannah wasn't really listening. She seemed very perturbed. 'There's something wrong with this village, Kit, and I never realised until you came last night. It's like I've woken up. It's been the same for years: nobody's born and no one ever dies. It all came upon me in a rush as I was lying abed after you'd gone. No births, no deaths. That's not natural, is it?'

'No,' said Kit. 'The wedding always seems like 'tis just around the corner but it never happens. People talk and talk about it but they don't seem to realise, it never comes.'

'That's right,' she cried. 'I can see it all now; it's like you've woken me up, Kit. I've been lying low since all this talk about me being a witch. Then this morning I took a walk down the road and saw Meggy Baker and she was jawing on about Alys' wedding. She's not happy 'cos I was the one to take Col's fancy when he first come here and everyone knows it. So then, suddenly I couldn't stand her prattling. "Pray tell the date of this wedding?" says I. "For the weeks and months and years go by and it ne'er comes any nearer, do it?"'

'What did she say?'

'Oh, she cursed me and called me jealous, the hedge-born ronyon! Then she called me witch again and disappeared inside the bakehouse. But in truth, Kit, she did not know what I meant, I could see it in her eyes. None of them do. It's like everyone in this village is living in a dream. You must speak to them Kit. Then they'll see what I now see. Then mayhap, we can all work out what's happening here.'

'Zannah, 'tis too dangerous.' Kit was alarmed, all the more so now he'd had time to think through her plan. 'Seeing me there will give them such a fright, they'll refuse to admit they know me, lest they get called witch

140

too. And what about when I fade away before their eyes, like I did last night? They'll be more scared and then they'll call you "witch" even more. Where do you think this is going to lead? I have a different plan in mind so hear me out. I will find some way to come and get you and bring you here, to my world. What do you think?'

'Me go with you?' she marvelled. 'I... I don't know, Kit. How would it work?'

'There might be some way I ain't thought of yet. There's always some way out of trouble, you have to believe that.' It was what Gabe had always said, all the times they had been in trouble... but this was a very different situation. Was he wrong to suggest this now when he had no idea if it were possible? 'I just want you out of there, Zan,' he said. 'I'm sorry but your village is under some kind of curse. As long as I've had this book, I've known there's something wrong with that place.'

'Book? What book?'

Kit took a deep breath and told her everything, from his first encounter with the wicked lord to his rescuing her page from Polley and, thereafter, the book from the library. Zannah remembered his Lordship and recalled how he was trying to get her to find some magical object which was hidden somewhere in the village. Her eyes widened as she tried to make sense of what he was saying.

'Kit, our lives here are a dream, ain't they? We rise in the morning, go about our work, go to bed just the same each evening but time never moves on. It's always

141

summer here and no one thinks it strange. Why should that be? As it turns out, we're just pages in a book and that's why. I always thought my life was real. I do remember being a child and likewise remember my ma on her death bed, that seemed real enough. What happened, Kit? Who put us in a book? The thought scares me so.'

Kit was nearly crying. It was torture to see Zannah so distressed and not be able to do anything about it. 'I should be there with you,' he said. 'But everything has become difficult for me here, suddenly. It will take time for me to find a way of getting to you, Zan. You'll have to wait. Then I'll try to bring you back here, out of that village and out of the book.'

Zannah was shaking her head slowly. 'How can I come with you? These are my people, Kit, even if they hate me right now. I can't just run away.' She reached out her hand and placed it on her side of the page, while Kit reached his out, too. There was no human skin or warmth beneath his fingertips, just papery bumps and yet he knew what Zannah's hand felt like and tried to keep that feeling in his mind.

Kit spent longer talking to Zannah than he'd intended and had to race back to the Abbey Yard where the late afternoon performance had already begun. Saroni glared at him as he arrived panting and he dropped the oilskin bag amongst the pile of marionettes behind the stage. He picked up Columbina and straightened her costume ready for her entrance. It was a bright afternoon and an unexpectedly large crowd had gathered with many fine ladies and gentlemen amongst them. Kit could see why Saroni hadn't waited for him to return before commencing the performance.

'Where were you?' his master hissed at him while the crowd applauded the end of the first scene.

'I went for a walk,' said Kit. 'I'm sorry. I had a headache.'

'*Cavolo!*' Saroni muttered under his breath, then turning razor-eyes on Kit said, 'Later, you and I will talk, huh?'

There was no time for Kit to do more than nod before Saroni began the next scene with the arrival of the first of the three lovers. Columbina met him at the gateway of the castle and soon, Kit and Saroni were going through the familiar routines, although Kit noticed how his master's performance was lacking its usual sparkle. For the first time Kit could remember, Saroni looked really tired. Still, the crowd laughed politely and 'Oo'd' and 'Aah'd' appropriately. When Punchinello emerged and began waving his stick around, they seemed delighted. At this point, Kit usually took his chance to peek around the side of the stage and watch the spectacle of his master playing with the audience.

Kit could see the spectators enjoying themselves, the children diving out of the way of Punchinello's stick and laughing. Then his blood froze. There was a familiar face in the middle of the crowd, belonging to a sombrely but expensively dressed gentleman in black whose left hand rested on a silver-topped walking stick and whose other arm was in a sling. Kit remembered that arm protruding limply from the sunrise window as the stained glass reformed around it, biting into it. The glass must have squeezed it to breaking point. His Lordship's eyes wore the same sardonic expression and there was someone with him, a dark suited servant to whom he was whispering from the side of his mouth.

Colewich must have heard Kit was in Bath. Not content with sending his spies, he'd come in person to seek him out and re-claim the book and now he'd found exactly what he'd been searching for. Kit looked around, expecting to see Pinches watching the side of the stage, waiting for the performance to end so he could grab him, but Pinches was nowhere in sight and Kit gradually managed to pull himself together and reason out what was happening. Lord Colewich was a wealthy society gentleman; was it such a surprise to find him spending time in Bath during the season? As he was recovering from his injuries, his doctor may have recommended a rest in the spa town where he could bathe in hot springs and take the waters for his health. Moreover, Kit looked very different from the London thief he had been, in his smart coat and boots with his hair powdered and tied back. If Colewich saw him, he most likely wouldn't recognise him but Kit would remain backstage just in case. When he got the chance, he would explain quickly to Saroni that his headache was worse, so he could avoid taking his usual bow at the end of the show.

With his eye to a small gap in the side curtain, Kit studied Colewich. His Lordship seemed thoroughly bored with the performance and didn't so much as smile. Kit saw him consult a pocket watch and guessed he was merely passing the time before attending some other appointment. Finally, and to Kit's profound relief, Colewich turned and he and the well-dressed servant began to walk away.

It was Columbina's cue to sing her comic song about the hopelessness of men. From the corner of his eye Kit saw Saroni taking his chance to rest as he usually did at this point, wiping the sweat from his brow with a large spotted handkerchief as he squatted amongst the marionettes. Kit sang in a high voice while he used the wire to move Columbina's hand from her heart to her head to show despair, then flung it out in an appeal to the audience. He was so busy, he didn't notice Saroni slip his hand inside the oilskin bag and remove the book. Suddenly, in the middle of the fourth verse, Kit heard a commotion behind him and when he turned, he saw his master backing away from the pages which had come loose and were lying all over the pavement. The upturned faces were shouting in an angry chorus and the magical light curls were beginning to swell upward and outward. Kit dropped Columbina and darted to retrieve the pages but the magic lashed out and battered him away. There was a huge gasp from the audience and some surprised laughter. Someone shouted 'Fireworks!' The magic manacled Kit's hands together and he felt himself being dragged backwards by Saroni. 'Let go!' he cried. 'We must get them back into the book!'

Something horrible was happening, horrible but not surprising to Kit who had already seen what the magic was capable of. The magical curls were beginning to animate the marionettes and first to get to her invisible feet was Columbina who whirled around on the spot. When that audience saw her perform this pirouette with her skirts billowing out all around her, they began to applaud, thinking it was part of the show. One by one, Scarramouccia, Pantalone, the Devil and all the others came to life and began dancing about on the stage, whirling around like spinning tops and crashing into each other. At first, the audience seemed to enjoy it, but their approval soon turned to alarm. The marionettes were destroying one another. Wooden arms, ears and noses were flying off and hitting members of the audience who began to turn and run. Punchinello woke up and the magic seemed to realise that his character was different to the others, wilder and more ready to break the rules. To Kit's and Saroni's helpless horror, the hook-nose marionette began to inflate until it was twice the size of the others and its head rose above the top of the stage like a giant, wicked baby peeping malevolently from the side of its crib. True to form, Punchinello began to use his stick, first to strike at the other marionettes, then violently at the stage itself. All the magic now seemed to concentrate upon Punchinello. As he continued to grow, he proceeded to wreck the stage in a furious frenzy, like a toddler in a rage, determined to reduce it to matchwood. The front panel boasting the bright, splendid painting of the Bay of Naples was smashed beyond recognition. Next, he turned his attention to the ladies, gentlemen and children who were screaming and scattering to the three other sides of the Abbey Yard, terrified and mesmerised by what they were witnessing. Punchinello was now as tall as the Abbey doors but had retained his marionette proportions with his head and hands still much bigger than the rest of him. It made him look truly monstrous.

Punchinello let out a terrific, inhuman roar and went racing round the Yard in his legless costume, aiming at anybody and anything with his stick like he was playing a hellish game of golf. His smile had collapsed into a terrible, downward curving grimace. When they weren't dodging out of his way, the ladies, gentlemen and children were shrieking and fainting in doorways. Worshippers and tradespeople emerged from the Abbey to see what the commotion was about, then wisely hung back in the shadowy doorway. The marionette was like a whirlwind, tearing up everything that crossed its path, including the booths and stages of other street entertainers. It was the first time Kit had seen the magic work from such a distance; perhaps it was because it had found such a suitable subject in the wicked Punchinello. Windows shattered and stalls were upended but it was never enough for the devilish puppet, who was delighting in his furious rampage. His evil energy seemed to double and re-double with each object he destroyed.

Kit shook himself free from Saroni's grasp and somehow managed to snatch up the pages and stuff them between the covers of the book, battling the sensation of fire and ice in his fingers. The book struggled to be free of his grasp and Kit had to use all his strength to force it into the oilskin bag and keep the bag closed, pinning it to his chest. Cut from the source of magic at last, Punchinello shrank back to his normal size in mid-air and dropped to the floor in the middle of the Abbey Yard like a dead bird.

For a moment which felt like forever, a tremendous silence fell over the Abbey Yard. Kit remained rooted to the spot, holding the bag and trembling.

CHAPTER 15

Footsteps could be heard running towards the Abbey Yard. Folk had heard the screams and were coming to see what was wrong. They were amazed to find dumbstruck ladies and gentlemen crouching in terror in a wide circle about a tattered marionette lying broken on the ground. Nobody wanted to go near it. Kit was the first to move. He couldn't see Colewich or his servant, but they couldn't have missed what had just happened. He stammered out some feeble apologies to Saroni, who was as stunned as everyone else, and clutching the bag which was vibrating with a terrible, unpredictable fury, he turned and ran.

Kit ran until his heartbeat thumped louder in his ears than did the pounding of his feet. The whole of Bath seemed to have come to a standstill as news of the terrible event spread from the Abbey Yard like wildfire. Kit felt the eyes of the silent people all fixed upon him. Anyone racing from a scene looked guilty but what else could he do? Bath wasn't like London, the new streets were wide and elegant and there were fewer crooked side alleys down which you could lose yourself in an emergency. Kit feared that at any moment he would hear the sound of an angry mob behind him and knew his best chance was to get out of town. He headed towards Barton Fields.

Kit stopped to regain his breath under cover of the trees. He could still see the hurt and bewildered expression on his beloved master's face as he'd attempted his stupid apology. Saroni had offered Kit a chance in life by teaching him his craft, and how had Kit repaid him? By lying to him continually; lies which had just ended up destroying his livelihood and ruining him, maybe for good. When he thought about the marionettes and the brightly-painted stage lying smashed to pieces, Kit could not help but cry bitterly.

Kit had vowed he would never steal again, but wasn't lying just as bad as stealing? Wasn't it *worse*? When you lied, you stole the truth from another person, and that was more precious than money or belongings. When you lied as much as Kit had, to someone you loved so dearly, to someone to whom you owed everything, what did that make you?

'Clodpole book!' cried Kit. He felt like hurling the bag to the floor and kicking it and was only stopped by the thought that it might hurt Zannah. 'What kind of nickninny am I to try and help you all the time? Why do you have to be so stupid and difficult?'

He could feel the magic humming angrily beneath the oilskin like trapped bees. It was vital he should put as much distance between himself and Bath as possible, but he turned for one last look from the top of Barton Fields, tears streaming down his face. He could still hear Saroni's voice: 'No running out on me... You do that to me, I never will forgive you.'

'From my deepest heart, I am so sorry,' he whispered, devastated to think that his dear, wronged master would never know how sorry.

Kit walked for the rest of the afternoon and evening, only stopping for a drink of cold water from a brook. He didn't trust the open roads but kept heading north, crossing farmland and great empty stretches of wasteland. He didn't attempt to open the book, knowing from experience that the magic would take time to calm down. In any case, his hands were sore and blistered from handling the angry pages. He spent the night in a wooded valley but the leaves that looked so dry grew damp within seconds of being lain upon and every sound startled him from sleep. His greatest fear was of highwaymen and footpads, for the open countryside was a lawless place and it was dangerous to travel alone. He had roughed up his clothes to make himself look less wealthy but there was no disguising the oilskin bag. If he were caught, the book would certainly be taken, and he would be lucky to escape with his life.

The next morning, he set off again with no idea where he was heading. He had a few coins in his boot and would have asked to buy breakfast at the farmhouse he passed on the other side of a field but knew he couldn't take the risk. It was easy to imagine Colewich sending his servant on horseback to check all the farmhouses in the area and enquire if anyone had seen a strange boy carrying a bag. Kit's belly was crying out for food and was barely satisfied with the few wild strawberries he'd found in the hedgerow and some fat hen, a weed they'd fattened poultry on back in his village in Kent.

By late afternoon exhaustion had overtaken him. The air had cooled and it was beginning to rain so he sheltered below a bridge on the banks of a river. Hunger was making him light headed. He placed his hand, which still hurt, tentatively inside the bag and felt only the faintest hum from the book so he took it out. He had to check that Zannah was all right and explain his predicament, but he dreaded opening it. He was scared of finding that in the middle of all the confusion in the Abbey Yard, he had failed to gather up all the pages. His fingers trembled as he opened the book. If any of the scratched men climbing the ladder were missing, there was no way back to the village. Worse still, in his mind's eye, he could see Zannah's page sodden with rain, lying in the corner of the Yard, disintegrating.

Suddenly Kit's heart leapt because there was Zannah before him, but he could also see how frightened she was.

'Thanks be, there you are,' she said. 'Oh Kit, there was another bad storm. So much damage around the village. People are saying it's on account of me being a witch; now they're saying it openly.'

'Can they not think a storm's a storm?' said Kit. He had never seen her look so scared.

'You don't understand. We were heard the other night, you and I. Our neighbour, the widow Edith heard us from her cottage. Now people are saying I've been consorting with a demon and that's what brought the storm. Grandda's so deaf, he don't hear what they're saying, that's my only comfort.'

'Something they don't understand must be a demon, then? They are so stupid.'

'But do you understand the storm Kit? Do you?'

''Tis the book,' he said and he started trying to explain some of what had happened the previous day but it only seemed to frighten Zannah more.

'Books! Pages? I don't understand. Everyone else in this village is living in a dream whilst I am living in a nightmare!' she cried.

'I don't understand either,' said Kit. 'Zan, we must get you out of there. I am thinking up a plan. You need to get out of that village, soon as possible.'

'But I can't leave, Kit, I told you that. What will happen to my Grandda? What will happen to the others? Even the ones that hate me, and that's just about all of 'em. I'm the only one with any idea that anything's wrong here. I need to try and get them to see what I can see, or they're done for.'

'But if you're in danger?'

'Can we not go back to my first idea, Kit? Come here again. When the others see you, they'll have to admit they've been talking to you as well and that'll show them I ain't a witch. Between us, we can find out what's been happening here and do summat about it.'

Kit still thought it was a bad idea, but he felt too weak to argue.

'Whatever the plan I am sorry, but I can't come straight away. I promise I will soon. When the pages fell from the book, I had to stuff them back in and now they're in such disarray. I must get them back in the right order. 'Twill take a little time. A few days? If I try any quicker, it may conjure another storm.'

Zannah's face fell but she kept her clear, trusting eyes fixed upon him. 'I know you are doing your best, Kit.'

'Of course.' Their hands touched although the wary magic fizzled beneath Kit's fingers and stung him again. He meant to keep this promise to return to the village. Yet there'd been other times he'd meant promises and had been unable to keep them and his heart hurt at the thought. He'd promised never to run out on Saroni. He'd promised to get Gabe well again. Sometimes you couldn't hold onto promises, they slipped through your fingers like sand.

Kit turned a few more pages. Although he'd visited every one of the villagers at one time or another, he usually returned to the more talkative. Apart from Zannah, they all treated him as an imaginary friend, someone to confide in but not take terribly seriously. He didn't know which of the many faces belonged to the Widow Edith but it seemed unwise to seek her out. There seemed little point in pleading Zannah's case with Meggy either, who had her own reasons for disliking her. The only one Kit thought might listen to him was Judd the blacksmith who always seemed full of good, practical sense and it was to his page he turned next.

'A bad do,' Judd shook his head. 'There's been much destroyed in the village since last we spoke.'

'I know there was a terrible storm and a heap of damage done,' Kit said. 'But it weren't anyone's fault, Judd.'

'I don't know so much,' the blacksmith said darkly. 'There's many as say that bold wench Zannah knows more about it than she lets on.'

This was true but not in the way Judd meant and Kit began to protest.

'I can only say what I been told.' Judd was insistent. 'The night afore the storm, she was heard and seen consorting with a demon outside awl Robin's cottage.'

''Tis a wicked lie,' said Kit.

'How knowest thou?'

Kit weighed up how to answer. Was telling Judd the truth going to make matters better or worse? He failed to reach a decision and turned back to Zannah's page. He suggested she should stay at home for the next few days, then tried to rearrange a couple of pages in the right order but the simmering magic flashed a warning and he had to give up on that, too, for the time being.

At nightfall Kit came to a farm. Although he was unnerved by how close the cowshed was to the farmhouse, the rain was coming down in sheets and the hay looked warm, deep and inviting. He managed to get a little milk from one of the cows, catching it in a pail and this became his supper, together with the best parts of some spoiled potatoes collected in a pan by the door, probably intended as animal feed. The cows' breathing filled the shed with warmth and he was asleep as soon as he laid down his head.

Kit had a rude awakening the next morning, when he was found by one of the farm servants who chased him off with a pitchfork. After two days on the road, he knew he must look rough, like a footpad. Even so, the servant might easily give a description of Kit to Colewich's men and he vowed not to risk spending another night at a farm where he could be discovered. He headed north-west with some idea of settling in the first sizeable town he came across, where there would be more chance of finding food and of concealing himself and the book. The journey was slow going and he was still ravenously hungry but at least he'd benefited from a good night's rest.

Kit carried on walking for another four days, growing weaker and weaker. Sometimes he was lucky enough to find a decent place to sleep but at other times his bed was the shelter of a hedgerow where he would wake the next morning cold and stiff, as often as not sodden with dew. At least he hadn't been robbed and for that he gave thanks. Twice a day, at noon and nightfall, he would open the book and talk with Zannah. He found her either scared or angered by what people in the village

CHAPTER 16

He was aware of voices above his head. Were they real or just another fever-dream?

'*Bychan yw e.*'

'*Yn wir? Duw, duw.*'

It didn't sound like the language Saroni spoke. Kit's head hurt. He drifted off again.

He was riding a sea of grass, small as a ladybird, losing his footing and tumbling then caught by the wind and tossed into the sky. Zannah was sitting on top of a hill, ripping pages from the book, crumpling them into paper balls and throwing them into the air, where they changed into dandelion seeds and drifted away. He tried to catch them. He wanted to tell her to stop but thick clouds were forcing their way down his throat and gagging him.

Later, someone was holding him up and he could feel cold water moistening his lips. When he found the bottle with his mouth, like a weakling lamb, he drank with the smallest of gulps, but the water could not put out the fire which raged in his throat. Exhausted, he fell back onto the straw.

He was in the attic and Gabe was pointing and laughing at something he could see through the hole in the roof. When Kit looked up he saw the comet heading straight for them like a fiery cannonball, gathering speed. It was going to hit them any moment and Kit was furious with Gabe, shouting at him to stop laughing as he tried in vain to make him understand they would have to run to save their lives. After dragging him from the bed, Kit saw with horror that Gabe had turned into a puppet: a laughing dead monkey puppet.

Much later, there were movements around the shelter, voices and noises. Shadows darkened his closed eyelids as creatures came and went beyond the gaping planks of the back wall. He could sense many large bodies with steam rising off their backs. The sounds they made were hellish, like souls in torment, and the heat built and built. They thumped against the wall and bellowed. When he opened his eyes, Judd was crouching in front of him with a scarf tied around his nose and mouth. The blacksmith was offering him water and pressing a cold, wet cloth to his brow. There was a fire on the ground outside the shelter and shadowy human shapes were huddled around it. Kit began to fear for the book's safety. He had to get back to the village and persuade Zannah to leave. If he couldn't do that, he would have to appear before the villagers, like she wanted him to. He had to get into the book again soon…

When Kit woke properly, his fever had broken. He was alone, yet someone really had been there; he hadn't imagined it. A battered leather bottle lay at his side with a small hunk of bread and cheese lying next to it and someone had covered him with a rough blanket. Sweating with fear, he groped around for the oilskin

160

bag, but it was safe beneath his legs and concealed by the straw. He reached for the bottle with a shaky hand, drank half the water, ate some of the bread and cheese then lay back and shut his eyes.

When he woke later, Kit noticed the folded piece of paper which had been placed beside the food. He couldn't read what was written upon it, so he folded it up again and drank half of what remained of the water, then sank back to sleep.

Another day passed, although Kit had lost all sense of time. He was depressed to find that at some stage, he had drunk the rest of the water although he could not remember doing so. He sat up, leaning against the wooden planks of the back wall and opened the book. He needed to see Zannah and explain what had been happening.

'Kit, thank God!' she exclaimed. 'But... you do not look well. What has happened?'

'I was ill, Zan,' said Kit. 'For days and days, such a fever had I.'

'I was afeared something had happened to you.'

'I still fear for you. When I'm well again and strong enough...'

She didn't let him finish. 'Something terrible has happened, Kit, and the whole village is in turmoil. Our neighbour, the Widow Edith died these three days since. She sickened quickly and died.'

'Was she very old?' asked Kit.

Zannah nodded.

'There you are then,' he said, shutting his eyes. It took too much effort to both look and speak at the same time. ''Tis only natural she might die if she were old and ill, 'tis what you'd expect...'

'It is not what anyone expected here.'

Kit opened his eyes and Zannah was staring at him and biting her lip. 'But there's nothing natural in your village, is there? Nobody's died there for hundreds of years?'

'I suppose not. I don't remember the last time it happened.' Zannah shook her head. 'It's come as a shock to one and all here. And of course, the wagging tongues wag harder now. They're saying as how I put a curse on her for catching me with the demon that night you came. Even Grandda's caught wind of what they're saying. He tells me to stay inside but I feel like a prisoner. I don't feel safe anywhere.'

A horrible realisation was dawning on Kit, stealing over him bit by bit, making his flesh crawl.

'Zannah. I'm so sorry. 'Tis my fault after all. I never should have set foot in your village because it woke time up again. Nobody's been born or died there for hundreds of years, but then I turn up, someone from outside, and time begins again. Suddenly someone very old has died. 'Tis the same as you beginning to realise there's something wrong in your village; that only happened after I set foot there.'

'Do you really think that's true, Kit?'

'What else is there to think?'

Kit felt a hundred times worse following this conversation. The pages weren't all back in order and for now he felt too unwell to do anything about it. Removing the pages hurt his hands so much, he had to do it quickly and for now that was impossible. In any case, he wasn't strong enough to enter the book so what was the point? Before replacing it in the bag, he turned the pages and saw that one was blank where before, there had been an old woman. This was surely the Widow Edith's page. Now she was dead and in some way the villagers were right, he was to blame. He'd meddled in something that had been the same way for hundreds of years. It was his fault time had returned to the village.

Kit could stand and walk a little. He tried to search outside the shelter for food, but it was such wild countryside and there was no fat hen or strawberries, just tough, windswept grass. He was soon exhausted and had to return and lie down again.

When he woke next, a broad-shouldered figure was filling the doorway and blocking out the light. Kit couldn't see the man's face, but he'd been dreaming about Judd and wondered if this was another illusion. 'How are you now, then?' said the man.

'I'm...getting better,' stammered Kit.

'No fever?'

'No.'

The man turned slightly to hold the unfolded scrap of paper up to the light. Kit shaded his eyes and saw that

163

it wasn't Judd. The man's long, sandy-coloured hair was tied back, and his light blue eyes scoured the paper while his tanned skin spoke of much time spent out of doors. He wore a long coat which stopped just short of his boots. 'I know the one who wrote this,' he said. 'He thought you might have plague but if the fever's gone...' The stranger looked at the paper suspiciously and back at Kit several times before speaking again. 'What's your name?'

'Kit.' He wouldn't lie. From now on he would speak as much truth as possible to anyone who was kind enough to help him and he sensed that this was a good man, like the one who'd left him the food and written the note.

'Where've you come from then, Kit?'

'Bath.'

'Where you going?'

Kit didn't want to say he didn't know and he couldn't remember the names of any other towns. 'London,' he said and his spirits sank as he heard himself say it.

'Funny way to get to London? 'Tis dangerous out here on foot, all on your own.'

Kit nodded. The stranger carried on looking him over and frowning. 'Did someone attack you?'

'No, sir.'

'You a thief?'

'No, sir.' Not any more.

None of Kit's answers seemed to satisfy the stranger, who remained puzzled. 'Then what are you doing here, Kit?' he asked.

'I'm an actor, sir. I got separated from my company. I knew not where I was headed. I just carried on walking and hoped to catch them up.' Some of what he was saying was the truth and that felt good.

'An actor?' The man considered Kit's appearance again, and his expression changed. 'I suppose you could be. They're strange creatures, after all. Got money?'

'A little,' Kit began to fish inside his boot but the man signalled for him to stop. 'I don't want any, I just wondered. You're lucky to still have it, my lad. There's thieves out here that'll finish you off for thruppence, soon as look at you.' The man folded up the paper and put it in his pocket. He left the shelter, then returned with a chunk of bread in one hand and a bottle in the other. He handed the bread to Kit, who gnawed at it ravenously and offered him ale which Kit poured down his throat, so it barely touched the sides. He gave his thanks through another mouthful of bread.

'There'll be others along soon. I must get things ready. Stay here.' The stranger turned and left. Kit lay back and watched him coming and going through the doorway. He knew he had heard this man's accent before but couldn't place it. He liked the musical way he spoke and practised it in his mind, vowing to stow it away in his memory for use at another time. The man soon got a fire started in the ashes of the previous one and unpacked more bottles and bundles. For the first time in a long time, Kit recalled another story from the Bible, that of the Good Samaritan, and realised that these men were like that good fellow from Samaria, strangers who'd saved his life.

About an hour later, there was a rumbling sound in the west. Kit stood up and holding onto the sides of the shelter, crept around to the doorway. He looked up at the sky, thinking the sound he heard must be thunder but then in the distance he saw a dark cloud approaching by land: cattle, hundreds of black cattle, spread across the brow of the hill. They came at a slow and steady pace and kept coming, even after Kit thought several times there couldn't possibly be more. The ones at the edges of the herd were kept from breaking loose by a team of small brown dogs which raced back and fore, while the men who walked on either side whistled and whooped their orders to the dogs. The stranger knelt beside the fire and Kit noticed his brown horse cropping the grass a little way off. He called over to Kit, asking how he was feeling, and Kit answered that he was getting better. He knew of the cattle drovers who brought animals across the country for sale in the English markets, had heard their voices on the streets of London but had never seen any at work or could have guessed what a spectacular sight it would be. He also knew why the man sounded so different: he was Welsh.

Kit withdrew to the shelter and lay back down. Although still weak and tired, he felt some hope. For the first time he appreciated that the shelter was set on the edge of a large, fenced enclosure. After a while, the cattle arrived at the enclosure and the noise they made whilst being funnelled through the narrow gateway, along with the barking dogs, made Kit think a person would go deaf or mad amongst them. Once inside, they spread out and began to feed on the grass. Once this lengthy task was complete, the drovers themselves gathered round the fire to eat, and in ones and twos peeped in on Kit, although none of them set foot inside the shelter. Kit heard them talking, mainly in Welsh but he caught odd bits of English.

'...Might be a gentleman, look at the boots...'

'...An actor? *Diawch erioed*! What acting is there to do in this godforsaken place? Acting the goat, more like!'

'...If the fever's gone, 'tis unlikely to be plague but *Duw!* I wouldn't sleep in there tonight, even so.'

Kit felt uncomfortable about remaining in the shelter on his own while the others slept out in the open and came to the doorway to say so. 'Lie down, lad,' said the first man he'd met, obviously the leader. 'Don't mind us. 'Tis a fine evening. Rest tonight and we'll see how you are in the morning.' Kit went back inside the shelter and did as he was told. The drovers settled down before it was completely dark, and so he took the opportunity to rearrange a few more pages quickly. It wasn't too difficult a task now the magic had calmed down and he could actually remember the correct order they went in without having to check the stick man.

Kit felt a lot better the next morning and the leader, who was called Daniel Price, invited him to come and join the men around the fire. He gave his thanks for the bacon and bread he was offered and felt his strength returning. The drovers seemed more relaxed around him this morning, having assured themselves that he wasn't carrying the plague. They introduced themselves and then continued to talk quietly in Welsh. It was still very early, with mist rising in the fields all around.

The cattle were greeting the day with a lot of noise. The small dogs sat beside the men like their equals and ate their breakfasts too. They were wiry and tough looking but had gentle faces and pointed ears and the men petted them and fussed over them.

'You're heading for London, then?' said Daniel Price and the others quietened to listen to Kit's reply.

'Hopefully, sir,' said Kit.

'Hopefully? You said it, my boy. It doesn't do to be out here on your own with money in your pocket, or in your boot for that matter. I wouldn't want to reckon your chances of getting to London. We're headed for Smithfield Market and you're welcome to make your way with us, if you're feeling well enough. From time to time, we do escort young gentlemen across the country.'

'I haven't much money,' said Kit. 'You can have what I've got.'

'Just pay what you can. Pay for your food and lodging.' For the first time, Daniel smiled at him. Kit nodded at each of the dozen men in turn and they grunted and nodded back pleasantly enough but there was no time for further chat, the drovers were already getting to their feet and packing up. Kit wasn't sure about going with them. He'd promised himself he'd never return to London where he was bound to get caught up in his old thieving ways but if they passed any smaller towns, he could make his excuses and leave at that point. In one way, it seemed a good plan to go with the drovers. Burying yourself amongst four hundred head of Welsh Black Cattle was one of the best disguises he could think of and Colewich would still be searching for him. Also, just as Daniel said, there was the very real risk of being robbed.

Kit set off walking beside Daniel's horse. The progress of the cattle across the land was very slow. Kit imagined that from a bird's-eye view, it might look like spilt ink trickling down a green page although that bird could never imagine the deafening din at ground level. When one started its bellowing, those around it would follow suit and the noise would spread and spread. If there was ever a lull, you knew one animal would soon smack into another and start them all off again. The constant noise, the rumbling of hooves upon the earth and sensation of being carried along in a sea of hundreds of hot, heavy bodies was exhausting. Steam rose from the backs of the great square beasts, tails whipped, and their heavy stench increased as the day went on, but it was the clashing together of the heaving ribcages which frightened Kit most. He was scared to imagine what might happen if he became caught up in the middle of these monsters.

When Daniel noticed Kit tiring, he let him ride the horse. They didn't stop all day and by late afternoon, had arrived at an inn in the middle of nowhere which had a smithy attached and a field into which the cattle were herded and where they could feed. Daniel explained patiently that the next few hours would be spent shoeing the cattle that needed it and each one would have to be checked. Kit learnt that because they were walking long distances and sometimes over stony ground, the Welsh Blacks were fitted with iron shoes like horses. After stopping briefly for a mug of ale, the drovers hitched up their sleeves and began checking each of the cattle while Kit entered the inn and bought a plate of stewed meat and vegetables. He was already in awe of the drovers who, after such a long day traipsing the hills, had to get through this job again before the light failed and they could step inside and enjoy their own suppers. At least they would sleep comfortably at the inn that night and thankfully, Kit had been given his own tiny, cupboard-sized room. He retired to this dark, wood-panelled chamber straight after his meal, even though it was still light. If he could get some sleep now, he would wake later, while everyone else slept. He still had the ball of thread in his bag and before he lay down, he rearranged the last few pages in what he hoped was the right order. Although he did not feel completely well, in all other respects it seemed like a perfect opportunity to attempt to re-enter the book. He hadn't seen Zannah in days. Had anything happened since the death of Widow Edith? Had the villagers' accusations of witchcraft led to anything worse? It wasn't enough to speak with Zannah, he needed to go to the village and see for himself. On the journey to the inn, he'd finally come up with a plan for getting her out of the book, should she agree to it. He hoped, with all his heart, that he wasn't too late.

It was dark when he awoke, and it took him a while to make out shapes in the room. The small window was set deep into the wall and was a paler sort of dark. Kit had to feel his way around. He peed into the pot and replaced it under the bed before taking the book and ball of thread from the bag. He tied one end of the thread to the bedrail and the other to himself but this time he left a long end dangling from his wrist. His plan for getting Zannah out of the book was to tie the thread to her wrist, too. It was a simple enough plan and he was amazed it had taken him so long to come up with it. Of course, he had no idea if it would work.

Kit sat on the bed with the book beside him. It was going to be difficult to flip the pages when he couldn't see the climbing man and he prayed he'd got it right and they were all back in their correct order. After five attempts, with time to calm down and collect himself in between, the sixth worked.

It was night-time in the village. Kit had landed on a different roof and didn't recognise the view at all. He wondered how he was going to get to Zannah. Should he wait until he faded and try again? But what if the same thing happened and he just ended up somewhere else? Perhaps he'd just been lucky that first time to land on Zannah's own roof and there was no guarantee of repeating it.

Zounds! Each time he felt he was getting somewhere, fate threw up some new barrier. If he hadn't felt so frustrated he might not have done it, but Kit untied the thread from his wrist and secured it to a wooden spar holding the thatch to the roof. It could stay there until he returned. Last time a strong tingling in his fingers had warned him he was about to disappear. The village wasn't large and if he hurried he would probably be able to find Zannah and bring her back before the tingling began.

Kit jumped to the ground and upset a bucket, sending it clattering across the yard in front of the building. A dog barked nearby and another answered, further off. On his hands and knees, Kit was startled when the door behind him opened.

'Who's there?' said a gruff bass voice. It belonged to a large and imposing figure dressed in a long shirt and holding a candle in his fist. The man looked down and saw Kit on the ground. Recognition dawned for the pair of them at exactly the same moment.

'Judd?'

'Kit!'

The coals in the smithy were still aglow and Kit stretched his hands out to warm them. Although he was shaking with fright rather than cold, the warmth was soothing. Tools which lay higgledy-piggledy on the rough workbench, the smoke blackened beams, Judd's leather apron hanging from a bent nail, all struggled to embrace the dim orange light. The walls of the room might not have existed, it was so dark beyond a few feet.

Judd loomed up on the other side of the furnace. His black hair was chopped short but his beard was long and wild and he reminded Kit of someone else from the Bible – the giant Goliath with his features lit eerily from below, taunting the boy David to throw stones with his slingshot. Wasn't it strange how many of these old stories he'd heard long ago in church were now returning to him? Kit could have sworn that Judd hadn't blinked once since they'd entered the room. His dark eyes didn't move from Kit's face, not even when he took a swig from the large flagon of ale in his hand, not even when he swayed from side to side on unsteady legs.

'Don't get drunk,' pleaded Kit. He had already been talking for some time. 'Just don't, I beg you. Soon I must go. I need you to remember what I say.' Kit feared that the tingling in his fingers would start at any moment,

173

prompting him to leave. He couldn't risk the thread on the roof disappearing without him.

Now he'd been seen, Kit was forced to tell the blacksmith everything. He had always thought of Judd as one of the more reasonable folk in the book. If he could only get him on side... but Judd's way of coping was the flagon in his hand and each mighty swig made it less likely he'd listen to reason.

'Please tell me, you're quite sure Zannah's not harmed?'

'Zannah the witch?' muttered Judd. 'Not yet she's not.'

'She's not a witch!' How many more times did Kit have to say it?

'Be that so? And art thou not some demon from... that other place?' Judd stopped waving his finger at Kit and pointed at the floor.

This was such an odd echo of all those Thursday evenings at Mr Steen's, except in this case, Kit had to convince his audience that he was very much not a demon. 'Look at me. I'm a boy, flesh and blood.' He stretched his hands out to the blacksmith. 'Touch me, I am really here. This is not bad magic, Judd, although 'tis magic of some kind. Truth is, 'tis as much of a mystery to me as to you.'

Judd did not seem ready to take Kit up on his offer. Slowly, Kit walked around the workbench. He allowed Judd to take one more swig from the flagon before he lifted the blacksmith's free hand and placed it on his own arm. 'See, I am but a boy,' he said.

'A demon may take many forms,' Judd snatched back his hand.

'Oh, what can I do to prove it to you, man?' Kit was trying not to lose his temper. 'I know! The holy Lord's Prayer. A demon would never be able to recite that. If I can say the prayer, then you have to believe me, right?' Kit launched into 'Our Father, Who art in heaven...' secretly praying that he might be able to remember it all. Fortunately, when he ran out at 'Lead us not into temptation...' he could see a hint of belief in Judd's eyes.

'Thou sayest thou weren't with Zannah the night of the last storm? The Widow Edith swore it were a demon. She said she seen this demon dancing with Awl Robin's granddaughter.'

Kit remembered his tussle with Zannah when she tried to drag him away from her cottage door. 'Yes. I am the one Zannah was talking to that night when the widow Edith saw...what she thought she saw. But we weren't dancing, we were having an argument, you understand? She was trying to drag me down here to meet you all, but I couldn't go with her. You see? People are blaming her for nothing, Judd. Nothing. She's not a witch; that's nonsense. If she's a witch, you're a witch. You're all witches, come to that, talking to me in your puddles and scrying mirrors and what not. I'm just an ordinary lad. But I bring a warning and I'm going to need your help.'

'The Widow Edith died after she seen thee with

Zannah.' Judd swayed and looked gloomy. 'How'd'ee account for that?'

Kit swallowed. Right then, he didn't fancy admitting it was his fault that time had kicked off again. 'People die!' he cried ''Tis natural. But you lot have forgotten what's normal and natural. This village isn't right, Judd. There's something very wrong here.'

Judd's eyes darted around the room as though he were, in a lucid moment, remembering something. 'That armour I'm making his Lordship?' He stopped and shut his eyes, screwed up his face as though he were groping for some truth which was moving around like a slow animal in the darkness.

'How long have you been making that armour, Judd? How far have you got with it? When's his Lordship returning for it?'

'I don't know,' wailed Judd and when he opened his eyes, Kit saw real fear in them. 'I seem to have been making it…for ever.'

Kit shook his head. 'Not right, is it?'

Judd rubbed his forehead hard with the heel of his hand and snarled through his teeth. 'I can't talk about this any more. Prithee, go hence!'

Kit knew he could do no more. He turned for the door. ''Tis not Zannah's fault. You're the only one here with the sense to see that,' he said over his shoulder, but the blacksmith didn't answer. It was understandable. The truth of the strangeness of the village was only just dawning on him, the same way it had with Zannah. The realisation was frightening. Kit closed the door behind him but the tingling calling him back to the thread had not yet begun and he was wondering if he still had time to go in search of her, when he heard someone cry out loudly.

For a moment, Kit couldn't place the voice which was shrieking and praying to God to defend the village but when he arrived at the door of the bakehouse, he discovered it was Meggy making the commotion. Her whole attention was fixed upon a sight high above. Kit looked up and saw a comet with a long tail powering its way through the night sky. It looked for all the world like the one which had left his own sky so recently. He gasped and without looking his way, Meggy reached out and grabbed his arm.

'See there!' she cried. He could feel her trembling with fright. 'What evil is this come to plague us?'

Kit wasn't sure what to do but Meggy's shouting had roused others from their beds and shadowy figures came running. They spoke with voices Kit knew from the book. He was also aware that the tingling had begun in his fingertips but the more he tried to squirm out of Meggy's grasp, the tighter she held on. She slumped her whole weight against him and he was forced to lean in to support her. Meanwhile he could see all too well that the onlookers' shrieking and panic was not just a response to the comet in the sky. One moment they were looking up at it, the next they were staring at Meggy and himself and every mouth was open in horror. The tingling sensation was spreading rapidly up his arm and he knew he had to get back to Judd's roof quickly. He tried to shift Meggy towards the doorpost and as he did so, he saw the man he knew as Aldith take a nervous step forward. 'Mayhap we have been wrong about Zannah,' said Aldith in a shaky voice. 'For surely here is the real witch.'

Kit's right arm vanished beneath Meggy's hand and she stumbled forwards before turning to face him. The sight proved too much for her. Her face became a mask of horror and she dropped to the ground in a cold faint while the low chanting of 'Witch…witch… witch…' began. The timing could not have been worse, with the sudden appearance of both Kit and the comet. These people were bound to think he had caused it to appear, but there was no time for him to try and reason with them. The small crowd screamed louder as he ran past and as he climbed back onto Judd's roof, the only distinct voice he could hear was Aldith's, ranting on like a street preacher about how the demon was now flying back to hell.

Kit was tired the next day and grateful to Daniel for letting him ride the horse again. He was still shocked by what had taken place the previous evening and needed to be alone with his thoughts. He had tried to enter the book once more before daybreak but found he was too exhausted. Now all he could do was replay the terrible scene in his mind and wonder what would happen next? Had Aldith or any of the others recognised him as the person they had been talking to for weeks and months? He guessed not. Not only had it been dark, but their attention had been divided between the sight of him and the appearance of the comet. The crowd believed that they were witnessing Meggy consorting with a demon. If only he'd had a chance to show himself properly and confront them all, as Zannah had always wanted. Although the incident might have stopped the mob going for Zannah, what would happen to Meggy now?

A drover's life was hard, walking as much as twenty miles a day, but there was a steady rhythm to it. They stopped at another shelter that night, just as rain was beginning to fall. By the time everyone else was asleep, it was pouring and there was no way he could sneak off the way he'd planned. The book would have become sodden in no time if it were opened out of doors. Yet Kit's fears for Meggy were increasing and he was desperate to speak with Zannah and find out what was happening. When he lay down amongst the others, he found it impossible to sleep.

The weather had turned and it continued to rain for the next two days and nights, so there was no chance to open the book. The rain made their progress slower than usual and by the second day, the cattle were slipping in the mud and complaining loudly. The drovers trudged on and didn't grumble much. They might be gruff on the surface, but they were kind-hearted underneath and would do anything to spare their animals pain or distress. Daniel was an impressive leader with a quiet, calm authority and Kit never heard him so much as raise his voice at the other men. The dogs were just as committed to their work, racing back and fore with their heads lowered against the rain. All the men wore wide-brimmed hats and long coats and Daniel had fashioned Kit a kind of cape from a piece of oilcloth. Several times Kit had seen Daniel down on his knees, muttering his prayers before going to sleep at night. Perhaps his faith led him to perform these acts of kindness? Whatever the reason, Kit was very grateful to the head drover.

At the same time, Kit's fears continued to plague him, keeping him awake at night as the rain fell endlessly. He wished he knew for sure that Judd had believed him. He wished he could feel confident that the blacksmith was now on Zannah's side. Together, the two of them might stand some chance of making the others see sense. But what if Judd had just carried on drinking? And what if Meggy was shut in some makeshift prison, frightened and alone, awaiting trial or even death? Even though Meggy had been needling Zannah for weeks, Kit guessed Zannah would speak up for the poor woman and what would happen then?

The drovers were somewhere in the belly of England and he could only hope that, before long, they would come near some town and he could say he'd changed his mind about going to London. He still had a few coins left to pay for a couple of night's lodgings and be alone with the book. He was starting to come around to the idea of confronting the villagers the way Zannah had always wanted. If he said the Lord's Prayer, they would know he wasn't a demon and there were no witches in the village. Finally, they could get together and help one another.

On Kit's fifth afternoon with the drovers the weather changed back. The rain stopped and by late afternoon it was really warm and humid and Kit started making plans to sneak off with the book. That evening's place of rest was yet another shelter on an exposed hillside and there didn't seem any obvious places to hide but that wasn't going to stop him.

For once, the drovers were in high spirits. Maybe the opportunity to light another fire and eat a hot meal was making them jolly. Whatever the reason, when it turned dark they didn't seem in any rush to get to bed and sat around the fire smoking their pipes, telling stories in Welsh, slapping their knees and laughing their heads off. Kit got the impression they were telling stories about people and places they all knew. The dogs barked and wagged their tails. Kit sat quietly with his guts in a knot. From time to time he rubbed his eyes and made himself yawn, but none of them took any notice. Surely they weren't planning on staying up all night, were they?

'Come, Kit,' said Daniel, teasingly, the firelight twinkling in his blue eyes like the sun in a summer sky. 'You're a fine actor, so you say. Can't you give us some entertainment tonight? Tell us a story, lad.'

At first, Kit shook his head. Putting on a performance

was the last thing on his mind. But the men's cries of: 'Yes, Kit, a story!' and *'Dere 'mlaen 'ychan!'* made it hard to refuse. In any case, a sad tale might depress their high spirits and make them want to head for bed. It was worth a try. There was a ballad Saroni often sang, telling the tale of a soldier who is rejected in love and rushes to his death on the battlefield because his heart is already broken. Il Capitano would sometimes sing it just before the next hilarious scene. With a wink, Saroni had explained to Kit how it made that scene funnier if the audience had been close to tears moments before. Even though it was an English song, Kit had heard his old master sing the song so many times, he could only sing it Saroni's way:

> *I am a simple soldier–o*
> *I've fought in many wars*
> *I fire with my musket-o*
> *I fire with my musket-o*
> *I fire with my musket-o*
> *Where 'ere the battle roars*

> *I fear not the enemy*
> *As I my cutlass wield*
> *So why do I lay dying-o*
> *Why do I lay dying-o*
> *Why do I lay dying-o*
> *Upon the battlefield?*

Over many verses, the soldier related his tragic tale of love and betrayal. The men listened with stony faces and Kit knew his performance was hitting the mark when the eyes of William John Jones, who was normally so gruff and bullish, filled with tears. The dogs seemed to catch wind of the change in their masters' spirits and began to whimper. By the final verse, there wasn't a dry eye around the circle:

And now the light is failing fast
Yet do not weep for me
For my heart was broken long ago
My heart was broken long ago
My heart was broken long ago
By Evangelina Lee

When the song ended, there were coughs and attempts by the men to disguise their tears.

'Thank you, Kit,' said Daniel. He seemed keen to turn the subject away from dying soldiers and broken hearts. 'I was trying to place that voice you used when you sang?'

'I know. There was a man in London last year, singing in the middle of Covent Garden,' Twm Pwll Gwyn broke in. 'That's right, I remember him saying he came from a place called Napoli. You sounded the same as him, boy.'

There were a few mutters of, 'Yes, that's right' around the circle but Kit said nothing.

'Well,' William John blew his nose and rose to his feet. 'I'll away to my bed. *Nos da.*'

Several of the others got up and shook themselves. Kit's plan for getting them into the shelter had worked. Before long, only Daniel remained staring into the dwindling flames and frowning. Something seemed to be bothering him.

'You're a young lad, Kit,' he said. 'Have you performed in many countries then?'

Kit was getting to his feet, ready to take his own place inside the shelter. 'No,' he replied. 'But I've worked with many actors. Some of them come from over the seas.'

Daniel nodded slowly. 'Actors travel a lot then,' he said. 'A bit like us, really?'

'Always on the road.' Kit nodded back. He was starting to fear it had been a mistake to copy Saroni's voice. But why should he worry? What was the harm? Beyond the fact that by recalling his old master singing the sad song, he had depressed his own spirits thoroughly. Once again, he wondered what had happened to Saroni after the terrible scene in the Abbey Yard. Where was his dear old master now?

''Tis a wonder you got lost the way you did,' Daniel's voice roused him from his thoughts. 'Separated from your friends like that? So far from anywhere?'

The head drover hadn't questioned him in this way since they'd first met. 'Some business detained me in Bath. I tried to catch up with them.'

'Yet the road from Bath to London's plain as can be. Is it not strange you did not stick to the road?'

'I suppose the fever came upon me and I began to wander?' Nothing Kit heard himself say sounded any good. He didn't like it that Daniel seemed suddenly suspicious. He decided to cut his losses and say goodnight.

Kit lay as still as he could, his nerves jangling as he waited for Daniel to come to bed. Eventually the head drover stumbled in and settled himself in the straw. Kit heard a few whispered prayers, but it was a good half hour before Kit heard gentle snoring from Daniel's corner and another half hour before he felt brave enough to venture out, clutching the bag containing the book. Some of the dogs slept inside the shelter with their masters but Kit already had a plan to distract those on watch outside and produced scraps of food from his pocket to keep them quiet. While the dogs were busy eating, he slipped past and proceeded down the hillside with the oilskin bag in his arms, seeking a place where he wouldn't be seen from the shelter. The land was rolling and featureless, with no trees or bushes in sight and Kit trudged on awhile until he came to a dip in the ground. When he crouched in the dip, he could no longer see the shelter, and reasoned that if he couldn't see it, the drovers wouldn't see him if they woke, which seemed unlikely now. In any case, by this time he was too exhausted to walk much further; the dip in the ground would have to do.

CHAPTER 18

Kit was itching to get back into the book and the oilskin bag was the only object in sight to which he could secure the thread. Without the book inside, the bag wasn't heavy, but neither was it a windy night and he was willing to take a chance.

The time of day was always the same inside the book as it was outside, and he landed in the churchyard yew tree at dead of night. The comet was still burning brightly overhead, but he didn't have time to stop and wonder. With all speed, Kit wound the thread around an ancient branch and jumped to the ground, landing softly on all fours like a cat. He sensed movement nearby. The grey goat was watching him, but it wasn't the low, munching sounds it made that put Kit on high alert. The movements he could hear were coming from inside the church. It was the sound of furniture being dragged about, accompanied by the low hum of voices. In one corner of an arched window, a candle flickered. Suddenly a voice within cried out in distress. Kit padded towards the church door, keeping well in the shadows but he turned when he heard footsteps running up behind him.

'Kit, you must help me.' Zannah didn't even express surprise at seeing him, there was no time. She was out of breath and several figures were about to catch up with her. One of them called out, 'Enter not the house of God,' but Kit didn't see who it was before he'd been thrust inside and Zannah was slamming and barring the door. Her pursuers banged on the heavy oak, cursing and shouting: Did Zannah want to suffer the same fate as Meggy Baker the witch? Perhaps the two should be tried together? Yet it was not what he could hear outside, but the sight within that turned Kit to stone.

There were no wooden pews, the kind Kit was used to seeing in a church. A fire was glowing on the floor in the middle of the empty nave and upon it stood a small cauldron. All but one of those standing around the fire looked up the moment Kit burst in and froze at the sight of him, as though some magic had turned them to painted statues. Only the bent figure of Meggy dressed in a loose shift, her long grey hair falling over her bowed head, continued to cry for mercy as she writhed and twisted away from the steaming pot before which she was being held. It was full to the brim with boiling water while the damp firewood smoked and hissed beneath. Tall, white candles stood in niches around the walls and their flames guttered with the rush of incoming air.

A villager Kit knew as Margery, also known as Goody Clarke, was standing witness-like, a rosary clasped in her hands and she screamed first at the sight of Kit. 'God in Heaven!' exclaimed Aldith, letting go of Meggy's bare right arm, which he had been trying to force towards the bubbling cauldron. John Farmer relaxed his grip on Meggy's other arm and she battered both men off with flailing limbs and ran to the back of the church. 'There,' Aldith pointed at Kit with a shaky finger and spoke in an even shakier voice. 'See how the demon comes to take his own.' He began crossing himself, as did John and Margery, repeatedly and frenziedly. Margery raised her face to the ceiling and began to chant in Latin.

Kit was struck dumb but Zannah's voice rang out strongly. 'What evil work is this?' she demanded. 'To take a blameless woman and claim that everything that's going wrong is somehow her fault, is beyond stupid. Let her go!' Kit had never seen her so angry. 'They dragged her here tonight,' she explained to him. 'Meggy's been no friend to me, but I cannot stand by and see her tortured so. They claim if she can pull a stone from the boiling water without blistering her skin, it will show her innocence. Have you ever heard such foolishness? When I found out, I protested and Aldith got his friends to hold me back, but God gave me strength to escape.' She shouted at Aldith, Margery and John again. 'God is not on your side in this matter!' For a moment, all was silent, except for Meggy who continued to cry softly, crouching by the back wall and Margery still muttering her Latin prayers. The banging had stopped, as though those outside the door were listening.

'We see there was no need for this trial after all,' yelled Aldith. 'See how this heretic witch stands by her demon and curses all that is holy.' The group on the other side of the fire were now huddled together. Margery's eyes were no longer turned up to heaven but staring fearfully at Kit, as though expecting him to sprout horns and hooves at any moment. Aldith grabbed one of the flaming candles and brandished it before him like a weapon. Perspiration poured down his face and he was trembling from head to foot. 'Take her and be off. Back to hell with the pair of you,' he shouted hoarsely.

For a moment in his frustration, Kit was tempted, so tempted, to launch into his Ashentoth routine. These three believed him to be some infernal demon so why shouldn't he terrify them out of their wits? What better punishment than what they were expecting? Then he remembered where he was, in God the Maker's house where he should show respect. He took a few deep breaths and emerged from the shadows and closer to the fire so the three of them could get their first clear view of his face.

'But you all know me.' Kit began speaking in a gentle tone and he watched with satisfaction as their faces turned from one kind of horror to another. 'We have been conversing for weeks, have we not? We've had the most marvellous talks. I know you, Aldith, and you, Margery, don't I? As for you, John Farmer, I know all your little secrets, do I not? Do you swear all the sheep in your flock belong to you? I know otherwise.'

'At long last you see,' Zannah stepped forward and pointed at each of them in turn. She was still furious.

'You have spoken with him just as I have. Therefore if Meggy and I be witches, so be you all. Why don't the three of you stick your arms in the boiling water to see if they blister, eh? You Aldith, why don't you reach in and grab the stone if you're so innocent. There's nothing to fear, isn't that the truth? Nothing to fear if you've done nothing wrong. And you, John Farmer, who's the witch now, say you?'

The three accused stared at one another, dumbfounded. Margery began to deny that she had ever seen Kit before, until he reminded her of their conversations about her bitter feud with Goody Payne over which of them was the owner of a white cat. She turned her head away in fear and shame, holding her rosary beads to her mouth and began to cry.

Zannah continued to goad them until John, his face pale as ashes, began preparing himself to do as she demanded, hitching up the sleeve of his shirt and holding his trembling arm over the water. Zannah dived towards him and pushed him away from the cauldron in time. He stumbled and fell to the floor where he cowered in shame. Meanwhile, Margery continued to cry loudly while Aldith was trying to hide behind a pillar.

'If I really was a demon, how could I stand here, in God's house?' Kit did his best to keep a reasonable tone to his voice. There had to be some way to turn the situation around and make peace. 'See how I cross myself. I will say the "Our Father" to prove it to you once and for all. I am not a demon; in fact I have come to help your village.' He began to say the Lord's Prayer and the scene quietened. Zannah ran to comfort Meggy, who wrapped her arms around her and howled. Neither Aldith, Margery nor John would meet Kit's eye as he carried on reciting the prayer. The fire and candlelight lit the brightly painted walls which told Kit of the beliefs of those who worshipped there, including the terrible figure of the Devil himself, studded with horns and fangs, presiding over his pitchfork wielding demons who were busy tossing a procession of naked sinners off a cliff into a fiery lake. No wonder these villagers were so scared and ready to believe that he was from that place. It was so different to the plain whitewashed church he remembered from his youth.

Kit was almost at the end of the prayer when there was more banging on the door and a faint voice called out Zannah's name. Zannah left Meggy and walked hesitantly to the door. She and Kit looked at one another. 'Grandda,' she shouted as loudly as she could. 'Go home now. The danger has passed.'

'Zannah my child,' came Awl Robin's thin voice. 'I must speak with thee. I have remained silent too long. It is my mistake and I must put it right.'

'Open the door.' Now Judd's voice rang out, and Kit held his breath. 'The danger has passed from this side too. We must all listen to Awl Robin.'

After a moment's hesitation, Zannah removed the wooden post barring the door and opened it. In stumbled Awl Robin dressed only in his long shirt, his feet bare as though he had come straight from bed. Judd was close behind and three other men who backed off the moment they saw Kit. From their stammering apologies to Aldith, Kit understood that they had been standing guard over Zannah's grandfather but incredibly, the frail-looking old man had fought like a lion and escaped. Zannah cried out and ran to embrace him but he held her at arm's length, his eyes travelling over her to make sure she'd suffered no physical harm. 'Meggy?' he asked urgently.

'We were in time,' replied Zannah and the old man sagged with relief.

Judd explained how they had met at the lychgate and their brief conversation had convinced him that Awl Robin had something important to tell them all. It was Judd who had held off the villagers who would have stopped Awl Robin approaching the church. Judd gave Kit a brief nod and for the first time since he'd arrived, Kit felt some relief. Father Bernard appeared in the doorway next. He was shocked at the sight of Kit who had no choice but to recite the Lord's Prayer all over again. Judd coaxed the priest to step into the church where he was equally horrified to find out about Meggy's trial, which he clearly hadn't known about. 'Fie upon thee, Aldith, and thee, John, for wishing harm to Meggy. Margery, I am surprised at thee,' said Father Bernard. 'This is barbaric and cannot be God's way.'

'We wished her no harm,' protested Margery. 'We

thought we could prove her innocence. We were giving her a chance. We were thinking of her, as well as the rest of us.' Meanwhile, more and more faces appeared in the doorway, although the villagers gasped and crossed themselves at the sight of Kit.

Father Bernard turned to Awl Robin. 'This person who accompanies thy granddaughter, is he a demon or merely a boy say thee? Dost thou know him, Robin?'

Awl Robin was watching the priest's lips and understood what he said. 'I know him no better than thou dost Bernard, but anyone can see he's flesh and blood, man,' he snapped before adding, 'If there be any sin to confess here, it be mine own.'

Kit wondered what the old man meant but for the first time, Father Bernard was addressing him directly. 'Where camest thou from? Speak! Dost thou come from some neighbouring village? How hast thou appeared to us in our waking dreams?'

'Aye, what trickery was that?' cried John Farmer angrily, risen to his feet again.

'Damn, what were we supposed to think?' said Aldith, looking thoroughly shamefaced. 'Appearing and disappearing, for all the world like witchcraft.'

'Strange things have taken place, as every Christian soul here knows,' Margery joined in. 'And it all began when he first appeared.' She pointed straight at Kit and he swallowed, fully aware that there was truth in what Margery was saying. When he'd entered the book, time had begun again, and he couldn't say different.

'He cometh not from these parts.' Judd spoke up. 'We have all talked with this lad and there's no denying it. Flesh and blood he is without doubt and from whence he comes, he'd best tell without delay. I am willing to listen now.' This last he said quietly and directly to Kit.

'You believe me then, Judd?' asked Kit.

For a moment, the blacksmith's eyes roamed the church as though seeking out some invisible flagon of ale, which might help him cope with the situation. 'What choice have I? Before, I was unwilling to listen. Yet I know what thou sayest to be true. Something is wrong with our village and if we stand any chance of putting it right, we should mayhap listen to thee.'

Kit could have hugged the blacksmith. 'What made you change your mind?' he asked.

Judd took a few more steps into the middle of the nave and turned to face the crowd in the doorway. 'You had all better hear this.' He spoke loudly. 'Kit opened my eyes to the strangeness in our midst, and your eyes must open too. As the good Lord says, the beam of wood in my own eye is removed, I can see clearly and so should you all. Life is not normal here, nor has it been for some time. Time hasn't passed as normal this many a year and so, when there is a death, we are so unused to it happening, it shocks us. When I began to realise the truth of what he told me, I grew afeared. I tried shutting it from my mind with ale. I failed at that and so I ran. I attempted to leave by the road to the east, then by the road to the west, then I crossed the fields and headed north, then south. I walked around in one big circle and finished where I'd began. Have any of you left this village lately? Just try it and see how far you get. There's something wrong here and this lad Kit speaks the truth. He is not at fault, something else is.'

'Even I had almost succeeded in forgetting.' Awl Robin's voice suddenly lost all its strength. Letting go of Zannah, he sat heavily on the stone bench next to the wall and screened his eyes with his hand. 'I wanted to forget and carry on as though nothing was amiss. But I knew the truth, deep down. I chose not to think of it. That's why I say again, if anyone's to blame, it is I. My worst shame is that what I have kept hidden has endangered my precious grandchild. Yet...what else could I have done? What else?'

Only those near Robin heard these words. Father Bernard approached Judd, whispered something, then turned and ordered the others to return to their beds. Those gathered round the door left first, followed by a stunned looking Aldith, Margery and John. A cousin of Meggy's wrapped her in a shawl and guided her out. As she passed by, Meggy squeezed Zannah's hand and whispered her thanks.

As the crowd left, Judd used a bucket to half-empty the heavy cauldron of water, then he took it off the fire and set it to one side. Father Bernard found some fusty vestments, beat the dust out of them and with tender care, Zannah helped her grandfather put them on. The five figures huddled on stools around the fire and Awl

Robin began: 'The fewer the better to hear this. The more folk remember, the worse it will get, for the faster the changes will happen. At least, such is my fear.' The orange flames reflected in the old man's eyes as though a more ancient fire burnt within. Kit was bursting with questions but held his tongue. He prayed there'd be time enough to hear this speech before the tingling began and he must run back to the thread tied to the yew branch.

'It might have been yesterday, My Lady Pearl called me to her and told me what I now tell you. I was her only servant and she trusted me with knowledge of her power. Her house, which once stood in the woods, down the path which runs opposite our home, is vanished. So also is her magic hidden. Now thou rememberest, my dear?'

Zannah was frowning hard and staring into the fire. 'The Lady Pearl, of course...' her voice trailed off and then she looked straight at her grandfather, her expression full of wonder. 'How could I have forgotten, Grandda? The Lady Pearl. She taught me to read and write as a small child, lent me books, took me for walks and taught me the names of flowers and herbs. How could I have forgotten her?' The tears trickling down her cheeks held their own tiny flames.

'And thou Bernard?' said the old man. 'Stir the embers of thy memory, thou shalt find her there. She was a good friend to us all and a strong magician, although the magic she wielded was protective and good. I miss her so, and I've only just remembered how much.' Kit could tell by the others' reactions that they were starting to remember this person and were equally astonished, but Awl Robin carried on. 'Yesterday morning, for it may as well have been yesterday morning, she called me to her and said she could not hold back his Lordship's power and anger much longer. She had grown weak and ill from years of protecting us all. Now she was dying just as his wickedness was in the ascent, but she had cast one last spell, of which she must tell me. For years, you remember, she had stood up to the man whose heavy taxes threatened to destroy us and who would trample underfoot anyone who would stop him getting what he wanted. His desires were selfish and sick and to speak truth, if any walked hand in hand with the Devil, it was he. When he sent his men to plunder or take some revenge, she would cast spells to make them sick or conjure a fog and voices in that fog would send them the wrong way. Whenever his Lordship came, he found himself without protection, for his weapons would shatter, his sword of steel would snap as easily as a dry husk of corn. His armour would break to pieces.'

'So he gave me the order to fashion him a new suit,' said Judd.

'Aye, and thou hadst no choice but so to do,' nodded Awl Robin. 'Yet the Lady Pearl's magic would have destroyed his next suit of armour, that much is certain. He could not burn our dwellings neither, for any fire he lit would kindle with a strange blue flame and die in seconds. He knew this was her doing. Once, she had been his wife and knew well his cruelty and malice. His hatred for this village stemmed from his hatred for her but when his vile attentions turned to thee my granddaughter, the final battle began.'

Zannah closed her hands over her mouth and spoke behind them. 'That man,' she said. 'That hateful man. I remember all now.'

'Before the Lady Pearl settled amongst us, he had assaulted many daughters – and sons – of this village. Then one morning, he dragged thee screaming from our cottage while his sergeant held me back with his sword. He ripped thy hands from the doorpost and attempted to throw thee on his horse, intending to remove thee to his manor house. I knew I should never see thee again but then a sudden flash appeared in the air and the beast bolted. The Lady Pearl's doing of course. She emerged from the silence of the wood and threw a charm hoop which paralysed both him and his sergeant. Thou didst escape into the wood and when he regained movement, they battled, but the effort of producing spell after spell sapped her strength. This time his sword remained in one piece and he dealt her such a blow as she could not recover from, here between neck and shoulder. He was injured, but not as badly and crept away vowing to return.

'We stayed with her that night and I could hear her pacing slowly in her chamber. When I knocked her door, she shooed me away but early next morning she called for me. She lay stricken upon her pallet and as I watched, the grey dawn unveiled the fearful pallor of death upon her. Some secrets would die with her, she said, for she feared his Lordship might find some way of torturing them out of us, if she were to tell. Zannah, thou and I were to return home. She had thrown a mighty charm about our little village which would keep him out and us safely within. But the charm would only hold if we were ignorant of it. We'd remain safe in our ignorance but if a true and honourable soul should find their way into our village and if, by the light of a great travelling star, that soul should learn the secret of the charm, our village would return to its proper place, in proper time. That person, a stranger, would need to find a magical object she had hidden which she called the key to the charm. From what I understood it is not, in truth, a key. That person would need to make haste because this would be the most dangerous time. That's as much as she said.' The old man's eyes moistened, and his voice dried up completely.

'Then thou art the one of whom the Lady Pearl spoke?' Father Bernard addressed Kit, gravely. 'The one true soul who can help us.'

'I don't know.' Kit wondered how someone who had been a common thief could be the one this great lady meant? 'My time here is never long. This very evening, I feel it begin already, the call to return to my own time and place.' The tingling in his fingers had begun and he had to fight the panic rising in his chest. 'I know what your lady did. She put you all in a book and simply opening that book and turning the pages is the way I have been able to speak with you. You are all in that book, a face on each page. From the outside, I have tried my best to keep you safe from those who seek you harm.' He remembered how Colewich threatened the villagers and insisted they search for an object. It seemed as though Colewich was the only other person to know of its existence. But how could Kit continue to protect the book from the outside and hunt for this object on the inside? Wasn't there another, more sure way of saving everyone?

'Faith, there isn't long to find the object,' said Awl Robin. 'Remember My Lady Pearl's words, this is the most dangerous time. Our ignorance has held her charm in place. As the whole village starts to remember, it will grow more dangerous.'

'Aye and what I have discovered on the edge of our village makes me agree with thee,' Judd added.

Kit wanted to ask Judd what he meant but there wasn't time. 'You must come with me, Zan,' he said urgently but she was already shaking her head.

'I cannot leave my people, Kit,' she said. 'Not if danger lies ahead. They need me.'

'But if you come with me tonight, your Grandda can come the next night. Then another, and another. If it works, we can remove the villagers one by one from the book and all will be safe.'

Awl Robin was shaking his head. 'This would take

too long,' he said. 'And such was not My Lady Pearl's intention.'

'Then come with me please, Zan, and help me keep the book safe at least? You can guard it in my time while I return each day to seek out the object.'

'He may be right,' said Judd.

'Yes, go with him, my child,' Awl Robin took Zannah's hands in his own.

'How canst thou ask me to leave thee, Grandda?' she pleaded. 'I must stay and search for this object with the rest of you.'

'No,' Awl Robin turned back to Kit. His voice was stronger again. 'For the hidden object can only be found by the stranger. This was to prevent any of us stumbling across it and corrupting the charm.'

'Do you know what the object is? Did the Lady Pearl leave any clue?' asked Kit.

'No,' said the old man. 'Its discovery is thy business.'

The tingling was growing stronger and reluctantly, Zannah agreed to accompany Kit back to the yew tree, where, while the others stared up at them, they sat in the broadest bough and Kit tied the end of the thread around her wrist as well as his own. They clung to each other and waited. Overhead the comet burned, and Kit prayed that it might actually be a good sign, a sign that his plans were about to succeed at last. Kit felt himself melt out of the world. The wind in his face told him he was back on the bare hillside but there was no Zannah by his side and a second loop of thread hung slack on the grass.

He wasn't alone though. A dark figure was walking towards him and Kit closed the cover of the book with all speed. There was uncertainty, amounting to fear in Daniel Price's voice when he spoke:

'What are you doing here, Kit? What light was that I saw?'

'Twas nothing, Daniel.' Caught so off guard, Kit hoped it was too dark for Daniel to see his doubtless guilty expression. He had to think fast, faster than fast. 'I…felt unwell. Too much ale by the fireside, like as not. I needed a breath of air. I din't want to wake any of you so I came down here.'

'But that light I saw, that glowing light? Then a mighty flash, for all the world like ten flintlocks going off at once? And one moment the ground was empty I could have sworn but when I looked again, there you were.' Kit guessed the flash of light Daniel had seen was what happened the moment he re-entered the real world but what a time to discover it. Daniel had seen everything, and this chilled Kit, so much so his teeth began to chatter. He considered making a joke about Daniel drinking too much but feared speaking in such a flippant way to the leader of the drovers, someone who commanded such respect and someone to whom he owed his life. This and the fact that Daniel had not been the slightest bit drunk earlier and seemed to have all his wits about him now.

Kit rose unsteadily to his feet with the light-headedness he always experienced straight after returning from the village. He couldn't show Daniel how scared he was. 'Mayhap you were still dreaming?' he suggested, trying to laugh while keeping his chattering teeth still. Daniel didn't respond to this. Instead he turned his attention to the book Kit was clutching to his chest. 'What is that?' he asked, with a hard edge to his voice Kit had never heard before. ''Tis never far from your side. We've all noticed it.'

It wasn't good to hear that the drovers had been discussing the book. Kit began to replace it in the bag. 'This? Just... verses and such like,' he said. 'Songs and playscripts. Shakespeare, you know. They belong to the master of the travelling players I hope to catch up with. The company I was with before I got lost. You remember, I told you?'

'Ah?' The drover didn't budge, and Kit doubted he was swallowing the story. He wanted to turn and leave but Daniel spoke again. 'Lights which come from nowhere. Now, that's something people fear where I come from. *Cannwyll corff* they're called: corpse candles. Those are lights which foretell a death. They're seen travelling through the lanes towards the *mynwent* – the graveyard – the way the next funeral will pass.'

'I haven't seen anything like that,' said Kit, 'And I have been here all the time, faith! Anyway, there are no graveyards on this hillside, you must have been mistaken.' Daniel didn't answer. He didn't say anything when Kit said goodnight either. They walked back to the shelter in silence and lay down again on opposite sides of the entrance.

Now that other, huge wave of disappointment crashed

down upon Kit. His plan for releasing Zannah from the book may have been pitifully simple but it least it had been a plan. Any idea of removing her and the rest of the villagers now seemed hopeless. He wanted to speak to her right away but feared leaving the shelter a second time that night. What if Daniel woke again and came to find him? Instead, he would have to try and sleep. The effort of entering the book had exhausted him and it would take at least a day before he felt strong enough to attempt it again. That meant at least a day before he could get answers to all the questions prompted by what Awl Robin and Judd had revealed, questions which spun round and round in his head and exhausted his mind yet stopped him sleeping. It also meant he had to wait at least a day before beginning his search for the mysterious hidden object – the so-called key to the Lady Pearl's charm.

Kit was still pondering what to do as they set off on the next leg of their journey. It was usual now for him to walk alongside the other men while Daniel travelled ahead on horseback. The morning was bright, clear and chilly. Over breakfast, Daniel hadn't mentioned what had taken place the night before, but neither did he seem too ready to talk to Kit or even meet his eye and Kit wondered what was going through his mind.

Now he was well again, Kit had determined to leave the drovers as soon as they came near a town. He still had a few coins with which to pay for a day or two's lodgings: maybe that's all it would take, a day or two to find the hidden object. All he needed was a room and no further disturbances. As soon as his shiners ran out, he would think again. He could always return to his old occupation.

No. Not thieving. Not that.

'But what else is there, Gabe?' he thought. The back of Daniel Price, rising and falling with the horse's steady rhythm, put him in mind of Gabe, riding their comet from star to star and finally, up to heaven. He felt a lump in his throat and had to turn his head away from William John Jones who was walking beside him.

Summer was giving way to early autumn. The sunlight had turned mellow and golden and there was an earthy, woody tang to the air. The rolling hills were clad in a soft haze of purple heather while dainty, mottled butterflies flittered from one patch to another, but the beauties of the landscape were lost on Kit, whose mind was stuck in a mire of worries and questions. The bellowing of the cattle, the heat of their rising breath and their stench, the ceaseless trampling of hooves was by now, so familiar, they didn't encroach upon his thoughts either. They'd been walking for a couple of hours along a wide track winding its way around the hillsides, when they came across a group of men on foot. These were drovers on their way back from market in London with wads of banknotes stuffing their waistcoats and their boots full of shiners, no doubt, and their hearty cries of greeting and waving of sticks showed that they and Daniel Price's men were well known to one another. The forward motion of the cattle made it impossible to stop and chat for long, but Daniel remained talking to them long after Kit and the others had passed and it was a full half-hour before the brown horse came trotting up beside him.

'Can we stop and talk?' said Daniel and without waiting for a reply, he veered off the track and down the gentle slope. Kit followed. With the wall of Welsh Black cattle proceeding along the ridge above them, Daniel dismounted, allowing the horse to crop the grass at his feet as he turned to speak to Kit while avoiding his eye.

'I've heard news which troubles me greatly,' Daniel began. 'And I'll not beat about the bush, no time for that. You said you might head off to a large town, well, Marlborough is in that direction and about a day's walk. 'Tis time you left us, Kit.'

It was what Kit had been meaning to do and yet it stung him that Daniel was suggesting it happen now. 'What news?' he asked, although he wasn't sure he wanted to hear the answer.

Daniel's blue eyes looked far off into the distance as he explained. 'Those men that passed by are heading back to Wales. They've met others along the way, and those others have spoken to others, and that's how news carries around this land. They said there was some commotion in Bath a few weeks back. Bath, where you said you'd come from.'

Kit felt his cheeks colour and he stared at the ground.

'Aye,' said Daniel with a heavy sigh. 'I can see how that hit home.'

'What did they say?' Daniel's horse was cropping the grass noisily and for a moment, Kit's quickening heartbeat fell in with the sounds in double time.

'That the Devil himself appeared in the middle of the city. He attempted to get into the Abbey church, you can still see the deep scratches down the door where he clawed at it, but when he failed at that, he slaughtered the ladies and gentlemen who were gathered. At least twenty were killed and the street was awash with their blood. They say a young lad conjured the Devil up right there in broad daylight for all to see. Afterwards, this lad gave them the slip and hasn't been seen since. They say he was a travelling player. An actor, Kit, an actor like yourself.'

Kit almost laughed. Another story about him being in league with the Devil: why did everyone seem to assume he was guilty of this?

''Tis something to do with that, isn't it?' Daniel pointed at the bag on his shoulder and Kit held tighter onto its strap.

''Tis not what you think and the story you heard was wrong,' protested Kit. Daniel shook his head more in confusion than anything else. They stood in silence for a full minute. Even though the drover was a sympathetic soul, it was clear to Kit that their time together really was over.

'There's a reward upon your head,' Daniel went on. 'And though I don't care a hang about that, by rights I should turn you in. I should march you to Marlborough myself and hand you to the watchman.'

'Please don't,' Kit looked the drover full in the face and pleaded. 'I'll go right now, just don't tell anyone where I went, I beg you. There's a man after me and if there's any such thing as the Devil, 'tis he. Don't believe what they say about me, Daniel, 'tis not at all the same as what you heard. I cannot conjure a devil: how would I do that? I was present but there was no slaughter. I didn't see anyone get killed but the whole thing's too hard to explain.'

'Even if I believe what you say, there's something else. 'Tis what I saw last night,' Daniel nodded, sadly. 'And I know what I saw, there's no use denying it. You need to be careful my boy. Here…' He reached into his pocket and produced a bright shilling which he tossed over and Kit caught. 'I know you don't have much. That's to help you on your way from here.'

'I should be paying you…' Kit began but Daniel waved away his words, took off his cap and removed from the band a small green sprig bearing a cluster of bright red berries. 'This is more important than the money: 'tis a sprig of rowan. It protects the wearer against the Devil and his followers and 'tis the best I can give you now, Kit. Wear it and my advice is, throw that old *beth yn galw* – whatever-it-is – away. Better still, burn it.' Daniel held out the rowan sprig but as Kit took it, he snatched back his hand as though he'd got too near a fire, then looked embarrassed for doing so.

Thanking him, Kit dropped the shilling down the side of his boot and tucked the rowan inside his shirt.

'Would it help if I said the "Our Father"…?' asked Kit. He was desperate, suddenly, not to let this good man go away thinking badly of him. Several different emotions were at play on Daniel's face, like a spinning dice and Kit wanted so badly for it to come down on the hopeful side, the side that believed against the odds that the lad standing before him was innocent of the terrible crime he had supposedly committed.

''Tis always good to say our Lord's Prayer. You can say it as you go,' said Daniel. Kit nodded, and the drover nodded briefly, yet Kit found it hard to decipher the look upon his face. With the heavy, familiar feeling of letting people down, he turned and began to walk in the direction in which the drover had pointed. He started reciting the prayer loudly, hoping that Daniel might hear but knowing that in all probability, his voice was being drowned out by the mighty thunder of cattle up on the ridge. As Kit walked on, he was too sad to turn and watch Daniel Price rejoin the great procession as it continued on its way to market.

Kit only stopped once to open the book and talk to Zannah and then but briefly. She was safely at home with Awl Robin and said she would remain there until Kit returned. No one could be sure how the villagers were going to react to what they'd seen the night before but from what her grandfather said, neither was it safe to reveal too much to them. There was no point in her or any of them hunting for the object in any case. Kit was the only one who'd be able to identify it. With haste, he explained that he was making his way to town because although the wild, open landscape seemed empty, if he stopped and entered the book right there and then, someone might happen by, perhaps some footpad who might take the book, snap the thread and imprison him within its pages.

Dusk was falling as he reached Marlborough and by that time it was also raining heavily. He had lost the sprig of rowan somewhere along the way, and this unsettled him. Kit had visited this fine town with Saroni, but he wouldn't allow himself to think of that now and become depressed; he had to find a safe place where he could spend time with the book, undisturbed. Somehow, he must rebuild his strength because he was determined to get back to the village that night. The first inn he came to could provide him with a room, although the giant of a landlord stood blocking the doorway, looking him up and down until he fished inside his wet boot and produced the shilling. Kit was wet through and knew he must look like a bedraggled rat. The landlord grew even more suspicious when he asked particularly that the room should have a lock on the door but led him down a corridor, to a small, wood-panelled closet which boasted a key almost as big as the door itself. It appeared there were few people staying at the inn that night, for Kit sat alone by the fireside to eat his supper of bread, cheese and ale while his boots steamed gently on the hearth. He ate without enthusiasm. Despite all the walking he'd done that day, worry had taken the place of hunger in his belly and he had to make a mighty effort to chew and swallow the food. He had to eat to give himself energy. He had noticed that the more energy he had, the longer his visits to the village lasted and he hoped that this time he would have long enough to conduct a proper search. After supper he took time to rest, lying still upon the bed in the cold little room until he could no longer sense the vibrations in the lower part of his legs from pounding over tussocky ground for the best part of that day. He needed to calm himself and pin his attention to the one important matter, strengthening his body, mind and soul for the great task which lay ahead. By the light of a single tallow candle he secured the thread to the back of a chair, opened the book and with his thumb, began moving the comical little man up the ladder.

'It is best you come at night.' Zannah was breathing hard from walking so fast beside him in the dark. 'At this hour, folk mostly keep indoors since their fear is so great.'

'Aye, were they to see thee, they might tear thee apart, the mood they're in,' added Judd although he too was panting from walking at such a pace. 'They're waking up, just like we did, and the truth is unbearable to them. They'd rather find someone to blame.'

'Again?' said Kit. Even as he answered, he realised

212

how predictable it was that the villagers would return to their pointless blaming.

'I would only venture out after dark for the same reason,' said Zannah and Kit briefly reached and squeezed her hand.

The three of them were heading west. They had passed by Zannah and Awl Robin's home a while back and were skirting the wood. Kit was in a hurry to begin the search for Lady Pearl's object at once but the other two had insisted he come and see first what Judd had discovered on the edge of the village. They found it hard to describe in words; Kit would have to see for himself. It wasn't long before they reached the place and Kit felt his knees buckle. He heard Judd say, 'It's moved again. Damn, but if it hasn't moved this way a good few feet since yesterday, I'd stake my life on it,' but the end of each word was sucked into the wall of shimmering light which extended right across the fields of barley, wheat, oats and grass from as far as he could see on one side, to as far as he could see on the other. A 'wall' was probably the best way of describing it, but it wasn't like any kind of wall Kit could ever have imagined. The trees and fields which should have been visible as blacker shapes against the inky sky were broken into pieces, like reflections in jagged shards of glass moving slowly and glowing strangely in the moonlight, so you caught glimpses of the branches of trees far away then suddenly so near you could see tiny insects crawling in the creases of the rough bark. There was no sense or pattern to the wall, it moved and changed continually like the sea, yet when you concentrated on one part, it seemed to fall still. Kit had never seen the sea, but Saroni had told him about it and for a moment, he wondered if that was what he was looking at. He drew closer to the shimmering, senseless mass. He was mesmerised by the way it seemed so near one moment, so far the next. He heard Judd shouting at him to stay clear of the wall but the end of each word disappeared into it, sucked into the swell. Kit picked up a stone and after a moment's hesitation, threw it, expecting a splash but instead hearing a flat kind of bang, almost deafening but over at once and leaving no trace of an echo. The sound was like nothing in nature, not even the loudest thunder. The moment it hit the wall, the stone rebounded off and burst apart, disintegrating into sandy particles which shivered to the ground. This was not the sea, nor was it the sky or the land. It was a flat but deep, near but far, still but moving, empty, deadly memory of what had once stood there.

An idea occurred to Kit: what if this was the comet, fallen to Earth with its tail lying across the fields? Then he looked up and saw the real comet burning in the sky. He turned to Zannah and Judd and they stared back blankly, lacking all understanding until Judd said in those strange half-words: 'Let us go. We'll do no good here.'

Back at Awl Robin's fireside, Kit asked questions which the others answered as best they could. Yes, the wall

214

completely encircled the village with no gaps and yes, Judd had walked all around in a complete circle. He would have dug down to see if there was any way to tunnel beneath, only he feared getting too close and his guess was, the attempt would be useless. For years, none had strayed from the village and there was no reason to suppose it hadn't stood there all that time, part of the Lady Pearl's charm, but now Judd was certain it was closing in further each day. It wasn't good to imagine what would happen to their village and everyone in it if the wall continued to move towards them.

'The more the people remember, the quicker the charm breaks down,' creaked Robin's voice. His small, rheumy eyes never left the burning log which sat in the grate with yellow flames dancing along its back. 'When first thou came, Kit, time began again. Now we're running out of it. Oh don't upset thyself, my boy. Thou wilt do thy best for us, I knowest thou wilt.' It was as though without looking, Awl Robin could see that Kit was becoming upset.

'I cannot but think I am to blame,' said Kit. 'If I hadn't come you would still be safe in your little world, safe in your dream.'

'But we would not have been safe.' Zannah moved nearer to him on the wooden settle and cradled his arm. 'Not while that evil man from your world sought the book we're all a-livin' inside of.' Her speech slowed and she looked around at the others. 'Aye, the fault's not thine,' agreed Judd, shaking his head in bewilderment.

Kit felt he could read the blacksmith's thoughts: first the wall and now talk of living inside a book? Life was not as it had once seemed, not at all.

'But what if I am not the person of whom the Lady Pearl spoke? What if the book was waiting for someone else? I am not that good a person, you know,' whispered Kit, turning to face Zannah.

'Of course you are,' she said. 'Look at all the risks you took to find me. Look at what you've suffered for our sakes.'

'I've tried. All my life I've tried to do my best, Zan.' His vision of her blurred through his tears. 'I've tried to keep the ones I love safe, but I've failed each and every time. My family all died; I promised Gabe I'd get him well again, but I din't; I promised you I'd keep you safe and look what's happened. I try my best but 'tis never good enough.'

'Now's not the time for this, lad.' He felt Judd pat his shoulder. 'We all try. When times are hard that's all we can do. It's trying that's the best part of us and when we do so on behalf of another human soul in distress, that's best of all. Now I pray God will give thee the strength to get up and try again.' Kit closed his eyes and swallowed the next measure of his tears. 'Then try I will,' he said.

CHAPTER 20

Awl Robin could tell them no more than he already had. The Lady Pearl had hidden the unknown object somewhere thereabouts, but what and where it was could only be discovered by the true soul who had come to rescue the village. Kit shuddered each time he heard himself described in this way because if he really was a true soul, wouldn't he already know what he was looking for? His thief's heart was corrupt, how could he know? That evening he was granted longer there than usual, but it did no good. He told Zannah he would search alone, and she returned to her fireside while he began roaming the streets, on the lookout for anything unusual, a glow in the darkness, because a magical object would glow just like the book, wouldn't it? This was another reason why it was better to search by night. He poked about in vegetable patches and peered up into the thatch of the cottage roofs. He hunted through the reeds by the millpond, disturbing the ducks, then took off his breeches and waded into the cold water to knee-height, churning up the mud at the bottom with a stick. There was no mysterious glow in its murky depths. It was a cloudy night, which didn't help in his search. After a while, he headed to the smithy where Judd awaited him. He began on one side of the room and worked his way around, picking up every single tool in turn to rub off the dirt to see if it was actually made of gold or some other precious metal, concentrating hard to see if he could feel any magical vibrations. There were no vibrations and they were all just ordinary tools. Father Bernard was ready and waiting to take Kit around the church, where his eyes roamed every inch of the gaudy wall paintings by candlelight. The priest let him touch the precious objects on the altar as well as the finger bones of the saint stowed beneath it, in a casket studded with gems which looked suspiciously like chunks of coloured glass. They climbed the tower and Kit leaned in as far as he dared to inspect the bells. The tower gave the best view of the village and his eyes roamed over every roof, checking for something, maybe something quite small, glittering on top of one of them. After working his way round the inside of the church for a second time, he left Father Bernard and went to check the lychgate over, even persuading the knowing-looking goat to move from its usual position, then smoothed his hand over the flattened grass where it had been lying. Turning back to the churchyard, he walked up and down with his eyes on the ground and visited each and every raised hump of earth. Very few upright stones or wooden crosses marked these graves, unlike his own time when every churchyard was thick with them, so it didn't take long to check each one for maybe a large jewel embedded in it, something no one else was able to see but him. Yet nothing Kit found that evening, nothing he touched spoke to him of being anything out of the ordinary and by the time the tingling began, which signalled his time to leave, he was no nearer solving the puzzle.

Kit spent the next day in a dream, not leaving the small chamber and asking for his meals to be brought there, which the landlord agreed to with a grunt once he'd been presented with another coin. He recalled Daniel the drover's words: there was a price on his head. Who knew who might stop to drink at the inn, possibly someone who had heard the same cockeyed tale peddled to Daniel? Kit could just imagine himself sitting beside the fire and all eyes turning slowly towards him: a lad travelling on his own; a lad with an oilskin bag and a price on his head. How was he going to talk his way out of that? Worse, one of Colewich's men might arrive, asking questions. There was a small window in the wall behind the bed and Kit had already checked that it would open. The first sign of a rattling doorknob and he would be out of that window like a shot; he had scrambled through smaller openings and there was an alley directly outside.

He lay on the bed, shivering beneath the moth-eaten blanket with the book by his side. He went through the village in his mind, taking time to recall as much detail as he could, as though he were out for a stroll beginning at Zannah's cottage on the one side and ending at the smithy on the other; next he went from the church, past the millpond, down to the main cluster of dwellings, some old and tumbledown, others better cared for. He counted them and checked them off against the faces he remembered in order in the book, for he had a good idea where most of them lived. Zannah had told him. Now it seemed that the night before, he might have been too hasty, hunting here and there and leaving out less obvious places where the object could be hidden. Many old trees were hollow and made excellent hiding places, wasn't that the case? Was there an old fruit tree in someone's garden... or the yew tree in the churchyard which was so ancient and broad, doubtless full of cracks and crevices, wouldn't that be a good place to look? Night-time was still the best time to search, without suspicious eyes tracking his every move and he was still sure a magical object would glow in the dark or hum in the silence and therefore be easier to find. He would rest and gather energy that day, ready for another journey that evening.

When night-time came he had his plan ready, determining to start at the yew tree because he had convinced himself that's where the object would be. Yet when he got there, he failed to find anything magical amongst the ancient, flaky-barked boughs. He tried not to be too downhearted because he was sure he was right about it being hidden in some tree. He would work his way through the village and search the bigger, older trees. By now, Kit was glad of company, and Zannah stayed with him while Judd and Father Bernard came and went throughout the course of his search. There were no signs of life from the shuttered-up cottages, but they conducted their conversations in whispers. It was better the villagers stayed behind their shutters, and better for the shutters of their memories to remain in place as long as possible. At one stage, when Kit had stopped to rest on the large stone next to the millpond, which was used as a mounting block to get up on horseback, Judd told him that he had been to the edge of the village again that afternoon and was certain the wall had closed in by as much as twenty feet. It had completely swallowed a ruined hovel which had stood in the field ever since Judd was a boy. The news made Kit redouble his efforts but after climbing every tree in every garden and finding nothing, he was utterly despondent.

'What of the wood itself?' There was desperation in Zannah's voice, but Kit considered her suggestion and for the first time, noticed that the tail of the comet he now took for granted was pointing straight at the wood. Did this mean anything? The wood was a part of the village after all. 'Perhaps you wouldn't have to climb every tree,' Zannah went on. 'We can walk through, and you can see if any lights appear in the branches.' Kit's heart leapt with fresh hope: the wood was the place where the object was hidden, no doubt about it!

It was much darker in the wood, and they stumbled along hand in hand through the dense undergrowth. There were no paths visible and it was easy to trip over a root, or for a piece of bramble to whip past and hit the person behind in the face. Even though there were no villagers to rouse, they still spoke in whispers and froze at the slightest snap of a twig or the flap of startled wings. It didn't take long for Kit to scale a couple of the mighty oaks, but he was soon exhausted and feared that the old familiar tingle might begin at any moment. That evening, he had landed on the roof of the empty cottage belonging to the dead Widow Edith and now he prayed he would be able to find his way back there quickly.

There was nothing to be seen in any of the trees he climbed, not the faintest glimmer, and he had discovered some ideal hiding places. It was becoming clear just how much of a task this was going to be, even if he limited himself to climbing the biggest trees. There might be fifty or a hundred of them and the wood stretched away in all directions. Soon, the wall might have closed in so far there would be no wood, no village even. Stupidly, in their haste and excitement, they hadn't even thought to mark the trees he had already climbed. Zannah said she would look around for a sharp stone with which to scrape a mark across the bark.

'I don't think it's worth the bother,' Kit said with a heavy sigh. 'If I'm supposed to feel like the object's near, well I don't. I don't feel anything at all, not while searching here, nor when I was up by the church, nor in the gardens, nor standing in the pond. I felt nothing. I don't believe I am the one that's supposed to be searching for this. It's not me, Zan.'

'Don't say that,' she pleaded. 'It doesn't help. The Lady Pearl would not have made that kind of mistake. You are the one true soul, Kit, or you wouldn't be here. Whatever it is that's waiting to be found, is waiting for you.'

Kit leaned against an old oak. In a moment he would feel that tingle in his fingers and another night would be lost. 'The Lady Pearl would not have made a mistake,' repeated Zannah and then she added slowly, but with dawning excitement, 'The Lady Pearl... Kit, her house is here somewhere, in this wood.'

'Her house!' said Kit. Awl Robin had spoken of it, why hadn't it occurred to Kit that this was the obvious place to search? Although it lay within the wood, it was still in the village and if the Lady Pearl had been wounded the night she cast the charm, she might not have been able to stray far from home.

'Why didn't I think of it before!' cried Zannah, clapping her hands to her head. 'Such a dalcop am I, my brains must be addled! Or yet...not all my memories have fallen back into place. They almost seem to be dropping from the skies back into my head, Kit, but not in any good order. I was in that house every day as a child while Grandda waited on the Lady Pearl. I knew every corner of it; it was there she taught me my letters. And her library, full of books! Some I could read but many others were in different tongues I could not. I spent hours there each and every day.'

'Do you recall where the house stands?' said Kit, trying to contain his excitement.

'Stands?' Zannah looked around at the trees, puzzled for several moments and Kit had to hold his tongue and give her time to think. 'I would not know from here. Methinks we should go back and begin again.' She grabbed Kit's hand and it took surprisingly little time to find their way back to the entrance to the wood, opposite her home. 'Now,' said Zannah. 'I am a small wench again. I am walking hand in hand with Grandda to the Lady Pearl's house.' Kit felt her hand slide into his and said not a word, fearful of breaking whatever trick of remembrance she was using. 'We start down this track a little way.' She led him back down the main path between the trees but at the end where it divided, instead of turning left as they had done earlier, they turned right where the path was interrupted by a group of young alders before reappearing a few yards beyond. Unless you knew it, you would not have guessed the path began again and in the dark, Kit could only just make out the flattened earth snaking its way ahead through the trees. 'Just a little further now. She is waiting for us, Grandda. She told me today she would show me a book written by a great French lady and she would speak the words to me in our own tongue and then I should write them down.' Kit wondered if Zannah had done such a good job of tricking her own mind, she really believed she was accompanying Awl Robin; her voice had lightened and seemed more girlish, which in the dark seemed strange. No, not strange: chilling.

They came to a large clearing and she dropped Kit's hand suddenly. 'But where be My Lady's house?' she cried, distraught. 'Verily, here should it stand. What hath happened? Where be My Lady?' Kit placed his hand on her shoulder and felt her slump against him. 'Aye, Kit, aye,' she said in her usual voice, and spoke as though the newly recovered memory pained her. 'She is not here, and the house is not here because of what happened later. I was no longer a child, but fully grown on the day she left us. A fire began in the house and it burned with the strange blue flames of her magic. She set her beautiful house alight, Kit, with her poor ailing body inside and all Grandda and I could do was stand and watch. The trees around did not catch light and neither did the heat of it scorch us where we stood weeping. Within an hour, all was gone, the stone walls vanished, almost as though a giant hand had come down from the sky and pulled the whole thing off the earth like a musheron, not a trace left.' Kit realised she meant a mushroom and he looked up at the dark, cloudy sky above the clearing, imagining the hand might reappear and do the same to them. Yet there was no time to stand and ponder such fancies and just because the house didn't exist any more, it didn't mean a hiding place did not exist, some place where the stricken lady would just have had strength to conceal the object. Zannah went on speaking sadly: 'We turned and left and when we got back home, Kit, the strangest thing, we had forgotten it all. We had forgotten *her*. Yet, now it seems all this happened yesterday. How could I have forgotten? I feel so bad.'

225

'You mustn't feel bad,' said Kit, holding her. "Twas part of the Lady Pearl's plan that you should forget. 'Tis what's been keeping her charm in place all this time. Zan, we don't have long. I need to ask you about this place.'

Zannah pulled away from him and breathed in deeply. 'Yes,' she said, her voice suddenly strong again. 'The house is fully in my mind, now. I can tell you how it was.' She took Kit's arm and they began walking slowly round the clearing. For the first time, Kit could make out the large flagstones marking the floors of the downstairs rooms, and patterns of smaller stones running in straight lines showing where walls and doorways had stood. It was just as though a knife had sliced cleanly along the base of the house. No grass had sprung between the stones because time had stood still, and it was just as Zannah had said, the house might well have been removed yesterday. She guided him around and described each room in detail: the hall with its rich red and gold tapestries and painted gallery; the kitchen with its large pots and pans where Awl Robin did all the cooking and where the blackened hearth was still visible; the small wood-panelled library where the Lady Pearl had taught her to read and its window seat where she would sit dreaming for hours with a book in her lap. Many of the books were in languages unknown to her but there were others she knew well, including those of her favourite poet, Geoffrey Chaucer.

As she talked, Kit scanned the ground for the

smallest hint of a light but there was none. It was so dark underfoot, it would have been impossible to make out if something had been buried. 'I will have to return in daylight, Zan,' said Kit. 'I am sure this is the place and just as sure we don't have long to find the object. There could be some sign 'tis impossible to detect in the dark.'

'I fear for you so in daylight. I fear to go out myself,' Zannah replied. 'Judd says there is such anger in the village now. Fear is turning to anger and vexation. They'll blame you just as surely as they will me, for everything that's happened. And yet I would not have them remember the truth for then the village itself will get chewed up by the magic wall.'

'I believe what you say,' said Kit. 'But I fear we must take the chance. There's naught else we can do. 'Tis the only way of stopping that wall from closing in. I must find the Lady Pearl's object in daylight or this whole village is done for.'

They spent another fruitless half-hour searching the ground where the house once stood before the tingling began and Kit had to race back to the Widow Edith's roof and the thread joining their worlds together.

CHAPTER 21

He was on the floor of his chamber at the inn but the thunderous banging on the door made him jump to his feet, dizzy as he was. The doorknob was rattling and the large key was about to drop out onto the floor. Remembering Saroni's trick for gaining access to a locked room, Kit leapt to catch the key as it fell and flung it into the corner.

'Open up!' shouted the landlord and the thumping and rattling continued. Kit's head was spinning, but he knew he must put his escape plan into action. He grabbed the book, gathered up the thread and thrust both into the bag. He was making for the window when another voice froze him, momentarily.

'Get out here now, Kit, you hear me?' The familiar, commanding voice was raw with anger and the door shook even more violently as the loud, sharp rap of a hard object threatened to smash through the wooden panel. Kit was sure it was the silver ball at the end of a walking stick.

Perhaps they didn't imagine he'd be able to get out through the tiny window. He squeezed one shoulder out, then the other and squirmed the rest of himself through, perching precariously on the outside sill while he tugged at the bag. It was jammed so tightly in the frame, he was afraid of not getting it through in one piece but the idea of removing the pages to get it out bit by bit terrified him. He heaved at the strap, leaning his whole weight into empty space and it finally came through. Kit fell the five or so feet into the alleyway and hit the cobbles hard but before he could get up on his own, hands had laid hold of him and were dragging him to his feet.

'Gotcha,' rasped a voice and the low tide stink was worse than ever. The bag was somewhere on the ground and Pinches was attempting to pin his arms behind his back. Kit jumped and thrust backwards off the brick wall with both feet, catching Pinches off balance and propelling him into the opposite wall which he struck, letting go of Kit as he fell. In the length of a heartbeat, Pinches was on his feet again and he dived headfirst at Kit who was attempting to find the bag, forcing him down onto the dusty cobbles. In the midst of this ugly struggle, Kit heard voices at the street end of the alley and saw a lantern approaching. If he didn't escape in the next few seconds, Colewich and the landlord would be there too and all would be lost. Pinches was now practically sitting on top of him but at least Kit knew where the bag was because he could feel it with his foot. When he bit hard into Pinches' thigh, the henchman yelled in pain and relaxed his grip. Kit spotted his last chance to wriggle backwards out of the sleeves of his jacket which remained beneath Pinches, then snatched up the bag and hurtled down the alley away from the lantern light and voices. He didn't know where he was going, maybe a dead end awaited him but he could only run one way. The three men pursuing him were shouting, 'Stop, thief!'

The alley snaked between buildings and he could make out a wall at the end. He briefly considered taking the book from the bag and using it like a weapon, but the magic was unstable and in the small confines of the alley, he feared being attacked by it himself. In the darkness, it was difficult to find handholds in the brickwork but Kit managed to climb up to a low roof and when Pinches grabbed onto the heel of his boot, he was able to kick out. He saw the man fall on top of the others and heard their oaths. His heart was hammering and he knew he had been less than a second away from capture but he made it up and over the roof, dropping onto rough ground on the other side where he hoped the earth would muffle his footsteps so it would not be as easy for the men to tell in which direction he was heading.

After running as fast as he could for so long, Kit feared his heart might give out and he took refuge in a field. A hue and cry had gone up in the town and worryingly, hounds were barking and yelping excitedly, but he had already waded down a stream or open sewer which was swollen from all the rain and trusted that it would have thrown the dogs off his scent. He lay on his back on the damp ground, panting and shaking with cold and fear, aware that in a short while he would have to start moving again. Now at rest, the pain of his injuries hit him full on. There was blood leaking from the side of his head and his cheek and chin were scraped raw from his fall onto the cobbles. Pinches had punched him several times and it hurt each time he drew a breath, maybe a sign of a cracked rib. Apart from these, his worst pains, everything else ached from the effort of struggling out of the big ape's stifling grasp but it didn't feel like he'd broken or dislocated anything else, otherwise he was sure he would never have made it up the wall and over the roof.

The longer he lay there, the worse he felt but, before long, fear conquered pain and he knew he had to get moving. To stand was agony and he limped slowly along the hedgerow to the lane, holding his hand to his right-hand side and breathing in with every other step to try and limit the pain. The bag on his left shoulder felt ten times heavier than usual. At some point, he would need to wash the grit and dirt out of the cut on his head and clean up the rest of his face but for now, all his instincts were telling him to flee while it was still dark and find a proper place to hide before the sun rose.

That place was an ancient shepherd's cot or shelter which stood on the verge of a wood on a hillside. Kit almost hadn't chosen to go that way, the climb up the slope only adding to his difficulties, but he'd reasoned that the hill would be a good vantage point for spotting his pursuers should they begin searching the valley below. With the morning mist already rising, it was time to take cover. He nearly stumbled past without seeing the wooden cot hidden amongst the dense brambles. It was lying at an angle with one of its wheels off and it clearly hadn't been used in years, but Kit could have cried with joy at the sight of it and managed to squeeze in through the tiny door although the thorns tore at his arms. He managed to pull the door nearly shut, turning the inside dim. The cot was full of decaying leaves and there was a musty smell of rotting wood, but it seemed for the most part watertight. When it started to rain again, the water came in through one corner of the roof but trickled out through a hole in the floor. It seemed like the discovery of the tiny shelter might just have saved his life, but as time went by and the sun rose higher, Kit's fears returned worse than ever.

He was injured and exhausted and certainly wasn't well enough to return to the village that day or maybe the next. He'd been shivering for hours, his thin shirt little protection against the cold, and the damp weather meant there was no chance of him drying out. He lay on the leaves in a frozen, broken, wretched heap. Thankfully, the book seemed unharmed when he slipped his hand inside the bag to check. It lay quietly, not giving him any trouble, but soon he would have to open it and tell Zannah what had happened. She'd be expecting him to return by daylight, as he'd promised.

He fell into a doze and woke feeling worse than ever, wincing each time he took a breath, while his cheek throbbed and his head ached and to add to his more obvious injuries, there was a bad pain in his throat. Doubtless he had caught a chill and he remembered that time not long past when a fever had been upon him for days as he lay in the drovers' shelter, unable to move. He had to speak to Zannah soon in case he was coming down with the same kind of fever, so she'd know that he hadn't abandoned them all. At the same time, he didn't want to tell her what was wrong. How could he be ill now, at this most dangerous time and when he seemed about to discover the Lady Pearl's hiding place?

Chilled to the bone, with scarcely the strength to wonder what to do, Kit could only pray that each time he slept, he might wake up again. Slowly he came to a decision about speaking to Zannah and his hand returned to the bag, but his side hurt so much, he struggled to pull the book more than halfway out. With the page edges turned towards him, he opened the cover a fraction and felt warmth in his fingers. Soon, the heat spread up his hand and arm. His eyes were shut but he could imagine the light curls filling the cot and marvelled at the way the warmth began spreading itself around his entire body, unstiffening his muscles and unfreezing his bones. The book's magic was as good as a fire and soon his clothes were dry, and the inside of the cot was toasty and warm, and he sobbed for a while from sheer relief. Within an hour he was sitting upright against the wall of the cot, his senses stirred back to life and although he still hurt a lot, his fear had lessened, and he was ready to make a plan. It seemed that for the first time, the book's magic was on his side rather than fighting him and this was hopeful at least. Before the close of the day he had eaten blackberries from the brambles outside the door and licked rain from the leaves, a tiny meal but enough for him to feel food inside his belly and believe it wouldn't take long to gather the strength he'd need to journey back to the village. He listened in the doorway but not a sound, not a shout or bark led him to believe his enemies were in the area. If the dogs in Marlborough had lost his scent, Colewich and Pinches might have headed off in a dozen different directions and he hoped they were kicking themselves for missing their chance of catching him.

Before nightfall, Kit had pulled years' worth of leaves from under the cot inside, warming them in front of the book until they were cracklingly dry. He piled them up on the floor, a bed to bury himself in, since he feared keeping the book open at night. A light on the hill would be visible from miles around so he would have to try and keep out the cold like this. The last thing he did was talk with both Zannah and Judd, although he didn't tell either of them about his encounter with Colewich. They didn't need that to worry about too. He tried to sound positive and told them that although he had encountered some difficulties, he would aim to get back to them the very next day. He fell asleep praying he'd be able to do as he said.

Kit was stiff with cold when he awoke but warmth from the book helped him recover and after an even smaller breakfast of the feebler looking blackberries he hadn't bothered with the day before, he was ready to use whatever energy he had left to get back into the book. His hands were shaking with nerves and it was hard to flip the pages, but he finally managed it. Kit landed on the church tower and cursed himself for landing so far from the wood.

In the church Father Bernard was praying at the altar, but the moment he saw Kit he rose from his knees, crossed himself and looked around, as though checking to make sure no one else was present. His face was pale and strained. 'I feared thee coming by daylight,' he began. 'Many folk here are frightened and angry.'

'I haven't time to stop and talk,' said Kit. 'I must away to the wood.'

The priest carried on calling after Kit, but he had already left the church and was heading out of the lychgate and down the lane when Judd ran up and caught him by the arm. 'I've been looking out for thee,' he said, guiding Kit in the opposite direction. 'We go this way. The danger is great for us both. If anyone were to see thee now...'

Judd wasn't about to take no for an answer. Kit let the blacksmith walk him back through the churchyard but he stopped at the eastern wall. 'I haven't time for this,' he protested. 'Where are we going? I'm weak, Judd. I cannot stay long and the wood is in that direction.'

'Dost thou not understand?' Judd was growing angry. 'We're under threat. It won't just be a test this time, putting our hands in a pan of water. There's those who would kill thee as soon as look at thee, thinking it might ease matters. As they remember more and more it frightens them, Kit. More than ever, they want someone to blame. They're scared how time has gone out of shape. Look around, what season is this dost thou suppose?'

'Summer as always,' said Kit with certainty.

'Look again,' said Judd.

For the first time, Kit looked properly. Yes, there were dog roses tumbling over the churchyard wall and barley ripening in the fields beyond but there was something wrong with the trees: brown autumn leaves were blowing to the floor while fresh buds were already bursting into life upon their branches. Now he saw the snow lying in patches on the ground and in deeper drifts against the walls.

It was all getting worse.

He turned back to Judd. 'Then I need to get to the wood as quick as I can. The object's hidden where the Lady Pearl's house stood, I know it is.'

'This is the safest way to the wood,' said Judd. 'We'll skirt round the village.'

'No.' Kit hung back. 'I haven't time. As soon as we get there, I'll have to leave.'

Judd caught him by the arm. 'Go the quickest way and thou art dead, make no mistake. And once they've spilt thy blood and that don't work, they'll come for me and the priest: anyone who's been consorting with you. Zannah hath already flown from her home.'

'Zannah? Where is she? Is she safe?' asked Kit. Judd turned and vaulted the wall and Kit had to follow him to get a reply. The blacksmith walked quickly and when they arrived at the open fields, Kit saw the curve of the glowing ring which now seemed closer than ever, encircling the village. It was like a shimmering, tilted rainbow and above it, the sky Kit had taken for a cloudless blue that day looked darker, more solid, like the lid to a box.

'Has anyone else seen that?' Kit ran behind Judd, feeling tired and weak.

'I dunno. They're fearful of straying too far from home, so happen not,' Judd said grimly. 'Don't look at it. It's best not to. It'll drag thee toward it.'

'Mercy, tell me what's happened to Zannah,' begged Kit.

Judd didn't slacken his pace, if anything he seemed to speed up. 'Last night, I got wind that a gang of 'em were planning to fetch her from Awl Robin's cottage and I hastened to warn her,' he said. 'She escaped moments before they arrived. Even Aldith, he was there. The fool seems desperate to forget what he saw at the church that evening.'

'Margery, too?'

'No, not she,' replied Judd. 'She keeps to her house with the shutters up. She don't call for blood, but she don't help neither. Anyhow, at least they left the old man alone, once they'd searched his house and persuaded themselves she must be with thee somewhere. Then they seemed to take fright. I watched them go, from where I was hiding 'neath the trees. Zannah camped out in the wood for the rest of the night and that's where she is now, awaiting thee where the Lady Pearl's house stood. This is the safest way to the place, believe me.'

They were coming from a different direction with the western edge of the wood in sight when they saw a child standing in the middle of the field, staring at the shimmering wall. Judd ran up to her, crouched and took her by the shoulders, shaking her gently. 'Sarah, thou must away from here,' he said. 'Don't look at that thing. Go home to thy ma right now and keep thine eyes from it.'

It took Sarah a moment to wake from her dream and refocus her eyes upon Judd. She looked from Judd to Kit, then screamed and ran back to the village. Judd gave Kit a hard look. 'Come,' he said. Kit followed.

Zannah was waiting in the clearing and left off pacing and wringing her hands when they appeared. She had the grimy look of someone who had camped out overnight but there was a fierce energy about her. She barely greeted Kit before she started walking him back through the pattern of rooms marked out on the ground. They were there for one purpose and no one was going to admit out loud that this was probably their last chance. If Kit didn't find the magical object soon, they were as good as dead.

By daylight it was easy to see the footprint of the house, where every wall and hearth had stood, as though someone had drawn a map upon the earth. Kit's eyes swept the ground for anything which might give him a clue, but he was beginning to panic and once or twice he feared the tingling was about to start. Would he even make it back to the thread this time? He was trying to not think about it, trying to not think of the vicious sparkling wall closing in upon the village and smashing it all to dust, trying to not think of his remaining lucky chances like candle flames being snuffed out one by one. 'It's trying that's the best part of us.' That's what Judd had said but how much longer could Kit keep trying? As he walked around the ghost of the Lady Pearl's house, he tried to not think about his family, about his darling Gabe dying alone in the Portland Street attic. How long could he keep doing this? One thing was for sure, if after all this trying he failed to save the village, he would stay with Zannah, Judd and Father Bernard rather than return to the safety of his own time. Their fate would be his.

'Pray show me the library again,' he said. Zannah led him to one corner. Kit closed his eyes and concentrated. With despair he felt a tingling but then he realised this feeling was different to the one calling him back to his own time. This was more like a vibration in the air, a humming which he could feel most strongly through the palms of his hands. Every part of him now focused upon these vibrations and slowly, subtly, the scent of the woodland air changed to polished furniture and spice. Surely the vibrations were hardening and he could feel something beneath his fingertips? It took a huge effort to keep his eyes closed as he focused solely on the sensation which was now growing stronger. His heart leapt as he realised that what he could feel was the plasterwork of the library wall, warm and slightly grainy to the touch. 'Can you see this wall?' he cried and when the other two replied that they couldn't, he was sure he must not open his eyes in case what he could sense of the house disappeared. That he could feel the house had to be a sign, a definite sign at long last that he was closing in on the magical object.

Zannah and Judd held their tongues as Kit slowly worked his way around the room, his sense of it becoming stronger every second. He swept his hands over the invisible wall, searching for any clues. He found the window seat Zannah had spoken of, where she'd sat with a book in her lap for hours, but beneath his questing fingers, the knots and grain of the ancient oak told him nothing. It would have been easy to rush, and he had to steady his nerve and make himself take time. He stroked the rows of books, with their spines of ancient leather and their smell of deep learning. The temptation to open his eyes was very great but he kept them closed and kept on going, moving up and down the shelves, holding on to the last one as he worked his way between what he supposed was a chair his leg bumped against, and the wall. He came to the fireplace and felt the heat of a fire in the grate. There was the definite sense of someone just having left the room, but this was balanced by an absolute certainty that no one else was there, no phantom Lady Pearl about to come and tell him her secret. He was alone and would have to work out the puzzle for himself.

Kit checked all around the stone fireplace, then his hands travelled up to the plasterwork of the chimney breast. There was a picture made from plaster: a man's face with his mouth wide open and leaves spilling from it. It didn't take long for Kit's fingertips to recognise this as the same Green Man he had seen on many a tavern sign in the towns he had visited. His fingers stroked the curling leaves and worked their way down the man's nose and mouth to his chin. Just below the chin, Kit felt some cuts that had been made in the otherwise smooth plaster and his heart beat faster. As his fingers travelled over and over the scratches, he felt sure he'd been right the first time: someone had scratched a small stick man on top of a ladder and to one side of him, an arrow pointed down towards the floor.

"Tis here,' said Kit, opening his eyes and seeing trees rather than the fireplace. Zannah and Judd approached and the three of them stared at the hearthstone but not for long. With a stubby knife, Judd scratched out the earth from where the hearth met the neighbouring flagstones and the three of them grasped hold of the exposed edge. It took a while and Judd's patience appeared at breaking point when the blade snapped off his knife. He offered to run back to the smithy and fetch tools, but Kit stopped him, afraid he wouldn't have time to wait for his return. Together they strained to prise the heavy hearthstone out of the earth but in the end, it lifted and Judd held it up while Kit searched underneath. The fear of failure returned for a fleeting moment before his hand came across an object and he drew it out of the dry earth.

241

It was a red velvet bag, tied with a gold coloured cord. None dared speak as Kit untied the cord and drew out a white goose feather. Zannah broke the silence: 'Her quill! My Lady Pearl, faith it is one of the quills she would use to write and lend me, so I should write!'

'Wait,' said Kit. He could feel something else at the bottom of the bag and placed the quill in Zannah's upturned hands. She held it gently, marvelling at it while Judd smiled broadly with relief and lowered the hearthstone back into place. Kit removed the curved scrap of parchment which had been lying at the bottom and unrolled it but the squiggles upon it meant nothing to him.

'I can't read,' he said. Judd also shrugged his shoulders. The parchment was passed to Zannah, who read aloud, 'Here is one half of the key to this charm. Find the other and all is restored in good time.'

'Here is one half of the key to this charm…' Kit repeated.

'Don't say we must hunt this place over again? There is no time!' Judd blew up again.

'I know not,' said Kit. 'But we must keep the quill safe and mayhap 'tis safer with you than I. I shall go quickly but will return, you have my word.' The proper tingling, the one calling him back to his own time, had begun. Judd raced with him, all the way back to the church leaving Zannah sitting on the library floor with tears in her eyes, cradling the goose quill, the parchment and the velvet bag.

Kit felt worse that afternoon. That final run across the open fields with Judd had nearly broken him and all the while, he'd been aware of the hellish glowing rainbow on the edge of the land. It had taken extra strength not to look that way and lose himself in its shifting shapes. He was sure he'd only just made it back to the church tower in time because no sooner had he untied the thread, but he and it had disappeared at once.

Hunger was making him weak. He plucked up the courage to leave the shepherd's cot and go in search of food but there wasn't much in the wood that was edible, and he realised that he would have to search further afield for his next meal, under cover of night. Perhaps there was a farm on the other side of the hill with animal feed in the cowshed or vegetables growing in the garden? If so, he could take what he needed and return to the safety of the shepherd's cot to eat. Convincing himself that this was very likely, Kit rested for the remainder of the day, trying to conserve as much energy as he could. When he fell asleep, he had a terrible dream where he was fighting his way through Chi-Keen's scarves which were draped like curtains, then fell onto the stage of the Drury Lane theatre. There were no other actors and only one audience member, a faceless figure in the darkened box overlooking the stage. A hand reached over the side of the box and pointed at him with the silver ball end of a walking stick. In terror, Kit retreated through the tangle of scarves but on the other side he stepped out onto another stage, in the courtyard of a tavern he had once visited with Saroni. This time Colewich was watching from the otherwise-deserted gallery, striking his stick hard on the wooden boards in time with Kit's thumping heartbeat. Kit hastened back through the curtains and this time, found himself in the Portland Street attic which was piled high to the rafters with Chi-Keen's props and Saroni's puppets. Punchinello was suspended from one beam, smiling grotesquely and pointing at the comet which was visible through the hole in the roof. A figure lay on the bed, coughing and coughing. Convinced that Gabe was alive again, a pure, intense joy flowed through Kit but as he approached the bed in the half-light, the figure sat up slowly and it was not Gabe at all. His joy turned to dread, then horror, as Colewich opened wide his blood-rimmed eyes, reached out his hands, each finger tipped with a silver claw and bared the white spikes of his teeth. The grotesque figure of Colewich rose to his knees as though it were being pulled up with puppet strings and came shuffling jerkily across the bed, snarling and slobbering and clawing the air while Kit stood paralysed by fear. His own screaming woke him. He was too afraid to sleep again.

Kit left the shepherd's cot as the sun was going down,

with the bag on his shoulder. He had persuaded himself that on the other side of the hill, he would certainly find a farm or at least a cottage; he could practically smell the smoke rising from the chimney. Despite his horrible dream, he had to remember that he had succeeded in finding the Lady Pearl's magical object within the book. Things were starting to go his way at last. He was going to get the villagers out of this mess they had innocently found themselves in. Of course, there would be food on the other side of the hill, plenty of it. And drink, as much as he needed.

When he got to the top, there was nothing to be seen but another overgrown hillside. If he wanted to eat he was going to have to walk further but each shaky step he took through the knee-high grass and deep, watery ruts, sapped strength from his legs which soon felt like they didn't belong to him but were borrowed from some life-size doll. Down he stumbled into the moonlit valley, wondering if he would have the strength to climb back up to his hiding place, even if he chanced upon some amazing banquet of food, laid out before him on a polished table the same as on a Thursday evening at Mr Steen's. He was chilled through again and for the hundredth time, regretted leaving his jacket in the alley during his fight with Pinches.

There was a pond at the edge of a field, standing water left over from the rain and he drank from it. He was scared to rest, knowing that if he lay down, he might never get back up. He tried to give himself heart by repeating what was written on the parchment he'd found at the bottom of the red velvet bag, or what he could remember of it: 'Here is one half of the key to this charm…here is one half of the key to this charm…'

Soon he felt dizzy and sick and wished he had never left the shepherd's cot. Before he knew it, he was face down in the long grass and couldn't move while the stars he could see from the corner of one eye spun overhead. He was sick, but only foul-tasting water came up. There was nothing else in his belly. In a little while he made it to his feet again, picked up the bag and began to stumble along, only to collapse after a few short steps.

When day broke he wasn't sure if he was still alive or not. He was cold as death with no feeling in his body. He could only raise his head and open his eyes a little. Something went past, a blurry shape seen through a gateway, and he heard wheels trundling along a stony surface. Kit heard a snatch of a song being hummed and it was a tune he recognised.

After wiggling his toes to try and create some feeling, Kit got to his feet and picked up the bag, holding it in his arms like a baby. The song was growing fainter and he felt he should follow. After attempting a few steps and not falling over, he found himself in a lane between tall hedgerows, watching a figure retreating into the distance: a man pushing a handcart. The way he walked, the song he sang and the feather in his broad brimmed hat, signalled to Kit that the man could only be Saroni. At that moment, it felt like he had two options: die in the ditch or follow his old master. Not that he knew what to say if he caught up with him. No, he did know: he would ask forgiveness. What if heaven was giving him this chance to make things right with the person who'd been such a friend to him? He shuffled a step at a time, straining to hear the song and sometimes it started up again, although from much further off. Even though he was pushing a handcart, Saroni could travel much faster than Kit. He carried on placing one foot in front of the other as the sun rose higher. It was a fine autumn day, the kind that makes you wonder if you are witnessing the last good day of the year, but Kit didn't notice the golden light or fine weather and showing himself in broad daylight didn't worry him any more. He was past worrying about Colewich or even the book. The only reason for carrying on along that path was to catch up with Saroni and beg forgiveness.

After a while, Kit realised that he was the one humming the song. What he'd taken for his old master's voice was actually his own. Saroni was gone, if he'd been there at all. This was the final blow: he staggered a few more paces and collapsed. The world spun round and round again but before his eyes closed, a face did appear.

'Drink, drink.' A cup was being pressed to his lips and water ran into his dry mouth, making him splutter. Eventually he managed to swallow a little. He opened his eyes and immediately Saroni retreated to the other side of the fire. Kit tried to say the words 'forgive me' but only a few cracked sounds came out of his mouth.

Saroni said nothing but he was frowning. He crouched, picked up a stick and began poking the small fire.

Kit remembered the book and felt around him with a trembling hand.

'It's right there. Shh!' Saroni spoke in a whisper and pointed near Kit's feet. Kit lifted his head a fraction and saw the oilskin bag. 'Don't ask me to touch it,' Saroni went on. 'I suppose you realise the risk I am taking, saving you once more, huh? If those men find out I talked to you, who is going to save me? Who?'

Kit tried to raise himself but Saroni signalled that he should lie back down. 'How far do you think you'd get?' he whispered. 'Had I not stopped to rest, I would not have seen you fall in the lane. Anyway, here you are again…'

'My thanks…' Kit managed to say.

'I don't want your thanks,' Saroni whispered angrily. '*Gah!* I should take that book of *diavolo* and throw it in the river. Then ask pardon of the river.'

Kit shook his head. 'You don't understand,' he wheezed out the words.

'I know what I saw in Bath that day,' Saroni pointed at the book again then crossed himself and shook his head. 'I know what I saw.'

His old master had aged in the space of just a few weeks. His beard and hair were grey. He'd lost weight but the light in his eyes was still fierce. Kit was scared to ask the obvious, since Donatello was nowhere in sight and the covered handcart didn't seem laden with goods. Saroni saw his eyes stray to the handcart.

'I had to sell my horse,' he explained, 'my cart, everything. I had to pay for all the damage in Bath. What you see, this is all I have left. But that was not the worst. That fine gentleman with the stick ordered for them to beat me as he asked his questions: *Where has Kit gone? What do you know of the book?* I didn't know but it took a long time before he believed me. In the next days, I thought 'Why didn't they just kill me?' I had nothing left.' Kit shaped his mouth into another apology. 'Don't ask me to forgive you!' snapped Saroni. 'I don't feel like it.'

Not another word was spoken for hours. Saroni tossed over an old coat for Kit to cover himself with. He tore pieces of bread from a loaf and threw them across. Kit ate slowly and each mouthful was like a lead weight passing down his gullet to his shrunken belly. They were hiding in a wood and Saroni kept the fire small, flapping his hand to disperse the smoke. At times, he would rise and pace nervously this way and that, on the lookout. Most of the time, he sat on a tree stump and continued painting the head of a new Punchinello he had carved from a block of wood. It was small, about a quarter of the size of the original Punchinello, more the size of a glove, and Saroni had given it a red cape. Now he was painting on the features, the surprised blue eyes, ruddy cheeks and devilish grin. Kit shut his own eyes so he wouldn't have to look at it.

Kit would have left if he could, but he was too weak and ill. Saroni attended to him whilst keeping him at arm's length but presumably this was only to help him get better, so he would leave. Kit was afraid to sleep, in case Saroni did what he'd threatened – take the book and throw it in the river. He needed to persuade Saroni that the book was nothing to be scared of and he had to do it before nightfall. In the late afternoon, Kit's voice returned. 'I won't ask your forgiveness,' he whispered. Saroni didn't look up from his work but Kit could see that he was listening. 'But I need to tell you about the man who ordered you to be beaten. His name's Lord Colewich. He's rich and powerful and wicked. Blame him, not the book. 'Twas he I was running from when I first met you. You're right to fear him. You saw those faces, when the pages fell out in Bath? They belong to real people, people who are alive. He would think nothing of torturing them, just as he did you. That's why he wants to find it.'

Saroni gave a great sigh and laying aside his paints, he rose to his feet, put on his hat and prepared to leave. 'I cannot sleep here tonight,' he said, 'Not with that thing lying there. I will return in the morning to see how you are.'

'I beg you,' said Kit. 'I won't make you look at it. You don't have to go near it. Those faces you saw were faces of real people and they lived in a village, hundreds of years ago. They were put in the book by magic to keep them safe. Not bad magic, Saroni, 'twas a charm to look after them while they were under threat. They will all die soon, if I don't help them.'

Saroni covered his face with one hand. He remained motionless as Kit's words came tumbling out. 'That night you broke into our room in Bath, you wondered where I'd been? I'd been to the village. There are pictures scratched onto the sides of each page, little drawings of a man climbing a ladder...I won't show you, I promise...' Saroni was starting to back away again. Kit spoke faster. He had to make his old master understand. 'If you move the pages quickly, he climbs the ladder and that's the way into the book and to the village. Magic it is, yes, but not evil magic! There was a way I found to get back again.' Kit described how he used the thread.

He let Saroni digest the information. If he left, Kit guessed he would not return. At last and with another long and heavy sigh, Saroni squatted down and poked dispiritedly at the dying embers of the fire. He remained there while Kit told the whole story from the beginning. He told Saroni how Colewich had hired him to steal Zannah's page from the bookseller and how in turn, he had stolen the entire book from his Lordship. He explained the threat the whole village was under from the glowing wall and their discovery of the Lady Pearl's house and the quill which seemed to be the key to the charm.

'Very well. Is there danger in showing me?' Saroni nodded at the book, reluctantly. Kit shook his head and Saroni responded by nodding more slowly, which Kit read as a signal that he would see it. Kit had recovered enough to sit up and he pulled the book from the bag slowly, fearing that any sudden movement might still send his old master fleeing. Saroni rose to his feet but this time, stood his ground and watched nervously as Kit opened the book and found Zannah's page. She opened her eyes and Kit heard Saroni swallow. 'There you are, Kit,' she said. 'Times grow desperate here. Do not return, for verily it is too late.'

'No,' said Kit.

'Yes,' she insisted. 'Do not come back, you hear me? Finding the Lady Pearl's object has not worked. Judd and I stay hidden at her house, for we hear voices shouting in the village for our blood. We would be dead by now, if the crack-brains did not see lights glowing on the other side of the trees and fear to enter. The wall comes nearer Kit. Now it is just beyond the trees. It will be here soon.'

Kit was horrified. 'I must return,' he said. 'Mayhap there is something left to do. Oh, God, God *think*! The slip of parchment with the charm, what was written thereon? 'Here is one half of the key to this charm...' then what?'

'It is too late, Kit. Assuredly you will die with us if you return.'

'Tell me, Zan, what does it say on the parchment?'

Zannah's eyes were swimming with tears and she fought to say the words without crying: 'Find the other and all is restored in good time.'

Find the other? But surely there was only ever supposed to be one object.

'The Lady Pearl hid the object before she cast the charm and before her house disappeared.' Kit was thinking aloud. 'Meaning even if 'tis found in your time 'twill not yet have been found in mine. Zan, it might still be here in my time. 'Tis possible.'

'It is too late, Kit.'

'Zan, listen.' Kit felt stirrings of excitement. ''Tis exactly the same object we seek, the Lady Pearl's goose quill, but just as we found it there, so does it lie buried here, in the time in which I live. Put the two together and "all is restored in good time" as your lady wrote. I know not what that means but it sounds as though the village will be saved?'

But Zannah wouldn't listen and something happened that had never happened before – she turned her back upon Kit and her page turned dull, the shimmer of life extinguished. 'Zan? Zannah!' cried Kit. Saroni shushed him and slowly he closed the book. His old master was staring in disbelief.

'You see how 'tis?' said Kit. 'Yet I think I am right; the quill still lies buried in our time, below that hearthstone in what remains of the Lady Pearl's house, could I but find it. Were the two placed together to become one, so the village would be restored.'

The meaning of the Lady Pearl's words had just become clear and yet it seemed too late. How could Kit possibly roam the whole country to find the place where this unnamed village had once stood? How could he do so before the village in the book became swallowed up by the hellish wall? How long would he have left to find it: one day? Two?

Saroni crouched opposite Kit again. He looked shaken but he also appeared to be thinking. Suddenly, he rubbed his face with his hands as though waking himself and the strength was back in his voice. 'You say this village existed hundreds of years ago?'

'So I believe.'

'Where is it now?'

Kit shook his head hopelessly. 'That's the problem,' he said.

'Haven't you looked for it, Kit? Now would be a good time.'

Kit stared at Saroni. 'But how can we know if any trace of this village still stands?'

'There are ruins all over this land,' said Saroni. 'I travel past villages wiped out by plague and abandoned for hundreds of years. Where was it, you think? Somewhere it had to be, *certo*!' He spread his arms wide.

Kit thought about the Lady Pearl's house and how it had been sliced clean through at the base only leaving the floor and hearthstones. Had this happened to the rest of the village? He shook his head. 'There wouldn't be much to see,' he said. 'The markings of walls, the stones of hearths. I suppose the church, if that vanished, would leave a great sized floor. But what if newer buildings had been piled on top of those ruins?'

'This is strong magic,' Saroni frowned and nodded at the book. 'Do you think this lady would not have thought of this?' Now Kit nodded. It was true, there had to be a way of getting the quills together, the Lady Pearl would not have set a completely impossible task.

'What is the village like?' asked Saroni. 'Here...' He picked up the stick with which he'd been poking the fire and moved to kneel beside Kit, brushing away the twigs and leaves from the ground to expose smooth, bare earth. He put the stick in Kit's hand. 'Make a map,' he said.

Kit thought a moment, then began scratching into the earth with the charred end of the stick. 'There's a pond in the middle... on this side is the smithy; the blacksmith's name is Judd, and then there are dwellings here... and more here. The millpond, I suppose, is the middle, and there is a mounting block here. This lane takes you past more dwellings... here is the house of the Widow Edith who died... here is Zannah's cottage, where she lives with her grandfather and before it, the entrance to the wood. I would say the Lady Pearl's house stood about here.'

'The church?' prompted Saroni.

'Not far from the smithy, up this lane and there is a large yew tree, a very ancient one.'

'Ah?' Saroni stared at the map scratched into the

earth with a furrowed brow. He asked Kit to go over all the places again and kept returning to the church. Finally, he looked up at Kit and scratched his head. 'You know, I even think I know this place.'

Kit's mouth fell open but Saroni waved a hand to silence him before he could speak. 'The ruin is not far, about seven miles back down the road, then head north another three or four miles. I have never stopped long, for it is a kind of cold, forbidding place you want to hurry through. And though wild, the grass grown high, there are bare patches, as though the ground were scorched by some unnatural fire so nothing will grow there again. Square patches, mayhap where dwellings once stood? There is also a yew tree to one side of the road, on its own but *grande*, the biggest I have seen. They are like that in churchyards and oft have I thought: this one, why does it stand alone?'

'Is there a pond?' asked Kit.

'*Sicuramente*,' Saroni nodded vigorously.

'And the wood, here?' Kit pointed at the map.

'I think but there are trees all around, everywhere. The land belongs to no one, I would say. But most of all there is this feeling… this feeling of wanting to not be there, you understand? Clouds hang over this place on the brightest day. A snake slides over my shadow as I think of it.' He shuddered.

'The charm is still at work, keeping people away,' marvelled Kit. His excitement unlocked some inner chamber of strength and he felt fire in his belly again.

Each time he asked Saroni if he was sure, his old master studied the map and gave him so many assurances that his mind was soon free from doubt. Yet in his present state, how could he walk to this place, find the bag with the feather inside, walk back and enter the book?

'I will go,' said Saroni. 'I will find this quill if it is where you say it is. I can keep this map in my mind. When I return, you can save your friends, yes?'

'My deepest thanks,' said Kit, who could have wept with joy and for the first time, Saroni half smiled and shook his finger. 'You know what though, hey? No running out on me when I am gone. You do that one more time Kit, I will never forgive.' This was a joke, since the idea of Kit's running anywhere was ridiculous, but they stared at one another a moment, both remembering the first time Saroni had said this. Saroni asked Kit to draw one more map for him, a floorplan of the Lady Pearl's house. He studied it hard. Kit gave him as many details as possible about the wood itself, at least how it looked in Zannah's time. Saroni set out at once, leaving his belongings with Kit and ordering him to rest. If there wasn't enough light to find the quill when he got there, he would search early the following morning and promised only to return when he had found it.

Kit knew he had a nervous wait ahead and the earlier conversation with Zannah troubled him a great deal. How could he rest? As soon as Saroni left, he opened the book, only to find Zannah turned away and that same strange dullness across her page, as though it were a page in an ordinary book. Quickly, he turned to Judd's page and was relieved to find the blacksmith's eyes upon him as usual. 'Kit, do not return,' Judd said grimly before Kit could open his mouth. 'Our end grows near.'

'Listen,' said Kit. 'I think I have found a way to save you. 'Twill take but a little time.' Judd did not react with enthusiasm. 'And time is what we do not have. The wall of lights nears apace. Each hour it moves closer, smashing down trees. We do hear them being ripped apart and the sky rains fine white soot upon us. It is too late, too late.' Judd continued putting up his own wall, not listening to Kit and blocking him each time he tried to speak.

'Is Zannah well?' Kit finally broke through.

'She does not wish to see thee, Kit, and forbids your return. Her thoughts are fixed upon God now, as mine must also be. There's nought else left to us but death and pray God it is a painless kind. I bid you farewell.' In despair, Kit watched Judd turn just as Zannah had done and the same dullness fell across his page.

'No. No!' cried Kit. Judd and Zannah were giving up while there was still a chance! If only he could be sure Saroni would return with the quill in time... but what if the death wall chewed up the village before his return? Kit turned with urgency to Father Bernard's page and this time he was quick to speak first. The frightened looking priest seemed to be listening but finally, all he said was, 'My thanks for trying to help us,' before he turned his back just like the others.

The afternoon was growing cold and Kit had little time to decide what to do. It was impossible to lie there and rest with his friends facing their imminent deaths. He wished he hadn't left the quill with Zannah because if it was in his possession, he could have gone with Saroni and put the two quills together in his own time. If it were possible for the quills to meet in the modern time? Why not: there had to be some way of doing it! Kit needed to get back into the book at once and ask Zannah for the quill. Then he would head after Saroni and the quills could be united as soon as was humanly, or magically, possible. His friends would be saved.

CHAPTER 23

For once, luck was on Kit's side and he landed again on the low roof of the late Widow Edith's house. There was no one around, but he could hear distant voices shouting and wailing. The sky was not pretending to look real any more, it looked like a faded backdrop to a play at the theatre, daubed with clouds and swallows that didn't move, while over in the west, a theatrically painted sun radiated wavy fronds of light. The comet had been painted at the highest point above his head with the long tail streaming behind it. Again, Kit thought of the real comet that had flown in his own sky, the one Gabe had said looked magical, the one Kit had imagined him riding up to heaven. Was this a picture of the same comet? The comet from his own time had been predicted to return by Sir Edmond Halley, which meant it came and went. From what the Lady Pearl had said, the village could only be rescued when this same comet returned to real-time Earth. Kit couldn't spend long thinking about this. The unearthly glow was pounding like a heartbeat on the margins of the wood and revealing the falseness of the sky for the first time. When Kit jumped from the roof, he caught sight of himself in a barrel of rainwater, its dark surface acting like a mirror. Saroni wasn't the only one who had lost weight: Kit looked like a skeleton, his cheekbones sharp and his eyes set in two dark circles. He had tied the thread to a broken section of the roof and didn't plan to leave it there long: surely in his weakened state the tingling would start soon.

'Zan, prithee, the quill.' Kit was panting when he arrived at the Lady Pearl's house, despite barely having the strength to run. Zannah was alone and when she turned, he stared at her in shock. The dullness which had descended upon her page had also descended upon her; no, it was not even that, her skin, her clothes, everything had a flat look, as though she were made of paper.

Zannah cried out when she saw him, but her voice seemed to come from a long way off. With a pained expression she fumbled in her bodice and produced the velvet bag which she passed to Kit. The bag had the semblance of paper and the hand which reached for it did too, even though it still felt as much like his own hand as ever.

'I must bind it to my body, to secure it. Can you cut me a ribbon from the hem of your skirt?' Kit was remembering all the times he had climbed up to the Portland Street attic, with precious items held fast to his chest.

'Aye, Kit, for what good it will do,' Zannah's flat voice skimmed across the surface of the air. She bent and after a few attempts, tore a strip from the bottom of her skirt, then another and another, which she knotted together. As she was handing it over, there came a deafening roar from the other side of the trees. 'It draws near!' shouted Zannah and the two of them ducked and crouched with their arms around one another, shielding their heads as the earth shook and the smashing of trees began. Fine, sticky wood pulp rained down, landing all around them in clots. Kit held Zannah but was afraid of holding her tightly in case his arms went right through her, she felt so insubstantial. It was like holding a bunch of fragile flowers. They crouched low until the aftershocks died down.

'I told you not to return!' Zannah began to cry.

'We can still save the village!' Kit removed his shirt, but his fingers were trembling badly. 'Come, help bind this to me,' he said. He held the velvet bag in place while Zannah wound the strip of cloth around his chest. He could feel the bag humming with the magic of the quill. It was just as he was putting his shirt back on that the tingling began in his hands. 'I must away,' he said. 'But I believe we can still do it. Tell Judd that too. Keep my words in your heart and I will see you soon.' He couldn't bear to look her in the face, when it looked more like a face in an illuminated book, crinkle-browed and open-mouthed in fear. He ran back through the wood with its two-dimensional trees and the Widow Edith's house was already in sight when the tingling stopped. This had never happened before. He climbed up to the roof, where he found the tail end of the thread, broken.

'Kit? Kit!' A voice was calling him, a voice he recognised, then came horrible laughter and he recognised his worst fear. As he leaned over the edge of the low roof, his eyes were drawn down to the barrel of water. The edges of his vision misted as his attention concentrated on the mirrored surface. Colewich's face appeared.

'Here is a change in your fortunes, Kit,' the wicked face sneered. Besides the heart-stopping shock of seeing him again, there was the terrible sense that Colewich's face was the only real thing left in an otherwise papery world. Kit felt sick and faint and was lost for words. 'Now I have you, you must tell me the secret of how to enter the book,' said Colewich. Kit shook his head but his Lordship persisted, growing angrier. 'I have Saroni here. I will have him killed if you don't tell me.'

Colewich was a bad actor and Kit knew he was lying. 'If you have Saroni, show him to me,' said Kit. He thought about turning his back on Colewich, the way Zannah and Judd had turned their backs on him, and in his insubstantial, papery form it would have been easy to do so.

'Very well. But I know Saroni has been here recently; he left his belongings. It will be a simple matter to get the information out of him when he returns. Pinches will be more than happy to oblige.' Colewich smiled when he saw the effect these words had upon Kit. If Kit turned his back on Colewich, he would also be abandoning Saroni.

Colewich pressed home his advantage. 'Let's start again. Tell me how to enter this book?'

'You cannot,' said Kit. 'Only one of us can be in here at one time. See, there are no pages left for you, where would you go?'

The surface of the water darkened a moment and Kit imagined Colewich turning the pages to check them. Kit guessed that he was appearing on the page which had belonged to the Widow Edith, that had gone blank after her death. There had been no further deaths that he knew of. Colewich obviously hadn't noticed the scratchy little stick man or if he had, hadn't guessed its significance.

Colewich reappeared, and it seemed as though Kit had convinced him that there was no way in. He didn't seem disheartened. 'How about finding the magical object for me, Kit? 'Tis hidden somewhere in that place and the other dullards have failed to find it. Oh-ho!' He laughed again. 'How like old times this is! Remember when I sent you to the bookseller on such a mission? You succeeded then, and you will again. For you are an excellent thief, Kit. The best. Here is my final task for you.'

'I won't do it,' said Kit, aware of the velvet bag strapped to his chest, beneath his shirt.

'You think of me as your enemy,' Colewich tried a friendlier tone. 'But I can be such a friend to you, Kit. There'll be no more running and hiding once you've found what I am looking for. I will reward you handsomely. You will live in splendour. I can introduce you to the best in society, set you up in a fine way. 'Tis not even stealing, for the magical object belongs to me. It belonged to my ancestor, given to him by his first wife, a woman called Pearl. He was heartbroken when she died, and this was his one treasured possession, a remembrance of her.'

It made perfect sense that the cruel lord who had been married to the Lady Pearl was Colewich's ancestor. 'What am I looking for, then?' asked Kit.

'I know not,' Colewich spoke the words through gritted teeth then immediately softened his tone. 'But 'tis my birthright, Kit. That's why it pains me to be so cheated. When I found the book, I thought locating the object would be a simple matter, yet it does not prove so easy. With great magic comes great power, Kit, and I am the man who would use it for the good of the world. Should I really be cheated out of this great opportunity?'

The good of the world? Such smooth words and yet so hollow. Kit said nothing. He pretended to listen as Colewich poured out more empty promises. What he thought about was Gabe and Zannah, how far he had travelled and that this was the end of the story. Colewich had the book and all hope was gone. Saroni would return and Kit had no power to help him, unless he could find some way of tricking Colewich. Above everything else, he could not allow the quill to fall into his hands. He didn't know what to do so decided to play for time.

'I hear what you say,' Kit replied in his strange, paper-thin voice. 'Let me go now and I will do as you ask, your Lordship. I will do my best to find the object which belongs to you.'

'I thank you, Kit. I have every faith in you and will speak with you anon.' Kit could see the relief on Colewich's face before he disappeared from the mirrored surface. He couldn't know of the immediate danger facing the village.

Kit walked back into the wood. When she saw his expression, Zannah buried her face in her hands. 'At least I can clear up one mystery,' he said. 'The Lady Pearl was married to an ancestor of the man I have been running from. He was the one who questioned you over and over about the object. Now he's trapped me here. His name is Lord Colewich.'

'Colewich?' Zannah's thin voice suddenly exclaimed, 'Colewichton! Of course, that is the name of our village. Colewichton. Judd? Father Bernard?' She turned to the men who were just entering the clearing and were to Kit's eyes, painted paper versions of themselves. Judd's frown deepened upon seeing him. 'Colewichton,' Zannah repeated. 'To think we had all forgotten the name.'

'Aye, Colewichton it was,' said Judd. 'A wonder we forgot it. Kit, I see thou hast returned, but I wish to God thou hadst not.'

'Your fate is mine,' said Kit. 'In truth, if I handed the quill to the man who has trapped me, this Lord Colewich, who is every bit as bad as his ancestor, he might let us all go. Yet such evil would he wreak with its

266

magic, I dare not.' Judd just managed to grab the arm of Father Bernard before the priest collapsed and led him to a tree stump, where he sat, still clutching the altar crucifix to his chest. 'I kept watch on the village from the other side of the wood,' explained Judd. 'And saw the church destroyed, smashed to nothing.' Silent tears rolled down Father Bernard's cheeks as the blacksmith carried on. 'Now do the villagers cry and wail, although some are drawn to the glowing wall and must be held back from rushing headlong into it. One man, John Gregory, did and he was destroyed in an instant. Each hour it draws nearer. Many dwellings have been taken and each time it moves, the folk head further this way. They are scared of the wood and sense the magic here, but soon they will have to enter.'

Kit realised that now there was at least one empty page since John Gregory's death, and he hoped Colewich would not discover it, in case he changed his mind about trying to get into the book.

'The others mustn't see you, Kit,' cried Zannah. 'They will take you and throw you into the wall, I am certain. They will make some sacrifice of you.'

'Or thee, Zannah, or I. Any or all of us,' sighed Judd. 'They would sooner blame us than listen to sense.'

Kit walked into the Lady Pearl's house and stood in the library, as before. He closed his eyes, reached out his hands and felt vibrations in the air at once. Within moments, like an old tune returning, he could feel the wall and bookshelves which now seemed more solid and substantial than anything he would see if his eyes were open. It was warmer in the house and the old leathery smell of the books was strangely comforting. He left the walls and slowly walked into the middle of the room. 'Mayhap this place will protect us,' he said out loud. ''Tis still here. If I keep my eyes closed 'tis all around me. Come inside I pray.' He heard the others walk towards him. Zannah's light footsteps entered the study first, followed by the slow shuffle of Father Bernard being led by Judd.

'Sit you down,' said Kit. 'Here will we stay.'

They sat without argument. 'Do you not join us, Kit?' asked Zannah.

'No. I must walk.' Kit felt the need to keep touching the house, so he could see it in his mind. If he could conjure it up, it would protect them. If he opened his eyes, his three friends and the wood itself would seem no livelier than the highly coloured drawings in a Book of Hours. With his eyes closed, the world had three dimensions again. Kit worked his way around the room, feeling every object. He sensed the negative space around his friends and avoided it, but he could talk to them, although their voices were thin and distant. Back inside the Lady Pearl's house, it was easy to forget that they were facing death and the tension left him. Soon he was taking books from the shelves and opening them, feeling their weight in his hands. When Zannah asked what he was doing, he told her. There were quills, ink and paper on a low table. The fire was lit again, and he stooped to warm his hands. In a while he explained that he had finished with that room and would explore the rest of the house.

As he set foot in the kitchen, the wall moved again. The earth shook with greater ferocity, trees were smashed, and their pulp was hurled high into the sky then fell upon the roof. Kit heard it all, along with his friends' cries, and screams from the villagers. He did not feel a thing and the ground beneath his feet remained firm and steady. He continued to work his way around the room, to the great fireplace where a fire was smoking gently. There was a loaf of bread and dishes of cold meat, vegetables and herbs upon the table in the middle of the room. He broke off a piece of bread, smelt it, then placed it in his mouth. The bread was freshly baked and flavoursome; the flour clung to his lips and it was the best sign so far that the house was there to nurture and protect. Kit wished he might share some of the delicious food with his friends. He returned to the library with another piece of bread which he offered to Zannah and was disappointed that she could not taste it. Now he began to fear: was the house only protecting him? If so, he might as well open his eyes and make it vanish because whatever happened, he was determined to stay with his friends.

The food was good though, and he ate more, seizing the opportunity to stoke his strength. Once he had finished with the downstairs rooms, he came to the foot of the stairs, reached out his hand and smoothed the grainy oak of the carved newel post. Here was another test, another way to build his trust in the house and make it more real, perhaps real enough to provide shelter for others as well as himself.

'Faith, how you do rise through the air, Kit, like a spirit!' cried Zannah. It was true, his feet were ascending the wooden stairs rubbed smooth by years of tread, he heard and felt them creak beneath his weight. He rose to the upstairs landing and turned into a chamber where there was a large bed, furnished with thick embroidered curtains. There were smaller chambers and a tiny privy, with a hole upon which you could sit to do your business in style. This was indeed a fine house. When he found something new, he would call to Zannah, who agreed with everything he said, remembering exactly how her mistress' house had looked. He kept his mind on the building and away from the idea that he was walking on air. He smoothed the walls with his hands, reached up to touch the rafters and felt the reality of the house, its timber bones and plaster skin. It was so real, he almost, *almost* felt as though he could open his eyes and see it.

Time came and went. Each hour, the wall drew closer, but Kit kept his eyes shut, scared of breaking the protective spell. It worried him that Zannah, Judd and Father Bernard still reported feeling the sticky, powdery pulp descending. The villagers sounded nearer too. Kit returned to the kitchen to eat and again, offered some of the food to the others but they could feel nothing in their hands and taste nothing in their mouths. He walked around every inch of the Lady Pearl's house touching and smelling, tasting and listening until he was as sure of its existence as he'd ever been sure of anything.

Finally, after one long bout of smashing, which seemed to come from just beyond the nearest trees, the villagers burst into the clearing. 'Look, the demon!' yelled the voice Kit recognised as Aldith's, even though it seemed so thin and distant.

'Kill him! Kill him!' shouted several more. Kit could sense them closing in on him and, knowing his way around the house, ran straight for the staircase and ascended to the landing. There was a collective gasp. Kit was tempted to cavort about in mid-air: if they expected a demonic show, it would serve them right if he laid one on just to terrify them; he still remembered the dance he had invented for Mr Steen and his friends.

Kit heard Father Bernard's voice drift over from the library. 'Blame not the outsider,' he said. 'That is the way of ignorance, of cowardice. There is much of which we are ignorant but let us not turn into devils ourselves. The time has come to pray and ask God's forgiveness for our sins.' The crowd fell silent, overawed by the spectacle of Kit in mid-air.

The silence was broken by Father Bernard's voice again. 'Mutton, Kit, I can taste mutton! That was what you gave me – a piece of mutton!'

271

Kit opened his eyes and saw the staircase, at the bottom of which stood a dim passageway where a mass of faces stared up at him in shock. There was Aldith, Joan and Coswonked Jem amongst them. Despite cries of alarm, most of the villagers were simply stunned at finding themselves in the old house which had just sprung up out of nowhere. They gazed around fearfully but also in wonder and began touching the walls and floor to make sure they were real. Zannah squeezed through the crowd and climbed up to him. She looked like her real self again and when she reached Kit's step, they locked hands. When he looked down, his own hands also looked real.

'This is the Lady Pearl's house, just as I remember,' whispered Zannah in breathless excitement.

Judd appeared at the bottom of the stairs, looking and sounding like himself, and called up 'Thou hast done it!' Then he turned to the rest. 'Now will you not see, you bunch of fools, this fellow is here to aid us? He is on our side.' Judd continued shaming the villagers, some of whom muttered apologies. Most were still stunned and tongue-tied.

At that moment, a blinding light appeared both in the window at the top of the stairs and in the open doorway. It illuminated the whole passage. A deafening roar heralded the arrival of the wall which was now right up against the house. The building didn't move but the villagers were so in the habit of cowering, they threw themselves to the floor. Kit and Zannah clung to each other and covered their ears. By squinting, Kit could see the wall attempting to grind the small diamonds of leaded glass to powder, yet the window held firm. The Lady Pearl's house was strong enough to hold up against its power and protect all those seeking sanctuary within.

As soon as the light and noise died down, someone shut the front door and threw the bolt across. The frightened eyes returned to Kit. What was he supposed to say? That the house would protect them for now but there was no way to save them ultimately, because they could never leave? Well, if he handed the quill to Colewich, his Lordship might save them, but he wasn't about to suggest that.

'There is food, for the children.' Father Bernard squeezed into the passage and began rounding up the younger children, persuading them in his kind, comforting way to follow him to the kitchen. When they had gone, Kit and Zannah descended a few steps, side by side and hand in hand. 'I haven't much to say,' began Kit. 'Except I fear we are likely to perish, even if the Lady Pearl's house acts as protection for now. 'Tis as Judd says; I have always been your friend. If you only knew what I have been through for your sakes, but all that is past. I beseech every one of you, find a place to sit somewhere in the house for these are our final hours. Think upon God and pray for your souls as Father Bernard has said.' The stunned villagers did as he asked and dispersed. Zannah ran down to find her grandfather and returned, saying Awl Robin was sitting beside the fire in the kitchen, entertaining the little ones with tales of the old times. Judd joined Kit and Zannah on the stairs and the three of them sat side by side. At last, Kit had time to describe how he'd been trapped by Colewich. Although his Lordship had succeeded in tracking him down, he couldn't have seen him enter the book or he would already know the way in. Kit felt sick when he imagined how delighted Colewich must have been to come across the book in the clearing, and how quick to sever the thread which was obviously helping Kit in some way. Most of all, how overjoyed to open it and find Kit staring back at him. What if, when Saroni returned, he was forced to hand over the quill and reveal how to enter the book? According to the parchment, the village would be 'restored in good time' once the two quills came together. It would also leave the magical object in Colewich's possession. Zannah and Judd agreed, they could not allow that to happen.

Kit went back to the very beginning and told the whole story, fleshing out parts he had kept from his friends for fear of worrying them at the time. 'Faith, you have gone through much for our sakes,' said Zannah. She squeezed his hand and Judd clapped him on the shoulder.

'And I would have done more,' Kit replied simply and sincerely. 'For when my beloved Gabe died, who had I to comfort me but you, Zan? You offered me such friendship, though you were but a face on a page to me then. And you, my friend Judd. I would go to the ends of the earth for you both. You've made this village feel like a home to me.'

After that, they fell silent. Considering the house was so crowded, it was eerily quiet with folk speaking in whispers. Even Awl Robin's storytelling had dried up. There were still cries of fear and dismay each time the wall tried to move. It was like a restless animal being held at bay. They had to plug their ears to the noise and hide their eyes from the light which flooded the windows. At other times, the lights shifted this way and that behind the diamond-leaded panes like angry fish, building up for another attack.

The three friends rested awhile, or tried to, while people came and went, stepping over them on their way to the privy. Kit's brain was churning over the problem. Might there still be some way of tricking Colewich into saving the village without having to give him the quill? If there was, he couldn't think of it.

As time went on, the villagers grew more anxious and restless. When the food ran out, the younger children became upset, and their parents found it difficult to stop their crying. Kit feared being asked by someone like Aldith what was going to happen to them all.

The moment arrived that Kit had been both expecting and dreading. Colewich was summoning him to the window, and he sounded horribly triumphant. Kit approached, remembering that other time he'd seen his Lordship's face stuck in a window and being cut to pieces. This time was very different: Colewich's eyes crinkled with mirth and his mouth twisted into the nastiest kind of smile. 'Well? Have you found it?' he asked, and Kit shook his head. 'Really? I expected some such reply. No matter, no matter at all. For, my dear Kit, point one: I notice there is an empty page in the book, and point two: your master Saroni has returned and he has been most helpful. Mayhap in future you should choose your friends more wisely. They may not turn out to be such good friends after all.'

Kit froze at these words. Colewich didn't appear to be bluffing this time. How willingly had his old master given up the information Colewich had demanded of him? He remembered Saroni's words before leaving for the ruined village:

No running out on me when I am gone. You do that one more time Kit, I will never forgive.

Was it possible Saroni had returned to the clearing, seen that Kit was gone and assumed the worst? In his anger and disappointment, had he told Colewich everything?

Colewich stepped aside and Saroni took his place in the window. His smile was broad and his eyes twinkled below the brim of his hat. Kit's heart sank. Betrayal by his old master wasn't something he had considered, yet he'd seen for himself how embittered Saroni had become and how hard he found it to forgive.

'This serves you right, Kit,' Saroni cackled. 'Thanks to you, I lose everything. Have you any idea what that did to me? But now, thanks to you, I gain it all back. That seems fair, yes? Lord Colewich and I have made friends as you see. *Bravo* Lord Colewich! All is good between us!' At this point Kit heard both Colewich and Pinches laughing in the background. Saroni carried on, 'What did you expect me to do, my little Angelo? I tell him exactly what he wants to know, how to get into that damn book of yours. And he has paid me handsomely as you see.' He held up a jingling purse. 'So I must thank you, Kit. That information you entrusted me with, it has turned out to be a real "feather in my hat" as is the expression. Hahaha!' Saroni was being unnecessarily dramatic. He bowed to show Kit the feather decorating his well-worn and familiar hat. Except this time, the black cockerel's feather had been replaced by a grey goose feather, the duplicate of the one in the velvet bag which was at that moment strapped to Kit's chest. Saroni was showing him he had the quill and with relief and mounting excitement, Kit realised that all this was simply a performance, a piece of theatre with which to trick Colewich.

'I understand,' said Kit, sadly. To make it more convincing, he added, 'To think you have betrayed me, after all our travels together.'

'Huh! That is nothing to me,' Saroni rolled his eyes. 'I have told his Lordship everything, *everything*. How at the last minute he must put on your magic coat,' here he held up the old coat Kit had used as a blanket, '…before flipping the little man up the ladder on the side of the pages. I hope you are ready for what will happen, Kit.' As he watched with giddy excitement, he saw his old master begin to help Colewich on with the tattered old coat. Pinches stepped in to assist but Saroni gestured politely that he didn't need help. As Saroni bent down, Kit saw him remove the quill from his hat and slide it into the pocket of the coat.

Colewich turned back to Kit and held up the thread, rolled once more into a ball. 'And now I know what this is for,' he said. 'Pinches will make sure it remains in place on this side of the book.' Colewich tied one end around his wrist and Pinches took the ball from his hand. ''Twill be such a pleasure to see you again, Kit,' Colewich continued to gloat. 'It has been so long. Don't make any plans to attack me, for I bring weapons. I am sure you and the others will be more than happy to follow my orders and help me find the magical object. It belongs to me, after all. And when I do find it…' It was as though he couldn't sum up his happiness in mere words. His voice trailed off and he smiled horribly.

Kit wondered what weapons Colewich was bringing. A sword, pistols maybe? 'Oh, you can go now,' smiled Colewich. 'I will be there very soon.' His face disappeared from the window and was replaced by the blinding flash and ear-splitting grinding of the wall, squeezing the house on all sides.

Kit knew he didn't have long, only as long as it took Colewich to perfect the trick of getting the little man to climb the ladder. When the light and noise abated, he ran down to Zannah and Judd. 'Colewich is coming. He has the quill, the very same as this.' He touched the place where the bag was strapped beneath his shirt. 'If there were some way of getting it from him and placing them together, we should be saved.'

'...all is restored in good time,' recited Zannah.

'Exactly,' said Kit. 'But he has weapons...'

'We must fight him then?' said Judd. 'When does he get here?'

'Soon,' said Kit, knowing a better question was, where would he land? Inside the house, certainly because there was no outside now. At that moment, there came screams from one of the bedchambers. 'He's here,' said Kit. They heard heavy footsteps and angry shouts. There didn't seem any point in trying to hide. Colewich emerged onto the landing and strode to the top of the stairs. He was carrying a sword in one hand and a pistol in the other and immediately, his eyes fell upon Kit.

'There you are,' he said triumphantly but that's all he had time to say. Kit could feel something struggling beneath his shirt, pulling tightly at the strips of cloth wound about his chest. Moment by moment, the force grew stronger and he had to catch hold of a stair post to stop himself being dragged up the stairs. Some unseen force was also acting on Colewich, who stumbled sideways, losing his sword which came clattering down the stairs. His Lordship also caught hold of a stair post to prevent himself being whisked off his feet, while the pocket of his coat bulged as though something inside was trying to escape. Colewich cried out in terror and confusion.

'Hold onto me!' yelled Kit and Zannah and Judd did so, clutching him around the waist and legs. Kit hoped that Zannah had tied the strip of cloth tightly because the force threatening to pull him up the stairs was unbelievable and the strips of material bit into his flesh. Only he knew what was happening, that the quills, being in reality the same quill, were pulling toward one another like the opposite poles of a magnet. If it wasn't for his friends, he would have been flying through the air to meet Colewich.

His Lordship had wrapped his arms tightly around the stair post. His face was red and raging. He managed to wrap one leg around the post, allowing him to raise the hand holding the pistol. He fired at the group at the bottom of the stairs, but the bullet missed, shattering the wood near Kit's foot. There were screams from the villagers who peered down from the landing and out of the downstairs rooms.

'Can you not help us?' yelled Zannah.

'Aldith, Hamon? Where are you?' shouted Judd.

Aldith, Hamon and several others emerged and

added their weight to the pack attempting to stop Kit flying up the stairs. The force was unbelievably strong, and Kit feared that soon, his ribs would crack and all the air would be squashed out of his lungs. Colewich's pistol fell from his hand and bounced loudly down the wooden steps as he redoubled his efforts to hang onto the post. It was as though a whirlwind had entered the house and was sucking them into its contracting vortex.

"Tis not the wall, 'tis the Lady Pearl's quill,' Kit cried out. Zannah was closest and she heard what he said. Like Kit, she could see the pocket of Colewich's coat coming loose but this was as nothing compared to the shock of what was happening behind his Lordship. A bulge that had been growing in the other pocket ripped it apart and Punchinello burst out of it, smiling like the devil as he swelled to human size and laid his wooden hands around the throat of the struggling lord. In his fright, Colewich let go of the stair post but now Punchinello had him firmly in his grasp. Colewich screamed and tried to fight off the appalling creature; he didn't see the quill finally escape his pocket and come shooting through the air, sticking itself flat upon Kit's chest. The force vanished and Kit fell backwards onto Zannah, Judd and the others, all collapsing like a house of cards.

The air was suddenly still and the lights at the window had gone. Kit looked down at the tattered remnants of the front of his shirt and the strips of material and at the single quill resting still and silent in his lap. He didn't dare touch it, afraid of its power, yet it looked perfectly normal, the most ordinary looking goose feather you could imagine.

'Thanks be, they have gone,' said Zannah. At the top of the stairs, Kit was met with a clear view of the diamond-paned window. Where Colewich and Punchinello had been, the book now lay silently with its covers closed, protruding slightly over the topmost step.

'God be praised for this miracle!' Coswonked Jem was standing in the open doorway at the end of the passage with his arms raised to embrace the light of day. There was green grass and trees in the clearing. The wall had disappeared. One by one, the wondering villagers stumbled outside and began to talk, laugh and sing hymns of praise and thanks.

'We did it,' Zannah whispered, tears flowing down her cheeks although Kit could barely see her through his own tears.

'I shall be a better man from now on,' Judd said solemnly. 'I have been given a second chance as have we all, thanks be to God.' The three of them sat in stunned wonder while the whooping and laughter continued outside. Then Zannah spoke again. 'Truth, for such a magic object, it do look for all the world like an ordinary quill.'

Indeed, the goose feather no longer gave off any strange vibrations. 'After all, I think that's what it is, now its task is done,' said Kit, picking it up and offering it to Zannah. 'Take it. The Lady Pearl would want you to have it. Its magic is what you will make of it from now on, Zan.' Zannah took the quill and stared at it in fascination, then another thought struck her. 'All is restored in good time. But Kit, what is good time? Our time or yourn?'

'Were it our time, it would be the year of our Lord 1456,' said Awl Robin. He had been standing in the doorway and watching what they were saying. 'That will become clear soon enough. Methinks Kit is right, the Lady Pearl would want thee to have her quill and her library. She would want thee living in her house. Thou were more like her own child to her.'

'She won't be coming back then?' said Zannah.

Awl Robin shook his head. 'She died,' he said simply.

Zannah stood up and walked around, gazing all about her. 'Were I to stay in Colewichton, here would I live, amongst her precious books where she did teach me my lessons. Yet Grandda, I cannot stay. And what will pain me most is not leaving this house but leaving thee.'

'I know it,' Awl Robin came up beside her and took her hand. 'Zannah my child, we have all been given a second chance at life today. Take thine own and live it well. If that means leaving Colewichton, so be it. Thou hast my blessing.'

Hamon returned from the village with the news that every dwelling was back in place, apparently unharmed. Father Bernard urged the stunned villagers to return home and they all left. After some discussion, Judd and Father Bernard left for their own homes, and Zannah said she would walk her Grandda back to his cottage, then return with food. It was mid-afternoon judging by the real sun shining up above.

When they had gone, Kit paced about the downstairs rooms several times before plucking up the courage to climb the stairs and approach the book. It lay absolutely still, absolutely quiet. Motes of dust danced in the sunbeams which filtered through the old glass diamond window panes. He knelt and with the tip of one finger, raised the cover: a light curl emerged which coiled into the air in such a sinister way, he decided not to investigate further. Instead, he went to the bedchamber to seek something in which to wrap it. He found two old shirts in a trunk. One he put on and the other he used to wrap the book, then he stowed it under the bed in the smallest chamber. Zannah returned with bread, cheese and beer and they ate at the kitchen table. Everything was quiet in the village, no answer to the burning question, were they in 1456 or 1759?

It was late in the afternoon when there came a shout at the front door. They were still sitting deep in conversation when Kit heard the voice and sprang to his feet. He collided in the passage with Saroni, who caught hold of him and lifted him off his feet, hugging him like a bear. The two of them laughed uproariously, and Kit barely had breath to introduce Saroni and Zannah to one another. 'Did you like the surprise I slipped into the other pocket of the "magic" coat?' cried Saroni. 'Did it work? Did Punchinello come to life? I can see from your faces he did! Haha! I have the feeling that little fellow will always want to be where the magic is.'

'Wait, wait, has our village been restored to your time?' Zannah tried to butt in but had to wait for her answer while Saroni continued to dance Kit around the room. 'It is the year 1759,' he declared at last, panting once he'd put Kit down. 'And you owe me a new feather for my hat, my friend!'

CHAPTER 25
London, December 1759

It was Christmas Eve and Kit and Zannah were walking back from Conduit Fields where they had been collecting holly and ivy with which to decorate their lodgings in Hart Street. For half an hour, fine, powdery snow had been falling and it clung to the pale blue hood of Zannah's cloak and settled into the grooves of Kit's fine new tricorn hat, her Christmas gift to him. In the dark, late afternoon the shouting hawkers and barrow boys were out in force, their stalls and carts laden with geese, turkeys and mince pies while ballad singers competed with one another in singing carols. Candles in shop windows lit up a colourful array of gloves and sweetmeats, tea bowls and silver spoons, patch boxes and other Christmas gifts. On one street corner, a boy was roasting chestnuts and they bought a paper wrapper full, which they peeled and ate, talking animatedly about the holiday. Saroni was coming to dinner the next day and on New Year's Eve, the three of them were going to the Theatre Royal, Drury Lane to watch Mr David Garrick's new play *Harlequin's Invasion*. As they stood on the corner, a sedan chair passed them, and Kit caught a flash of Lord Snitherton's haughty profile. As the chair carried on down the road he told Zannah the Ashentoth story, conjuring up the vision of Snitherton dancing by moonlight in his green silk breeches and bird's nest crown. By the end, Zannah was laughing so much, she nearly choked on a chestnut and had to spit it out at the side of the road.

Saroni had insisted upon splitting Colewich's reward money with Kit and Zannah and it was tiding them over while they set themselves up in different ways of earning a living. Saroni had taken a lease on a building near Covent Garden which he was transforming into a marionette theatre and had new puppets ready for its opening the next month. He had taken on an apprentice boy, since Kit had turned down his offer of work, but he understood that Kit's ambition was to tread the boards of a stage with his own two feet. Kit had been taken on as an actor at the Little Haymarket Theatre where he was currently rehearsing two plays by Edward Moore: *The Foundling*, a comedy and *The Gamester*, a tragedy. Meanwhile, the words of Zannah's latest play were flowing from the Lady Pearl's quill, a comedy entitled *The Comet*, about how a comet's magical powers cause several characters to fall in love with unexpected people. She had already introduced herself to Garrick who had asked her to bring him the finished play. All three friends felt alive, happy and confident about the future. News of Colewichton reached them from time to time, including the wedding of Alys and Col which had taken place at last. There was little change in the village, but it had gained a reputation for welcoming strangers. Travelling players flocked there, finding an audience hungry for entertainment reflecting the news and politics of the modern age. Later in the year, Zannah planned to return by coach, walking the last few miles to her Grandda's cottage. Her ambition was to turn the Lady Pearl's house into a school for the local children and employ a live-in teacher to look after the building and library. On her next visit she planned to ask Judd to manage the project.

The book had remained where Kit had put it the day they'd moved in, at the bottom of a chest in his bedchamber. As the weeks passed, there were days when he hadn't thought about the book and days when he had. This was one of the days he had.

'Kit, what's wrong?' said Zannah. They had arrived home, but for a moment Kit seemed reluctant to follow her through the street door.

'Forgive me, Zan, I was trying to forget about it. I didn't want to tell you,' he replied.

'Tell me what?'

'I cannot spend another night with the book under our roof.'

'The book? Come, tell me.'

Reluctantly, Kit followed her into the dark passage and shut the door. It wasn't until they were in the drawing room and had dumped the greenery upon the tea table, that he began to explain. 'My curiosity got the better of me this morning, while you were writing. Well, one of us would have looked inside it one day.' Zannah nodded gravely and didn't interrupt. Neither of them had spoken of the book for weeks. 'I have often wondered about Colewich, if he were still alive? And that monster Punchinello. So I went to the chest and took it out. I only half opened it. No lights emerged, yet such a scream burst forth, it fair froze my blood. It was Colewich. Of one thing I am certain, he is in torment, wherever he is now.'

'But where could that be?' said Zannah. 'It cannot be the village, that's certain.'

''Tis not the worst of it,' continued Kit. 'His scream was followed by a shriek of the most evil, unearthly laughter I'd not want to hear again.'

'Punchinello?'

Kit nodded. 'The monster's in there with him. It must be tormenting him night and day.' Zannah held her face in her hands as Kit went on. 'I cannot destroy the book, can I? I'd not have murder on my conscience. Am I a coward for that?'

'No, Kit, of course not!'

'Yet the thought of what might be going on inside… 'tis so dark and horrible, I'd not have it here. Neither do I wish to lug the dreadful thing round with us for the rest of our lives.'

Zannah waited. Knowing Kit, he had already made up his mind about what to do. After taking a deep breath, he went on. 'So tonight, I will return to Colewich's house and leave the book where I found it.'

'Oh, Kit,' cried Zannah. For weeks she had been speaking like a modern, eighteenth-century person;

now her accent thickened, and she was back in her old medieval way of speaking. 'Thou canst not! And if thou be seen breaking into that devil's house? Think about all thou hast now, what thou wouldst lose!'

'Forgive me,' he sighed. 'I cannot bear to think of another human soul suffering like that. Even Colewich. You should have heard what I heard! We must be rid of the book. So this is what I am going to do, but I promise I won't be caught.'

'Thou canst not promise such a thing, so do not.'

'Then I believe there is small danger of being caught,' he argued. 'I have passed by that house many a time and it looks deserted. The garden is overgrown, and no lights show at night. With Colewich gone and no one to pay them, the servants have abandoned the place.'

Zannah strode about the room, wringing her hands while Kit continued to try and reassure her. He would get into Colewich's house the same way he had before and leave as soon as he'd put the book on a high shelf in the library where it might not be discovered for years if the place remained abandoned. There was always the risk of its being found but Kit preferred to run that risk than live with the book any longer. In any case, there didn't seem any way for Colewich to escape now although each time he thought that, Kit shuddered.

It was nearly midnight when Zannah, watching from the window, saw Kit disappear around the street corner with a bag slung over his shoulder. With several watchmen patrolling the area, he needed to stick to the shadows. He was very aware of the book banging against his side as he half walked, half ran, and for the first time in all his travels, he couldn't wait to be rid of it. It was a windy night and clouds scudded across the moon. Snow from earlier swirled in powdery eddies in blind alleys and empty yards.

The house was just as he'd described it to Zannah. The front gates were locked, the garden overgrown and the dogs were gone while the darkened windows were like lifeless eyes. Quickly, Kit proceeded up the alley and mounted the wall at the end, recalling those other times he had crept in the same way. Yet he was no longer a thief, he was an actor. It was not the most respectable profession, but he could hold up his head in public. This was the very last time he would ever break into a building, he promised himself.

The house seemed even colder and more lifeless inside. The longcase clock in the hall had stopped and there was a profound and overwhelming stillness. Even though he knew the sound of his footsteps were being absorbed by the thick hall carpet, it was tempting to imagine they wouldn't have made a noise anyway, that sound itself had died when the house's clock heart had stopped beating. He was relieved to find the library unlocked. Inside, there were still signs of the magical fight that had taken place on his last visit, with holes in the floor and ceiling, but the furniture had been straightened and the books were all back on the shelves. Although it was dark, Kit could see that the stained-glass window had been mended at least; the rabbits were back on the daisy-strewn hillside while rays of morning sunshine spread across the sky.

Somehow, he hadn't expected to see the box again but where else would it be but chained to the table? Its lid was open and when he tested the lock pin, it sprang back against his finger. He remembered Colewich telling him the box would lock without the key. What if he placed the book inside and shut the lid right now? If Colewich still had the key, it might never see the light of day again. As Kit's eyes carried on adjusting to the dark, he could make out the complicated wheels and springs of the puzzle mechanics inside the lid and the horror of the idea hit him. Once that lid was closed, the iron bands around the box would trap Colewich inside with Punchinello for ever and ever. It would solve the problem of the book's ever being found again but could Kit really do that, even to his worst enemy?

The solution came to him in a flash, yet in order to carry it out, he would have to open the book. He placed the bag on the table next to the box, and slowly drew it out. His stomach flipped at the thought of hearing those terrible screams and even more chilling laughter but after steadying himself a moment, he opened it. There were no magical light curls now, just a pale grey static fuzz and all was quiet, until he turned a page and the red and black figure of Punchinello appeared, his smile wider and more horrible than ever. He began beating his stick violently and the laughter began. Kit turned the page quickly and it stopped, but a few pages on, it began again. Punchinello was following him through the book, jumping from page to page and although there was no real danger to Kit since the monster couldn't get out, it was frightening. He steeled himself and carried on going but didn't find Colewich until the final page. His Lordship's haunted face stared out from a grey, murky background. His skin was almost as grey and his eyes were bloodshot.

'Kit? Kit! You must get me out of here!' His voice was desperate. 'I beg you! I beseech you! I am trapped with this… this…' Before he could finish the sentence, the maniacal laughter began, and Punchinello appeared waving his stick, with which he proceeded to beat his Lordship. Colewich screamed and cried out to Kit again until the two of them disappeared from the page.

Kit turned the pages as fast as he dared, although he didn't want to risk moving the little man up the ladder too quickly. He didn't know if that way into the book would even work again but it was best to be careful. He needed to find Colewich alone on a page. As he turned and turned the pages, Kit caught sight of the two of them, Punchinello chasing Colewich, their laughter and screams mixed together in a dreadful cacophony. He closed the book and waited, hoping that things would settle down. When he opened it again, all was quiet, and he carried on searching. Finally, he found Colewich alone and out of breath and did what he'd been planning: he removed his Lordship's page. As he shut the book, he heard Punchinello's laughter for the last time, faintly, as though it were gurgling down a drain.

Kit sat on one of the high-backed chairs, holding the page between shaking hands. Colewich was scared out of his wits and it took a while for Kit to calm him and explain that the monster had gone for good. Even so, his Lordship kept jumping in fear and looking over his shoulder and it was difficult to make out what he was saying, he was stammering so much.

'Where are you?' asked Kit. 'What is that place?'

'I... know... not,' jabbered Colewich. 'Some place between heaven and hell... there is nothing, nothing but fog...'

'Yet you can see me?' said Kit.

'I can see you, yes... you are in... my library?' The fear in his voice was now replaced by such sadness and loss. It was easy for Kit to feel sorry for him and he had to remind himself that this was the same person who had threatened his life and the lives of his friends. Would Colewich have bothered saving Kit if their situations had been reversed? Of course not. Well, Kit may have rescued Colewich from the monstrous Punchinello but what was he going to do with him now? No way was he taking the page home.

All at once, the morning window was filled with moonlight and although there was no magic making the swallows fly or the rabbits jump, the colours glowed, and it was a beautiful sight. Kit turned the page to the window and he heard Colewich sigh, and weep and laugh with relief.

'The beauty of it... oh the beauty... my morning, my dawn, the dawning of the day...'

This was the answer. Without further thought, Kit climbed the tall bookcase next to the window, placed the page on top and weighted the top and bottom edges with books to make sure it stayed in place. As he climbed back down he could still hear Colewich sighing happily to himself. Back at ground level, the voice could barely be heard and sounded more like a twig scratching on the window pane. Having helped his old enemy, Kit could now forget all about him.

There was only one thing left to do. Kit returned to the table, picked up the book for the last time and placed it in the puzzle box. When he closed the lid, he could hear the whirring of coils and cogs and springs which suddenly stopped. All was silent. When Kit walked out of that library, he would be leaving the last of his old life behind. No longer a thief, his memories of Gabe were all he wanted from the past and he vowed that whatever good he did from now on, whatever success or happiness he achieved, would be for Gabe too. As he closed the library door behind him, Kit's heart soared at the thought of his bright, golden future.

Ruth Morgan lives with her partner Chris and son Gethin in Penarth, South Wales. She grew up loving time-travel stories, particularly 'Tom's Midnight Garden' and later in life she was lucky enough to be tutored by its author, the late, great Philippa Pearce at Tŷ Newydd Creative Writing Centre. Ruth has a passion for history and the idea of travelling in time between two of her favourite periods, Georgian and Medieval, was the spark which ignited this story.